Fallen

LIA MILLS

PENGUIN BOOKS

PENGUIN IRELAND

Published by the Penguin Group

Penguin Ireland, 25 St Stephen's Green, Dublin 2, Ireland (a division of Penguin Books Ltd)
Penguin Books Ltd, 80 Strand, London WC2R 0RL, England
Penguin Group (USA) Inc., 375 Hudson Street, New York, New York 10014, USA
Penguin Group (Australia), 707 Collins Street, Melbourne, Victoria 3008, Australia
(a division of Pearson Australia Group Pty Ltd)
Penguin Group (Canada), 90 Eglinton Avenue East, Suite 700, Toronto, Ontario, Canada M4P 2Y3
(a division of Pearson Penguin Canada Inc.)
Penguin Books India Pvt Ltd, 11 Community Centre, Panchsheel Park, New Delhi – 110 017, India
Penguin Group (NZ), 67 Apollo Drive, Rosedale, Auckland 0632, New Zealand
(a division of Pearson New Zealand Ltd)
Penguin Books (South Africa) (Pty) Ltd, Block D, Rosebank Office Park,
181 Jan Smuts Avenue, Parktown North, Gauteng 2193, South Africa

Penguin Books Ltd, Registered Offices: 80 Strand, London WC2R 0RL, England

www.penguin.com

First published 2014
001

Copyright © Lia Mills, 2014

Set in Garamond MT Std 13.5/16pt
Typeset by Jouve (UK), Milton Keynes
Printed in Great Britain by Clays Ltd, St Ives plc

A CIP catalogue record for this book is available from the British Library

ISBN: 978–1–844–88305–9

www.greenpenguin.co.uk

For the city

PART ONE

August 1914

That August was unnatural. We weren't used to so much sun-shine, softening the corners and warming the ruddy brick of the terraces and squares 'til they shimmered. It seemed to reach inside my bones the same way. At first I liked the sensation, but there's such a thing as too much heat.

One sweltering afternoon, three weeks after war broke out on the Continent, I arrived at Rutland Square dishevelled and out of sorts after walking across town from Earlsfort Terrace. Our many-paned sash windows gaped wide open on all five floors, like so many mouths gasping for air.

I'd pulled off the pale linen jacket that had tightened beyond endurance across my shoulders as I walked. It was bundled across one arm, its matching hat crumpled in hands that itched to be free of it. Our outer hall, with its high ceiling and lime-stone floor, could feel like a tomb in winter, but that day I was glad of its chill. I settled the jacket on the back of a chair to air and dropped my hat on to the corner table. I put the flat of a hand to the wall, then cupped it to the nape of my neck for the cold as I went through the double doors to the inner hall.

I heard my mother's voice coming from the breakfast room and assumed whoever else was home would be in there too, drinking one of Lockie's cordials if they were lucky. Our housekeeper could coax refreshment from the tartest of fruit, and I was parched, but I was mad to change out of my damp blouse into something lighter and looser. So I didn't call out to say I was home, but went upstairs instead, tugging my blouse free of the waistband of my skirt and fanning it to make some kind of breeze in the dead air.

3

At the second landing, I avoided looking at the cheval mirror in the darker, recessed area outside our parents' room. Mother had put it there so that we could see ourselves as we'd appear to others, before we reached the more public parts of the house, below. I barely had a foot on the landing when a shadow moved in the gloom, to my left. I stopped dead, looked at it sideways. The shadow had the shape of a soldier: peaked cap, waisted tunic, jodhpurs. Fine hairs stirred on my arms and spine. I retreated a step and looked around me, to see was I in the right house, though of course I was. There, on the flight below, was the watercolour of Mother and her three sisters as girls, all dressed in white, in their Wicklow garden; there was our worn blue carpet under my feet; there the broken stair rod.

I looked at the tunic again, then up, into a face I knew better than my own. Shadowed by the cap, my twin brother's expression was wary. We stared at each other. Neither of us moved.

I broke first. 'Liam?'

'Hello, Katie.'

'I didn't know you, in that rig-out.' I sat, too hard, on the blanket box at the wall. Pain flared in my bad tooth, then mercifully subsided. 'Why didn't you say something? You must have heard me coming. You put the heart across me.'

'I wanted to see how you'd take it, when you saw me.' He took off the daft-looking cap and ran the palm of his hand across the fresh stubble of his hair. An outline of pale, raw skin at its edges looked as though someone had traced a chalk line around his features, to sketch the stranger they'd turned him into.

'Please tell me you didn't,' I said – but why else would he be wearing the uniform?

The war was all most people were talking about – the war, and whether Irishmen should take England's side against the

Germans, or fight off Carson's Ulstermen if they came south, or not fight at all. We'd been on the brink of getting our own parliament, after a hundred-odd years without one. Now people said we'd likely have to wait. Again. And here was Liam, ready to plunge headlong into the thick of a fight that had nothing to do with us.

'I told you I was thinking of it.'

'I didn't think you'd really do it. Not so soon.'

'Why wait?' He ran his freckled hands down the ugly tunic, with its loud brass buttons and bulky pockets, held out his arms, flexed and then straightened his elbows. The khaki sleeves fell below his wrists.

'It doesn't even fit you.' I'd the strangest urge to slap his hands back down to his sides and to carry right on beating him, as though that uniform was a dusty old rug hung out on a line to air.

'Lockie will fix it.'

'Why, Liam?' This came out harsher than I'd meant. 'Why would you?'

He flushed. 'We can't stand idly by while Germany –'

'Oh, Liam, I've heard that said a million times! What are you, some sort of lackey? Don't you have a mind of your own? All that guff about the rights of small nations – what about us? Are we not a nation too?'

His face shut tight. He straightened, tugged on the ends of the tunic. 'And is that what passes for original thought, in your head?'

The full force of it hit me then. He would go away. He'd put himself in danger. What on earth had tipped him through the door of a recruiting office to sign an agreement that he would wear their uniform, go wherever they made him go, do whatever they made him do? I couldn't ask, because it was too late, and that was the answer to the other, childish, painful question: why didn't you tell me before you did it?

I'd never, not once, hesitated to say anything to Liam before. Suddenly afraid, I wrapped my arms around myself and held on but I couldn't prevent a shiver. I took a deep breath. 'When do you leave?'

'The day after tomorrow.'

'What will Dad say?'

'He knows.'

'But – what about the firm?'

'He'll hire someone else to do my work.'

'That's hardly the point.' Dad was so proud when Liam joined the firm – he'd dragged us all down to Arran Quay to have a look at the fresh brass plaque outside the office door: WM. CRILLY & SON, SOLICITORS. We'd barely finished our final examinations, and Liam was mortified, wondering what the clerks would make of it, and he only the most junior of trainees, with more exams ahead. But he settled into the firm as naturally as though he'd been reared in the filing cabinet, Dad said – with a significant look at Matt, who showed no such inclination.

'What about Isabel?' The girl he thought so much of.

'I'm seeing her later. And, before you ask, I'll go to Eva on the way.'

Eva, our eldest sister, lived with her husband and small daughter across the river, on Ely Place. Her health was poor, despite all the care and attention her husband Bartley, a surgeon, could come by. If Liam went dressed like that, he'd give her a stroke.

He filched the thought from my head before I could say it: 'Don't worry, I'll change.' He went into his room and shut the door. The latch clicked like a scold's tongue, made me wish I'd a more generous heart. The silence on the landing was so deep I heard my own pulse tick.

I went into the front bedroom I shared with our other sister, Florrie, and poured myself a glass of water from the jug on the nightstand. I drank it too fast, waking the nerve in my tooth. Mother had arranged for me to go to our dentist about it later that afternoon – it had been bothering me for days – but I had time to kill before the appointment. I changed out of my stale linen blouse into a loose, cream-coloured lawn tunic and let my hair out, brushed it quickly and twisted it up off my neck again. The weight of it was ridiculous in this weather, like wearing a woollen blanket on my head. I waited for Liam to come out of his room, so I could talk to him. Or, better still, keep my own mouth shut and listen.

Mine was the smaller bed, near the window. Florrie hated any kind of draught, and being six years older she had the choice. I'd have chosen mine anyhow, for the light and the view and the fresh air I could avail of when she wasn't in the room. But even Florrie wouldn't complain about an open window on a day like this.

I sat at the end of my bed and tried to take it in. Liam had signed up to be a soldier. He was going to an actual war, where men were wounded and killed as a matter of course. I couldn't see it. I wished I'd asked him how long the training would last. There must be a decent chance he'd miss the fighting altogether – everyone said it would be over soon.

There was nothing warlike about Liam, never had been, but he was a crack-shot, a gun-club champion, and had a collection of pewter tankards and trophies to prove it. He kept his hunting rifles locked away in a cupboard in the box room, but they'd be no use in a war. Or would they? My stomach flipped. I knew so little about it.

He'd given me an article to read, written by Tom Kettle, who'd taught him Economics when we were in college. Professor Kettle's style was informal. He'd bring his students out to Stephen's Green, to sprawl on the grass and listen – along with anyone else who chanced by – to his eloquence. He had stirring theories about Ireland's brilliant future as an independent nation among other European nations. It was he who gave Liam his taste for politics, his ambition to go into parliament one day. Now he'd pointed the way to war, and Liam had followed.

I picked up the *Daily News* Liam had given me, folded around an article the professor had written from Belgium, where he happened to be when the war began. It described the anti-German feeling that had swept through the streets of Brussels after the invasion; how the city flowered with the tricolours of Belgium and France, cockades and rosettes in the reds, whites and blues of France and England; he wrote about people in anxious queues at banks and post offices, waiting to withdraw currency they no longer had faith in, the departure of the Red Cross for the Front in commandeered taxis and trade-cars. Liam had underlined the last lines: *War is hell, but it is only a hell of suffering, not a hell of dishonour. And through it, over its flaming coals, Justice must walk, were it on bare feet.*

Fine words, but it was hard to concentrate, between the heat, the echoes of our argument, my uneasy tooth, and the strain of listening out for him to stir. What I heard instead was Mother's heavy tread on the stairs, her knock on his door, her complaint. 'What on earth is keeping you so long? Ah, Liam. Put it back on you, for heaven's sake, and come down. We're waiting – we're dying to see you in it.'

I listened to the rustle of her skirt and the creak of the stairs as she went back down again, and wondered who was there with her, waiting. Whoever it was, they'd likely gloat over him, tell him what a fine fellow he was in the uniform. I wouldn't be able to bear it.

It was galling. I wished she'd thrown a few barriers in Liam's path, the way she so often did in mine. My purpose in going to Earlsfort Terrace that day had been to decline the place I'd been offered in the History Department, to study for a higher degree. It would have been easier to write a letter, but Professor Hayden was not the sort of person who took the easy route herself. She deserved the courtesy of a face-to-face explanation.

The door to the Professor's office was open when I arrived. She was reading at her desk, but she put the book aside and seemed glad to see me, 'til I told her why I'd come.

She took a stub of yellow pencil out from behind her ear and rolled it over and back between her fingers. 'I don't understand, Miss Crilly. Do you not want the opportunity?'

'Of course I do.' I fidgeted, like a schoolgirl, in my seat. 'It's my parents, they won't allow it. I thought I could persuade them. But –'

'How old are you?'

Her tone drew blood to my face. 'Twenty-two.'

She stabbed a series of holes in her blotter with the pencil. 'Can you not reason with them? Are they not proud of you?'

I'd come third in my year, and won a medal for an essay on Wolfe Tone, but this was the absolute last thing likely to make my mother proud, she was as staunch a unionist as you could hope to find. 'My mother says one degree is bad enough, it's an utter waste of money.'

'Then why did they send you here at all?'

I looked at her cropped hair and plain clothes. 'My twin brother wouldn't come unless they let me come too.' In fact, she and Liam had won me the right to study here, between them. As recently as seven years earlier, being a woman, I wouldn't have been admitted to college in the first place. Professor Hayden and her clever friends had fought the larger battles that changed all that.

'You have a brother.' She looked out the window at the unnaturally blue sky, not a cloud in sight. 'Let's hope the war ends soon.'

In fact, I had two brothers. Best not to mention Matt, the

youngest, the baby of the house, who was about to sit for repeats of the first-year examinations he had spectacularly failed. He was no advertisement for the benefits of university, his only apparent interests being in its social life and student theatricals. If anything, his carry-on in the last year had stiffened Mother's resolve to stop me going back. 'Liam studied Law, and Economics,' I said. 'He's working now, for our father.'

She dropped her pencil. It rolled off the blotter and across the desk, picking up speed. We both watched its progress. She waited, caught it as it fell off the edge. 'I suppose your mother thinks we've ruined you.'

I tried to smile. 'Something like that.'

'Would it help if I spoke to her?'

'No.'

My conviction seemed to startle her. 'I can be diplomatic.'

I shook my head. 'It wouldn't help.'

'A thing you want is worth fighting for.'

There was nothing I wanted more, but it wasn't that simple, as she must have known. She and my mother were of an age, but they might as well have lived in different centuries, on different continents. I could hardly tell the professor that my mother despised women like her, who campaigned for the franchise.

She dropped the pencil into a chipped cup that held several others and got to her feet. 'Well. It's a shame. Come and see me if the situation changes.' She walked me to the door, shook my hand and turned back to her desk with what looked like relief.

At the bottom of the stairs I'd a notion to look into a lecture theatre, just to smell the wood and chalk, or to find the place where I'd marked my initials on a desk at the end of the last lecture I attended. I'd broken the nib of my pen doing it. But when I cracked the door open, a young man I didn't know was sitting up in the top tier of desks, making furious notes from a pile of textbooks spread around him. The surface creaked under the force he wrote with. He didn't look up. I let the door fall shut and walked back out through the tiled hall, the echo of my footsteps ringing in the eerie quiet of the summer hiatus.

I gave Mother enough time to get well out of earshot before going across the landing to Liam's door. I rolled my knuckles on the wood.

'No,' he said, through the door.

'It's me.'

'I'm changing.'

'I'm going out for a bit. Will you be here when I get back?'

'I might.'

'I'm sorry for being such a crank.'

Silence. I rapped the door one more time, with what I hoped he'd know were friendly knuckles, and went on down to the hall.

Lockie was running a feather duster around a picture-frame. She lowered her arms when she saw me. 'I suppose you've seen him?'

'I can't talk about it, Lockie.' My voice came out ragged. I read pity in her face and bolted past her, out into the glaring light and heat.

I'd known our Square all my life, but something was awry that afternoon. The spire of Findlater's Church threatened to pierce the blue of the sky, a blue so wide and high I felt it tilt when I looked up into it. The uneven roofline and crooked windows of the terrace on the side across from ours looked shambolic and rotten, rather than charming. An empty tram hissed past, on its way to the terminus near the Post Office; a full one went the other way. Down on the corner a newsboy called a headline about Japan. It all felt like someone else's dream, impossible to enter. I hesitated, appalled by a growing sense that I'd nowhere, in fact, to go.

I would have gone to Eva's, but that's where Liam was going, to break his news himself. I'd only be in the way. I could have called on any of our friends, but what would we talk about, other than things I'd sooner eat glass than say? There was always the Rotunda Gardens, right there in front of me, where I'd find a shaded bench, but it would feel like defeat to hide, and so close to home. I couldn't face an hour in a tea-rooms either, not with a bad tooth. A splinter of pride got in under my breast-bone and lodged there. There had to be something I could do on my own, even if it was only to walk, with no particular aim. If Liam could make a decision to change the shape and course of his life with so little hesitation, and without consulting anyone – well, without consulting me – then surely I could manage to put one foot in front of the other and keep moving.

If I followed my usual route down Sackville Street, Liam might well overtake me on his way to Eva. So I turned east, along Great Denmark Street. Not since Liam and I were children had I been out and about and aimless like this, no one knowing where I was.

The sun beat against my back. I turned down North Great George's Street to escape it. The street was oddly deserted apart from a dog asleep on a step, a cat curled up in a window. You could read the history of this area in these decaying terraces of large Georgian houses, whose rooms once offered comfortable homes to gentry families, now mostly run to offices, boarding houses and tenements. One or two were near-derelict, with gapped windows and missing doors. Our own terrace had been saved from dereliction by its position and the trams; it had boarding houses and a small hotel to keep it going. Mother objected to it all and hankered after the suburbs and the sea, but Dad was attached to our house, which had come down to us from his parents. I was attached to it too – I was a city person at heart.

A whiff from a drain checked my enthusiasm. Not even the most passionate Dubliner could admire the city's smells. Florrie devoted hours to concocting tricks to defeat them. She made pomanders, lotions and soaps, shaved lemon peel into the water our handkerchiefs were boiled in. Her latest venture was scented candles, but Mother put a quick stop to that, afraid for our lives if we left unattended flames around the house.

I turned left on to Parnell Street, then right on to Gardiner Street, with a vague notion of aiming for the river, where a person might reasonably stand idle at a quay wall and watch the water and the birds, the movement of ships and barges. So many people, so much industry – a reproach to my aimless, time-wasting existence. I envied Liam his easy entry to work in Dad's firm. He had a purpose and a pattern for his days. I'd none for mine. I was left casting around for something to occupy my mind while I endured Mother's many schemes for my improvement. I could read books 'til my eyes were near falling out of my head, but to what end? I loved the discipline of chasing an idea, assembling evidence, constructing an argument for college essays. I loved the almost physical sensation of learning, an expansive stirring and waking in my mind. When Professor Hayden suggested I go on for a Master's degree, I was glad of the chance to stay in college a little longer, while I made up my mind what to do in life. I knew I was expected to marry, but suppose I never met anyone I wanted? Suppose no one ever wanted me?

My schoolfriend Frieda Leamy had trained as a nurse after school, and Mother hadn't spoken well of her since. Mind you, she'd never been entirely happy about Frieda, whose father was a draper. Frieda's face was spoiled by a purple birthmark that reached from one eyebrow to her collar-bone, as though she'd been scalded. It would put off the paying customers, Mother said, no wonder she needed to do something else with herself. But the truth was that Frieda had no interest in the shop, and now she was doing something she loved.

Eva thought I'd like teaching, but I couldn't see myself standing up in front of crowds of people to speak. I liked learning for its own sake, and if that was indulgent or impractical, Professor Hayden thought no less of me for it. I still smarted from her perfunctory handshake, which made me feel like someone she used to know but no longer took an interest in.

A disturbance of air blurred in an arc in front of me. A child swinging out of a lamp-post on a rope just missed catching me with her feet. She bumped to a standstill and grinned. Her face was ruddy and freckled. She held out her rope. 'Have a go, missis?' A swarm of children on the step of a doorless house jeered me. I considered them with a mean eye, then stuck out my tongue. They roared and applauded. The tips of a few pink tongues poked back.

An empty dray drawn by two black horses lumbered towards us on loud, iron-rimmed wheels. The horses' hairy feet were heavy and slow, their breathing laboured in unison, as though, together, they made a single funereal beast. The child beside me hopped from one leg to the other, her mop of brown hair flopping in time to their steps. Looking at her, something in my own ribs rose to the memory of how it felt to launch myself into the air and fly around the post before spinning back to earth. Liam and I used to do it, whenever we managed to sneak away from the house to play on more casual streets than our own — back in the days when we barely needed words to know what was in the other's mind.

*

Rounding the Custom House, I was assailed by a low-tide stink of fish off the river. Seagulls crowded the sky, whinging and giving out. I was glad to turn back on to Beresford Place, where the windows of Liberty Hall were littered with green anti-recruitment posters. Good for them.

A little way along Abbey Street, near the paper stores, a small crowd was mocking a white-haired man on a step. He yelled back at them. He'd a bell in his hand he kept ringing. I couldn't hear what he said.

'What is it?' I asked an old woman who held the skinny bowl of a clay pipe near her chin, between a finger and a thumb. The stem of the pipe ran into the many grubby folds and creases of her mouth.

She looked at me with lively eyes. Her lips parted with a sucking sound and out came the pipe, causing her face to collapse around her chin. 'It's them vigilants as want us all to go round with our legs crossed and our knees in a knot, and the English papers banned because of their filth. Sure, why else would we read them at all?'

I moved away from the poison of her breath.

I dreaded Mr Hickey, the dentist, pulling out my own bad tooth, not only because it would hurt, but because Mother said it was a slippery slope. She should know – she was a mar-tyr to her teeth. Lockie had only the front ones left, four top and five bottom, and a pair she called gnashers at the back. Enough to be going on with, she said, trying to cheer me up.

A throb in the bad tooth sent a bitter taste through my mouth. I put a hand to my cheek to quell it. I'd forgotten to ask Mother for the money to pay the dentist. I could go home and hurry back, but his rooms were two short streets away and by now every step was driving a searing pain through my cheek and into my ear. I'd go along early and wait, beg his indulgence about the money. He knew Mother well; he'd surely let me put the visit on account.

I was near crying by the time the Hickeys' maid answered their door and let me into the waiting room. I apologized for being early. 'Sit yourself down. I'll tell him you're here,' she said, and went away. I supposed she saw people in a similar state, or worse, every day of the week.

Eventually Mr Hickey called me through. I hadn't been in his consulting room for years. It hadn't changed. A noxious smell I couldn't identify spread across the floor of my mind. I avoided looking at a chipped enamel dish with steel instruments, a pile of cut flannel, an angled light. His wife busied herself at a cupboard in the corner. She looked up and gave me a brief smile with little comfort in it.

The pain was overlaid by fright as I sat into the reclining chair, but there was no backing out now, with Mr Hickey looming over me. I'd forgotten how much I disliked his thick fingers, or the bushy yellow moustache that lay along his narrow lip. He wrapped a finger in a piece of gauze and poked at the tooth. I winced away from his hand.

He shook his head, scolding either me or the tooth. 'That fellow will have to go,' he said. 'You stay good and quiet, or I might pull the wrong one out.' He chortled.

'Will it hurt?'

'Not a bit.' His smile showed yellow teeth, big and square and strong-looking. He waved a rubber tube. 'I'll give you the gas.' He patted my knee, glanced over at his wife. 'Marguerite, I wonder would you . . .'

I didn't catch what he asked her for, but she went out of the room, leaving the door ajar. I watched her go with envy. Not having much option, I settled to my fate and the mask he held to my face.

'You won't feel a thing.'

There was a thick smell of rubber, a green-smelling gas. I struggled on the first few breaths and then it was easy and slow and Mr Hickey became something marvellous, a fine fellow altogether. The hairs that grew from his ears made me want to laugh, the idea of touching them threatened to give me the giggles. His hand arrived near my knee, a curious pleasant weight. Thoughts too heavy to speak formed in my mind and my knee was getting ready to answer his hand when Mrs Hickey came fussing back. 'I couldn't find it – is that not enough of that now?' Her voice boomed and stretched away, then snapped back to a point. Their voices swam, there were loud creaks, he was twisting something over and back against the stretched inside of my cheek. It creaked loud in my ear and then there was blood in my mouth and a nasty-tasting rag to bite on.

'Look at that!' Mr Hickey gazed with admiration at a disgusting, yellowed molar. A sac of greyish jelly wobbled at the end of a sharp-looking root. 'An abscess,' he said. 'No wonder it pained you. We're lucky it didn't burst. You'll be right as rain, now, once and you keep that socket clean and dry until it heals.'

Mrs Hickey passed me a rolled plug of cotton. 'Bite down on that and hold still, as long as you can. Then another.' She gave me a packet with a half a dozen or so more plugs. 'Your sister's here.'

Florrie waited in the hall, looking cross. She held an envelope addressed to Mr Hickey. 'You might have told us you were making your own way here, Katie. Mother sent me to apologize if you'd forgotten. Or to pay if you hadn't.'

Mrs Hickey patted my arm. 'There, now.' She took the envelope from Florrie. 'You'd best find a cab to take her home, she's a tad woozy.'

In the cab Florrie started on at me with questions, but I shook my head and gestured at my mouth. I couldn't say a single intelligible thing.

'You've blood on your chin.' She pointed to her own face to show me where. I held up a finger and she guided it into

17

place on my chin and dabbed it. 'There.' My efforts didn't satisfy her, though. She hesitated over a fresh hankie she pulled from her purse, shot a look at the slumped, indifferent back of the cabman, gave a corner of the hankie a quick lick and scrubbed the blood from my chin. 'Now you're decent.'

Sackville Street passed in a dizzy blur: the tram-lines, the Post Office, the flower- and fruit-sellers at the base of the Pillar, the hotels and shops, the curved sweep of the Rotunda, our Square.

Lockie opened the door. 'Let's get you up to bed.' She came up with me to the room I shared with Florrie, turned the bed down, brought me a mug of salt water to rinse my mouth, a bowl to spit into and a flannel to wipe with. 'But later,' she said. 'Give it time to harden first, or you'll set it to bleed all over again.'

By then Mother and Florrie had gathered into the room. 'Did he give you the gas?' Florrie asked. 'They say he takes it himself, more often than he gives it to his patients. I wouldn't go near him, myself.'

'Why didn't you say so sooner?' I lisped, clear as I could through the gauze packed into my enormous cheek. *Thay tho thooner.*

Florrie's laugh was rare and sudden, hard to resist. She let a kind of bark out of her and her whole body shook, setting me off too.

'Florrie!' Mother's mouth did a little jig of its own, then settled down. 'You could ruin a man's good name.'

That was a dreary evening. I didn't go down for supper; I'd a rotten taste in my mouth and my head ached. Instead, I lay on my bed, a flannel at my cheek, and tried not to let my tongue worry the place where the tooth had been. I went over all that had happened, feeling well and truly sorry for myself. Professor Hayden, Liam, the dentist – the day had been a slowly closing door. The rest of the world moved on out into the stream of life, while I was left stranded and forgotten on the riverbank, at low tide.

The war was real, men out there fighting and dying, while I lay on a comfortable bed moaning about a toothache. I'd missed a single meal, and there were children in tenements all around me who'd count themselves lucky if they saw a proper meal in a week. I'd little to complain about. I should pull myself together, get more involved with Eva's charitable groups – she was forever raising money for good causes, with bazaars and raffles and cake sales.

When Florrie came up, she sat in front of the dressing-table mirror and gave her hair its hundred strokes. I wondered when Liam would get in. I rehearsed an apology in my mind, while Florrie droned on about the afternoon she'd spent in the company of her fiancé, a paragon called Eugene Sheehan who sold religious artefacts for a living. As she told it, their conversation was entirely commercial, to do with advantageous positions for premises and the merits of a plate-glass window for a shopfront.

I'd say she bored me to sleep. The next morning I woke with an ache in my face and a thudding head, but my cheek wasn't swollen any more. I found Liam downstairs at the breakfast table, in his own clothes. He looked pale but happy. I sat across from him and steeled myself to apologize, but he jumped in ahead of me. 'Isabel and I are engaged.'

'I'm sorry?'

He repeated himself, and there was Florrie making little squeals of excitement and giving him a hug, then Lockie came in with a plate of rashers, and Matt behind her. Beck, Liam's spaniel, blundered around waving his tail saying hello to us all and getting in everyone's way. By the time order was restored our parents had joined us.

'What will you do for a ring?' Florrie asked, sprinkling demerara sugar on to her bread and butter.

And there in a wood a Piggy-wig stood . . . I must have been feeling the effects of the gas, still.

'Dad gave me one.'

So Dad knew, and I didn't.

Mother set the teapot back down on its trivet. 'Which ring?'

I took up the pot. While I poured, Matt held the cups with a little wink, as though it were a game of Tea Party. He passed them around the table with exaggerated care when they were full. I was glad of something to do, glad Matt was there as a buffer.

Dad cracked an egg open with his knife, sliced the top off it. 'One of my mother's – the squarish silver one, with green stones.'

Mother took in a sharp breath. 'Those are emerald chips.'

'Isabel's birthstone.' Liam looked pleased with himself. He was passing rasher rinds and the casing of a pudding to the dog under the table.

'Stop that,' Mother said. 'Or do it outside. I wish you'd discussed this with me beforehand, Bill.'

'Ah, Mildred, there wasn't time. You never wanted it. It's too small for you, and you didn't like it enough to get it sized. You said so yourself.'

'Come on, Beck.' Liam pushed back his chair and stood up. He dropped a kiss on the top of Mother's head as he passed her on his way out, the dog lumbering after him. Mother closed her eyes. The look of pain on her face gave me a lump in my throat. I mumbled an apology and followed Liam out.

Dad caught a hold of my arm as I passed his chair. 'You're very quiet, Catkin.'

'It's the tooth.'

'Is it? You wouldn't be out of sorts with Liam, would you?'

'I'm going after him now.'

'Good.' He gave my arm a little shake. 'Don't store up regrets for yourself. Tomorrow, he'll be gone.'

I caught up with Liam in the back garden. Beck had his nose in a bush. Half blind from cataracts, he was being taunted by a bee. He jerked his nose back, then shoved it into the bush again, wagging his tail.

'Has he finished the bacon?'

'He has.'

I caught Beck's tail in my hand, felt its urge against my palm and let it go. 'I'm happy for you, Liam. Isabel is lovely.'

'She is.' He gave me a sidelong look, and went back to watching Beck. 'You'll find someone too.'

'Who says I want to?' I was livid with him all over again, for sounding like a governess in some stupid romance. How could we be saying such stale, empty things to each other? 'What did her father say?'

The trace of a grin crossed his mouth. 'She didn't give him much chance to say anything, she'd it all worked out.' He shielded his eyes from the sun to look at me. 'She's twenty-five, she has money her mother left her. And she'd her mind made up. When Isabel sets her mind on something, she'd run rings around anyone, even the Judge –'

'That's all well and fine, Liam, but why didn't you tell me?'

Beck yelped and came over to bury his face in Liam's leg. 'You poor eejit,' Liam murmured. 'What did you expect?'

'Is that directed at me?'

'Should it be?' He grinned up at me. His eyes were light and clear.

Suddenly all the prickly resentment I'd been harbouring evaporated. 'I've been a brat,' I said. 'And I'm sorry. Can we stop this, now? I hate it.'

The relief in his face shamed me. He held out his hands and I took them. His clasp was warm and steady, unbearably dear and familiar. Then Lockie came out and said Liam was wanted, because Mother had it in mind to pay a visit to Isabel and her father. I let him go.

I helped Liam to pack when he came in again, and arranged his room so that I could move into it when he was gone. Matt had his eye on it, but Liam said no, I was to have it. 'Katie'll take better care of it,' he said.

'You mean, she's more likely to give it back,' was Matt's opinion.

Eva came in the afternoon and Bartley brought their daughter, Alanna, at suppertime. The conversation lurched along like a faulty train trying to leave a station. I stared at Liam, hard, whenever I thought I'd get away with it, tried to fix him in place in my mind. The men talked about guns. Liam said he'd leave his behind, except for the Webley. He pulled on Beck's ears. 'They'll give me a Lee-Enfield.' His eyes lit up. 'I've heard that a good marksman can fire twelve decent shots a minute with it.'

Eva busied herself with wiping Alanna's mouth. Liam sent his plate up for more of the ham Dad was carving. I said I didn't want any more. 'There's only a small bit left,' Mother said. 'Bartley?'

Bartley put his hand flat to his waistcoat. 'I couldn't, but thank you. It was delicious.' They were so polite to each other always, their excessive manners an indication of their mutual dislike.

Various people came to say their goodbyes after supper. Some of Liam's friends stood in a knot in the corner, talking about the war in low voices; Mother's sister Chrissie came in from Kingstown; Isabel was shy with us all and a little awkward, 'til Eva put her at ease by borrowing her ring to twist for a wish – after that we all had to try it. Some of the neighbours dropped in. They said they wouldn't stay long, but they showed no desire to leave 'til Eva announced that it was long past Alanna's bedtime, and her own. Liam said he would see Isabel home.

I didn't want to go to bed, but he told me not to wait up. I'd swear I was awake all night, listening to the birds sing their happy little hearts out over in the Gardens, 'til I longed for a cat to come along and silence them for good, but I never heard him come in.

The next morning when Liam came down for breakfast he was kitted out in the full regalia, minus the cap. Poor, half-blind Beck growled at him, his hackles raised. Everyone stopped what they were doing, like a peculiar version of musical statues, and looked at Liam, or at the dog.

'It's the smell off the belt,' Florrie said, making a face.

It was a strong smell all right. Liam squatted down in front of the dog and spoke to him, rubbing the fur behind his two chestnutty ears. 'It's still me inside in here, Beck.' Beck whined at the sound of his voice. He licked the air in front of Liam's face. His tail wavered, uncertain.

The letters of the regiment, RDF, gleamed on Liam's shoulder near a badge that showed a tiger and an elephant mounted on a flaming grenade. Everything he wore was so shiny and stiff and new, it reminded me of when he went away to boarding school. How miserable I was then, being left behind. How happily I'd have gone back, now, and reclaimed that early misery in exchange for this one.

He stood, patted the dog's head, took his place opposite mine and reached for an egg from the dish. Lockie had fixed his sleeves for him, they were just the right length.

Beck pushed himself in under the table and lay down at our feet. I saw all this as through a rain-lashed window. The chat was of the weather, and how it was such a lovely day for a crossing, and could you please pass the salt and would any-one like a hot drop in their tea? There was a soothing, familiar

23

clatter of cutlery on delft, cups lifted and set back on saucers, Beck's snores under the table. I couldn't speak. I was like a girl in a fairytale, under a spell that bound my tongue.

We said our goodbyes in the hall, and kept them short, as Liam had asked. He hugged me hard, as though we'd never fought about his going. 'Behave yourself,' he said, playing the lofty older brother, a game he liked, usually guaranteed to get me riled. He was older by all of ten minutes.

'Why should I?' I mocked, finding my voice at last. It was an act, we all knew it was an act, but we still had to play our parts, because what else was there to do – howl and shriek and cling to him?

'Then be sure and leave nothing out when you write. Write often.'

He looked around, at the false smiles and glittering eyes we'd all put on for his benefit: Dad, Mother, Florrie and Matt. Lockie stood further back, near the head of the stairs leading down to the kitchen, her face in shadow. Eva had said goodbye the night before. I nearly envied her, not having to stand around and watch him prise himself loose from us.

He cleared his throat. 'That goes for all of you. Full reports. Everything.'

I plucked at the stiff, foreign sleeve of his jacket. 'Liam, I –'

'Don't, Katie. I know.'

'I'm sorry,' I managed to blurt out, regardless. 'Be safe.' My fingers had found their way under his cuff to pinch the back of his wrist. Our old signal. He caught my hand and squeezed it, just the once, and he was gone, out into the bright, noisy street full of morning traffic. Dad walked him to the station. It was what Liam wanted. He'd sent his luggage on ahead.

Beck's blue-sheened eyes searched the hall. I got down on my hunkers and put my face in his fur. 'He'll be back.' He wagged his tail, panting in the heat, though it wasn't yet nine o'clock.

'He's only gone for training.' Matt stared through the open door at the empty step, the bright street and the Gardens beyond it, a jarvey passing by. The horse's hooves clopped along, a metronome. 'It'll be over before he has to fight.'

'Please God,' Mother said. Lockie closed the door and we all went our various ways.

Lockie and I went upstairs to strip Liam's bed and turn the mattress before making up the bed for me. It felt like treachery, even though it had been Liam's idea. Lockie watched me wrestle a pillowcase from the bolster. 'Don't fash yourself, girl.'

I couldn't help it – I was all thumbs. She unfolded a sheet and threw me a corner. We made the bed in silence. One of the things I loved about Lockie was that she never wasted words. Everything she did was smooth and large: the way she swept the broad palm of her hand across the surface of the crisp clean sheet to even out the creases, the easy way she lifted the heavy corners of the mattress to tuck in the edges.

'I'll leave you to it,' she said, when we'd finished. She looked around the room, then at me. 'Make the most of it, Katie. He didn't leave it for you to be miserable in. He thought you'd like it.' She swept her hand across the eider-down one last time, though it was perfectly smooth already. 'There's a mirror in the box room, behind the gun cupboard. I'll look it out for you later.'

After she'd gone back down to the kitchen, I moved my clothes from the chest of drawers I shared with Florrie in our room at the front of the house. I carried them, drawer by drawer, across the landing to Liam's room in the back, swapped their contents with his and returned them to Florrie's room. It didn't take long. It turned out there wasn't much in our room that was actually mine.

When everything was laid out and neat in Liam's room, I didn't want to stay there, cuckoo that I was. I should have let Matt have it, after all. I opened the window, as wide as it would go, and went downstairs after Lockie.

October 1914

'Did we make a mistake about the university?' Dad asked me as we walked across town together, on a fine evening early in October.

We were on our way to a lecture about Georgian Dublin, in the Mansion House. It was Dad's idea. 'Should be right up your street, Catkin,' he'd said. He most likely wanted to get me out from under Mother's feet to a respectable, fixed location where he could keep an eye on me to her satisfaction, but I was happy enough to go. There were worse ways to spend your time than thinking about the Georgians and their prosperous city.

How things change. Liam was in a training camp in Dorset. We liked knowing he was safe, but he was keen to get to France, or Flanders, somewhere that mattered. I want to do my part, he wrote in his letters home. To me, he wrote about the boredom and exhaustions of drill. He said he knew there were momentous tests in store; he wanted to get out and face them. The waiting, he said, was what kept him awake at night, in spite of days of more physical activity and fresh air than he'd ever known.

'I'm worried about you, Catkin,' Dad said. 'You spend too much time alone.'

'Far from it, I don't get enough time alone.'

The atmosphere in the house was horrible. Mother and I grated on each other's nerves. She said she wanted to stop me brooding, but I had my own ideas as to what she was at when she devised things to keep me busy. I had got into the habit, whenever I could escape the house, of going on long, aimless walks, and Mother objected. Tramping, she called it. No way for a solicitor's daughter to behave. I wished she'd leave me in peace to walk off my worry and loneliness my own way, but she wouldn't have it. It would give scandal, and wasn't it just absolutely typical of me, to be looking for notice and causing aggravation, when it was Liam we should all be thinking about and praying for.

She insisted I go to lessons in musical appreciation with Florrie, even though I was tone deaf. I'd spent the past week trying to learn the artistic arrangement of flowers from her friend Minnie Whelan, who boasted the best garden in Glasnevin outside of the Botanics. I didn't mind the music so much. I wished I could understand it, since other people got such pleasure from it. I didn't even mind Minnie and her flowers; they were lovely, and the way Minnie talked about them made them interesting. But I did mind having to join Mother's knitting circle every Friday after Mass, making socks and mufflers for soldiers at the Front. I'd ten thumbs when it came to any kind of needlework.

'Go easy on your mother,' Dad said. 'She does her best.'

I knew perfectly well that she was the one who'd objected to my return to college. She'd have stopped me going in the very first place, if she'd had her way, just as she'd prevented Eva from going to the School of Art. I sometimes wondered if she'd regretted that. Eva went on to marry Bartley, a Protestant, despite everything Mother did to try to stop her.

'Is it really the money?' I'd asked Dad, when he told me I couldn't go back for a higher degree.

He went pink in the face. 'It's not the only reason. You'll have to ask your mother.'

When I pressed her, she told me she'd seen Mary Corballis loitering in the porch of the National Library, a dozen laughing men grouped around her. 'What's more, no one seemed to think a thing about it. If that's the sort of carry-on we can expect from university women, you needn't think I'll ever give it my blessing!' She gave me an old-fashioned look. 'No daughter of mine.'

'It's too late. There's no sense talking about it.' I tucked my hand into the crook of my father's arm.

He lifted the hand further in and folded his arm around mine. 'I'll talk to her again. I'll bring her around for next year.'

Next year was too far away to be real. I doubted Professor Hayden would take a second application seriously. We'd arrived at the steps leading up to the Mansion House, where Dad was greeted by several acquaintances. Inside, the hall was nearly full. We found seats at the end of a row near the front.

The speaker, a stocky man who looked more suited to work behind a counter than public speaking, stood off to one side, waiting to be introduced. He shuffled his notes with trembling hands. I sympathized. Just as another man rose to the podium to introduce him, a thin woman dressed all in brown appeared at the end of our row. Dad and I moved up to make room for her. She settled a large bag on the floor, took off her soft hat and stuffed it inside the bag quickly, with no regard for its shape. 'Thank you,' she whispered, under cover of the applause that welcomed the speaker. Her hair was the colour of steel. Dad smiled and extended his hand. 'Miss Colclough! How are you?' He whispered introductions and we settled to listen.

So, there was Liam, off in another country, learning about firearms and explosives and the finer points of drill, and there was I, the youngest person in that room by at least twenty years, listening to a white-bearded antiquarian describe the distinguishing features of the house we lived in – and the thousands of houses like it that characterized the centre of Dublin, remnants of more prosperous times.

Despite my general distraction, I was drawn into the story of the Gardiners, and the development of Mountjoy Square, the next square over from our own. Luke Gardiner had controlled the look of the square by putting covenants in the builders' leases dictating the dimensions and proportions of the houses, the number of windows and types of door, the acceptable style of brickwork. Residents were prohibited from practising certain trades. No butchers, bakers or candlestick-makers. No distillers or soap-boilers either. I wondered what he'd make of those houses now, most of them crumbling and rotting tenements, and the residents lucky if they'd any kind of work at all.

When the lecture was over, we stood off to the side while people filed out. Dad spoke to Miss Colclough, the latecomer. I gathered that she was one of his clients.

'What did you think of the lecture, Miss Crilly?'

I'd been mulling it over. 'It's strange, that something as actual as a street can come out of one person's head.'

'Go on,' she said.

I groped for words to express what was, after all, quite obvious. 'To have vision is one thing, but the self-belief you'd need, to implement it – it seems extraordinary. To have so much – I don't even know the word for it. Potency?'

'What would it require, d'you imagine?' She'd tilted her head to listen. There was a slight squint in her small, lively eyes.

'Well, money.' But that was too easy. 'And – a sense of entitlement?'

'Entitled is right!' Dad chuckled. 'No shortage of titles, in that family. Not to mention wealth and lands. For all the good it did them in the end. Is Miss Wilson not with you this evening, Miss Colclough?'

'She wanted to come but she's been wretchedly ill, she wasn't quite up to it.'

Dad said he was sorry to hear it, and asked her to pass on his regards. I thought we were about to leave, but he told me Miss Colclough was writing a book, about the public monuments of the city.

'I've fallen terribly behind these last few weeks,' she said. 'I don't suppose . . . would you by any chance know of someone who'd like a small job as a research assistant?'

I fidgeted with my gloves. Dad's eyes creased at the corners, making pleats in the skin of his face. 'Our Katie has a degree in history – would that be of use?'

'It might.' She looked at me, longer than was comfortable. 'If it would be of interest to you, Miss Crilly?'

I hesitated. Was she offering me actual work? An excuse to get out and about without Mother breathing questions down my neck? But I didn't think I'd be much use to her. It was only fair to tell her so. 'I don't know the first thing about sculpture, I'm afraid.'

'That makes no matter,' Miss Colclough said. 'I suppose you can learn?' It was a challenge.

'Yes, I can learn.'

We made an arrangement for a trial, the following week.

Mother was livid when we went home and told her. 'Is that the Dorothy Colclough who used to be a radical?' she asked Dad.

'What kind of radical?' I asked. This was what she used to say about Professor Hayden, the most dignified and conservative of all our lecturers.

'Votes for women,' Dad said, smiling, teasing me. 'About as likely as the man in the moon.'

So Professor Hayden and Miss Colclough must know each other. There were several suffrage groups, each with different methods and affiliations, but their paths would surely have crossed at some stage.

'Didn't she –' Mother bit off the end of her sentence.

'"Didn't she" what?' I asked.

'Miss Colclough is perfectly respectable, Mildred,' Dad said. 'I won't hear a word against her. It'll be an interest for Katie. It'll take her out of herself. This book of hers is for the Academy. It's a serious business.'

She didn't look convinced. 'Mind you, don't go bringing any of that suffrage nonsense home with you, Katie. I won't have you turning out like those Sheehy girls.'

On the day we'd arranged, I went to the terraced house on Percy Place, a calm stretch of road on the far side of the Grand Canal, that Miss Colclough shared with May Wilson. Traffic was sleepy and slow there: barges and swans on the water, horses on the towpath. A little further up, the lock could be busy, but their part of the terrace, near the lane, was quiet. Their house was similar to ours but smaller, and of brown brick rather than red. Steep steps led up to their front door over a basement that was practically at street level.

The house belonged to May Wilson, and she was the one who let me in, that first day. Her skin had an unhealthy, yellowish colour, and she moved slowly, but she had kind eyes and lovely hair, perfectly white like the feathers of a swan. The parlour walls were crowded by all shapes and sizes of pictures: drawings and paintings, mostly of buildings and city streets. A collection of tiny exotic animals in mahogany and ivory filled a glass cabinet in one corner, and there were plants on stands in the other three corners and in front of windows.

May declared that we should all be on a first-name footing. 'Otherwise, we'd "Miss" each other always, and we can't have that, now, can we?' She hooted a laugh. I laughed too. She patted my hand. 'But don't you go calling Dote "Dorothy", my dear. She won't answer to it and I can't say I blame her, I wouldn't either. Now, you must come to the area door in future. We do most of our living downstairs, or out in the back garden.'

'Speak for yourself,' Dote said, taking me upstairs to look at the dining room she'd turned into a study. Books were piled in neat stacks on the floor and on chairs pushed back against the wall. A crammed bookcase blocked the double doors that would have led through to the parlour. The table was piled high with folders of notes. Two chairs, one on either side, faced each other across the middle. Historical maps were framed on the walls. 'It looks chaotic, but I assure you I have a system.'

'I've been wondering, would you know Professor Hayden?' I asked.

'Of course! You must have been one of her students. That makes you doubly welcome. You must know the debt your generation owes to her? The future is wide open to anyone with an education. No one worked harder than Mary to bring that about for women.' She sounded wistful.

Dote had hired a cab and a driver to bring us on a tour of the city, as though I were a foreigner. Before we set off, she wrapped a thick green, gold and black tartan rug around May's legs, in case the open air was too much for her.

I admired the strong neck and pricked ears of the glossy chestnut mare which pulled us briskly along. There were so many miserable nags harnessed to carts hauling goods and people around this city – ever since reading *Black Beauty* as a child, I could hardly bear to look at them.

'We hire Mr Dolan any time we can,' May said.

Dote pointed out statues and plaques I'd never paid heed to before, as well as the ones you couldn't miss, like the massive Victoria Memorial outside Leinster House. The figures below her included a dying Fusilier, who leaned his head against Hibernia's thigh.

'What do you think?'

'She seems rather – overblown.'

Dote laughed, getting down from the car. 'She's a buxom one, all right. Come on, we'll take a closer look.'

She linked her arm through May's and we went closer to the memorial. I squinted up at the massive bronze figure of Victoria, curiously spiked and warlike.

'Look at the lines of the minor figures, how graceful they are,' Dote said. 'And the detail, here – see the way the soldier's foot twists under?'

'It'd make you want to straighten it, poor lamb,' May said.

I could just about make out the lettering on the belt buckle: *Dieu et Mon Droit*. I recognized it. 'My brother is in the Dublins.'

'So is my nephew,' May said.

We looked at each other. This was still new to me, the sudden sense of kinship with a stranger that came with hearing they were missing someone too.

'Hubie is with the Seconds, in France,' she said.

'Liam is only in training. He's plaguing everyone he knows for a transfer. He's keen to get to the Front before it ends.'

'Pray he doesn't,' Dote said.

May reached her arm around my waist and squeezed it. She was smiling as wide a smile as I ever saw, but tears stood plain as pennies in her eyes.

When we had clambered back into the cab and were on our way again, Dote said, 'That Victoria commission changed John Hughes's life, you know.'

'How?'

'He gave up his job in the School of Art and went to Paris to make it. He's lived there ever since. It reminds me of what you said in the Mansion House, my dear, about vision and self-belief.'

I was flattered that she remembered.

As the cab brought us around the centre of town and then out along the quays to the Phoenix Park, she talked about the generals and patriots and statesmen the monuments commemorated, and about the men who designed and built them. She told us who had been paid for their work and who hadn't, who'd died before a monument could be completed, who'd made rival bids, what they all went on to do after. She made me climb down from the cab and walk around the statues while she commented on their scale and location. She spoke about them as though they were living, breathing characters who should be as well known to me as members of my own family. 'They're memory-aids,' she said. 'And if we lose our memory, how do we know who we are?'

They didn't feel a part of my memory, not at all. A likeness of Luke Gardiner, whose influence was still visible in the lines of the streets, would have made more sense to me than these dead politicians and generals. But Dote's enthusiasm for the statues and the men who had made them intrigued me. The notion of conceiving an idea and bringing something tangible into the world intrigued me too. There was something here I wanted, even if I couldn't put my finger on what it was.

In the Phoenix Park, we got down from the cab near the Wellington obelisk. The cabman said he'd come back for us in an hour, and left to water the horse. It was a vivid October day, unusually warm. We took a short walk, then spread the tartan rug on the ground and sat on it to watch schoolboys kick a ball around the tussocky grass. The light was glorious. Given one last chance to show off their finery before it was put away for winter, the trees took full advantage and blazed, bronze, crimson and copper, under a high blue vault of sky.

Dote sat on a sketching stool and drew blunt outlines of the obelisk with sticks of charcoal that turned her fingers black. 'Of course, Wellington wasn't liked in Dublin, any more than he liked it, or its citizens,' she said. 'The memorial committee ran out of money in the end. The monument stayed unfinished for years. They never did raise enough to pay for the horse that featured in the original design.'

'How did they finish it?' I asked.

'They held a fund-raising dinner, in the vault. After, they didn't bother to so much as clear the table before they closed it off. Huh!' She'd her own way of laughing, through her nose.

'You mean they left the dishes there, inside the monument?'

'My dear, I mean they left the whole entire table and its settings. Chairs, linen, delft, crystal and all. They closed the vault and sealed it.'

'And it's all still in there?' I wasn't sure whether to believe her or not. I stared hard at the solid stone, as though it could dissolve and reveal the forgotten feast rotting behind it.

'That's not all.' Her voice went thrillingly deep. 'It was months before anyone remembered the butler. No one had seen him since that dinner, and he was never seen again.'

'Did they not think to open it up and check?'

'And spoil a good story?' Dote looked at me over the half-rims of her glasses, her eyes very blue and alive under a charcoal smudge like a thumbprint on her forehead.

'Lucky for him there was food and wine in it, so.'

'Oh, you'll do,' May said. 'She'll do very nicely, Dote. Did you know, pet, we have fourteen nephews between us and not a single, solitary niece?'

It never felt like work, to go to Percy Place. From the outset, I felt at home with Dote and May. Their house was a cosier, more cluttered version of our own. It had the same sash windows, the fan-lit front door, the hall with its internal arch and mouldings, the high window in the stairwell – Dote and May's had stained-glass insets that added chips of colour to their already busy walls. Our rooms were bigger and our ceilings higher, but their basement kitchen was brighter and more open, and included a seating area. It opened directly on to a long back garden that led to a lane. Beyond the lane, longer back gardens led in their turn to the arrayed backs of a grander terrace, everything orderly and in proper proportions.

I wondered how long it had been since Dote and May had entertained anyone for dinner, their dining room had such a feel of a long-established study. The oval walnut table Dote had commandeered was always strewn with an organized chaos of notes, stacks of index cards. My chair faced an array of historical maps of Dublin – maps by Rocque, Duncan and Harvey. The looming black mountains in the last felt ominous, menacing the city. My favourite was the seventeenth-century Speed map, with its child-like illustrations of houses and chapels and arches, the curved boats sketched on the irregular lines of the river before the quays were built, recalling a time when the ground beneath the foundations of this house was most likely swamp, when the houses in High Street used to shake every time a carriage rolled by. I had a degree in history but I'd known none of this 'til I met Dote.

She paid for me to have typewriting lessons. She sent me to the National Library and to the readers' cages of Marsh's Library to confirm details, to the Registry of Deeds to check leases, even to Charlemont House, on my own Square, to establish dates of marriages and deaths. I had walked through the world blinkered, blind to its texture and deaf to its music; now I discovered cities within the city.

I was glad to have things to write about in my letters to Liam. Dad began to ask me to sit with him in his study after dinner, as Liam used to do. He'd smoke his pipe and listen while I brought him up to date with the latest tale from our researches. 'I'm glad you're happy, Catkin,' he said one night.

Was I happy? I missed Liam. I worried about him. I read the war news in the papers every day, following the disasters and reversals of the stalled campaign as best I could. Even while he was still in training, I tried to guess where he was, what he might be doing, at any given time. What kind of danger he might be in. He was never far from my mind. But I did enjoy being useful and busy, and I liked having other things to talk about.

April 1915

The day we got the news that Liam had been killed began like any other. We hadn't heard from him, not so much as a field postcard, for five days. I was uneasy, but it wasn't the first time he'd gone quiet. At breakfast that morning, Dad said five days was no time. He said Liam's silence meant nothing more than that he was busy. We all got up from the table and went about our separate business, not knowing that our life as a family – as that family – was over.

As I walked down Sackville Street towards the National Library under a heavy sky after breakfast, I wondered what, exactly, Liam was so busy doing that he couldn't write to us. I paid scant attention to the flower-sellers at the base of the Pillar, people waiting on trams, newsboys calling headlines, the smell of horses' dung.

Narrower streets stretched off to the left and the right of me, leading through the markets and past smaller, meaner shops to the tenements. Women in shawls and full skirts who sold fruit and potatoes from barrels were already setting out their wares. And as I passed those streets, the traffic, those women – was Liam, in that very minute, crawling through muck trying to keep his precious rifle out of the wet? Playing cards in a dug-out? Taking aim? Lines from his letters scrolled through my mind, evoking their strange images: a grey-coated figure falling like a tree in a clearing, causing birds to clack and flap into a wheeling sky and vanish; the ghosts of leaves tumbling among echoes of snapping branches; mud underfoot and everywhere you looked. Rock-solid mud.

Crossing the river, I glanced upstream at the Ha'penny Bridge, which would have been replaced by the Lutyens Gallery, if we'd had the money to build it. Designed to span the river so the light of the rising and setting sun would spill through its colonnade, it would have been a marvel. People would have come from all over to see it and the paintings it would have housed.

Well. Big dreams that come to nothing are something of a speciality in Dublin. It aspires to be a city, but has the habits of a village.

I went on across the bridge. The tide was high, so the river's habitual stench was subdued by the smell of the sea. The blackish water made small, choppy, charcoal peaks that jostled each other. Seagulls screeched overhead. Clouds rushed together in a bumpy grey sky, trailing threads of would-be rain. To think that all the rivers in the world poured out into one great bowl of ocean – this, the Liffey, making its way to meet all the rivers and tributaries of France and Germany and Flanders, where Liam was. If he happened to be looking at a river now, any river . . .

'Watch out!' A woman with flowers in her hat-band shook my elbow. She scolded a child with a grubby face, thin as famine. 'Gurrier,' she called after him. 'Guttersnipe!' The boy ran, showing us the soles of filthy feet. He must have been frozen.

She turned her attention to me then. 'You should keep your wits about you. That wretched boy all but had his hand inside your pocket.'

I walked on.

I managed to hold the many things that might be keeping Liam busy at the very back of my mind while I worked in the reading room, making notes in pencil from a book propped open on its rest, surrounded by priests and students at the same sort of task. The high domed ceiling put me in mind of a skull, a brain, a mind. What did that make us, the readers?

The *Report of the O'Connell Monument Committee* felt less than meaningless, but I spent all day with it. At half past five, my shoulders aching, I gathered my notes into my satchel and returned the *Report* to Mr Carton at the desk. Dandruff whitened the shoulders of his badly fitting jacket and his breath was meaty, but this man knew more about the holdings of the library than anyone else. I fancied that when the others went home at night, he stayed on, reading his way through the stacks by candlelight. There was no need for a catalogue when he was on duty.

The high windows shivered as I reached him, a sound as though the sky were about to fall. We both looked up. Grey a few minutes ago, the windows had turned black as night. It was about to lash rain.

'Filthy day, Miss Crilly. You should hurry on home. Will you be wanting this again?'

'I've finished with it, thanks. I'll need the Foundation prints tomorrow.' I showed him the request form.

He took it in a thin, age-spotted hand that had the faintest hint of a tremor. 'I'll have them ready when you come in. You can view them inside, in the Librarian's office.'

A massive clap of thunder rolled over his words. My mind flew to the guns on the Continent. It was said that people in some parts of England could hear them across the water. As if he knew what I was thinking, Mr Carton put his dry, papery hand on mine and patted it. 'It's only thunder.'

I swung my satchel to my shoulder and hurried out, down the curved stone staircase and across the beautiful mosaics of the main hall's floor, past the stained-glass windows, all without a second glance. I should have left sooner, to beat the weather, but I hadn't noticed the storm closing in.

Outside, I stood in the shelter of the portico and debated my options for getting home.

A passer-by walking briskly up Kildare Street turned his head towards the library, and stopped when he saw me. 'Katie!'

'Con? Shouldn't you be at the hospital?'

He spread his arms wide, embracing his freedom, the day, even the coming storm. 'Sure, I'm wasted there.'

I had to laugh. There was something endearing about his willingness to show me his vanity. I took it as a sign of friendship.

Con was more Liam's friend than mine. They'd been at boarding school together, they both played rugby and liked to fish. Liam left that school before Con did, but because Con's parents lived in Africa, he often came to stay with us for weekends and some school holidays. Mother had a soft spot for his big-framed good looks and his easy manners. She thought his floppy blond hair and pale blue eyes were angelic and she pitied his artificially parentless state.

Unusually for a Catholic, Con had gone to Trinity. Mother did not hold this against him. All through college he had a standing invitation to Sunday lunch at our house. You'd swear he never had a meal anywhere else, the way Mother used to pile his plate with food and insist he eat up every scrap. She thought he could do no wrong.

Con's set, the Trinity medical students, were wild. I envied their adventures. Liam, who went along on some of them, said they were nothing to write home about — money on horses and dogs, late-night drinking in smoky shebeens — they wouldn't suit me at all. I'd have liked the chance to decide for myself, but it never came.

I left the shelter of the portico and went out to Con. The street bristled, a sound like autumn leaves skittering away from a stiff wind.

There was something dishevelled about him, his coat unbuttoned. Straw-like curls fell across his forehead. He caught my hands in his. 'You're a sight for sore eyes, Katie! What have you been up to, setting fire to all the dry old learnings with that hair of yours?' He gave a loose strand of my hair a little tug.

I hooked the hair behind my ear. 'That's right. Have you come to put them out with your wit?' I turned down the street, towards Trinity.

He walked alongside me, even though he'd just come up that way. 'Have you heard from Liam?'

'Not since last week. Have you?'

'I'm not the best correspondent, I'm afraid. He'll be all right, Katie. It does no good to worry.'

'Don't you dare tell me I could make myself ill, I'm sick of hearing it.' A few angry paces later, I said, more calmly, 'Where have you been?'

He nodded at the windows of the Kildare Street Club. 'Lunch.'

'Long lunch.'

He laughed. 'And where are you off to, might I ask?'

'Home.'

'Would you be amenable to persuasion, distraction, deviation of any kind?'

'What did you have in mind?'

'Supper?'

'I thought you just finished lunch.'

We'd reached the corner. The air shivered and broke open in a sudden downpour. Con gripped my wrist and swept me in under a grocer's awning. I smelled wine on his breath. The world washed away in a storm of water that drummed like stones on the canvas, dripped down my neck and into my eyes. Its fall made a cave of the canopy that sheltered us, hiding us from the world — if the world had been watching, which it wasn't, everyone intent on finding their own shelter.

The street was suddenly empty but for a single, sway-backed horse, ears down and shivering in the shafts of a cart, one hind leg bent as though it had a bad shoe. A tram hissed past. We were surrounded by crates of apples, red and gold and green.

Inside our sudden tent, in the fermenting smell of apples and wine and rain, his warm fingers lifted my hand and turned it, palm up, to kiss the blue veins at my wrist. He gave my arm a gentle tug, bringing me closer to him. How very near he was. I had never stood so close to a man before, face to face and almost touching. I was hot sand in an hourglass, falling, his bulk there to contain me.

A sharp knock rattled the glass. From inside the shop, the grocer, in his dull brown apron, shook his fist at us. 'Mind that window! I'll be having ye, if it breaks. If ye're not buying . . .'

'Making a show of me.' I took my hand back to push Con away and went out into the rain. He let me go.

I kept my head down and hurried home, glad of the storm. It would explain the state I was in, soaked, breathless, loose hair clinging to my cheeks. My mind raced ahead of me.

I'd last seen Con at a supper party. I'd been put beside Danny Tobin, a famous bore, with a plea from our hostess to keep him entertained. I was spinning a yarn and Danny was smiling, loosening, so that I began to see possibilities in him, when I felt a tiny shock, as if something had reached across the table and touched my throat. I looked over at Con, whose face glowed out of the gloom directly opposite me. A candelabra burned between us, more candles on the mantel behind his head. Their light was doubled in the enormous mirror; it blazed around the pale blur of my own face, looking back at me from over his shoulder. I forgot what I'd been saying, turned my face to the plate. Con leaned back in his chair and laughed. Under the table, his foot came to rest beside mine.

But what did it mean? I'd seen Con flirt with other women, seen how they would turn to him, all smiles and glittering eyes. His touch, today, surprised me. There was the ordinary skin of my inner wrist, laid bare. When he turned it over and put his lips to its branching veins, something happened. His breath on my skin. My pulse at his mouth. My mind flowered with thoughts I'd never had in daylight, of other hinged places, how they might open.

Could I give my life over to Con, as Eva had to Bartley? I wasn't sure I wanted to marry anyone. But, if I didn't, what would I do with my life? The truth of it was that I didn't know what a person like me was *for*.

Near the end of Sackville Street, I walked the median, for the slight shelter of the young plane trees. I couldn't wait to get indoors, to run upstairs and peel off my wet clothes in front of the fire that would be waiting for me in Liam's room. Thank God for Lockie.

I'd arrived at the monument to Parnell. Dote despised it – Gaudy Gus, she called the sculptor, and said his conception was nonsensical, that the soaring granite blocks dwarfed everything else, distorted the perspective of a once lovely street, though admittedly the tram-lines had a head start on him there.

May said the figure of Parnell was just like a policeman directing traffic at a crossroads, making the congestion worse. I liked that about it. It got in our way. 'Isn't that the point?' I said. 'Like it or not, we can't ignore it.'

Actually, I liked the entire, solid structure. Parnell stood firm on his plinth, one arm raised, under a golden harp pinned to a soaring granite wall. Liam was fond of quoting the speech the inscription was taken from. I closed my eyes to let the words run through my mind. *No man has the right to say to his country, 'Thus far shalt thou go and no further'*. Liam and I were all for a free Ireland, but like Parnell we didn't believe it was worth shedding blood for. Liam preferred a gradual, planned, parliamentary route – and look, it took him to war just the same.

I crossed the road in front of the statue and moved quickly up past the Rotunda and its gardens, racing the rain, although there was little point, I was soaked through already. I could see the lit windows of our house, caught a glimpse of Matt's face at the downstairs window and waved to him to let me in. I took the shallow steps up from the street in two easy strides.

'You're a lifesaver, I'm drenched!' I said, when he opened the door. He stood still, blocked my way. I could hear voices in the breakfast room; there were coats piled on the boot box. Upstairs a door slammed. 'What is it? What's happened?'

He peered over my shoulder at the rain, then at his feet. His mouth was moving but no intelligible sounds came out of it. My clothes pressed, cold, against my skin. Impatient to get indoors – why would he not stand out of my way? – I turned to see what he was looking at, the sodden trees of the gardens, cowering under a sky as low and billowing as gun smoke. Then I looked back the way I'd come, at the plinth of Parnell's monument. *Thus far. No further.* And I knew.

My legs went from under me then. If he hadn't caught my arm and hauled me upright, I'd have fallen back into the road. 'Let me go,' I said, each word breaking in my mouth.

He held me up. A tram passed. A girl at a window stared out at us. I wanted to be her, to be on my way to wherever she was going, knowing anything but this. If not for the tears in Matt's eyes too, I'd have fought him. I'd have ripped his throat. But I let him drag me inside, and then I was in the parlour and there was Mother, already dressed in full black, receiving callers.

People came and went. Neighbours. Eva and Bartley. Liam's fiancée, Isabel, was away, visiting an aunt down in Cork. Eva sent her a telegram. Florrie's Eugene brought his mother, an enormously fat woman, to console ours. Father Carroll came from Marlborough Street and we knelt on the hearthrug to say the Rosary for Liam's soul. Lockie brought black arm-bands for us all. I stayed close to Dad, who was pale and quiet. If you looked closely enough, you'd see that he was quivering all over, vibrating like a plucked string. Like old Mr Carton in the library. A single idea echoed through the hollow chambers of my head, *No. It's not true. No.*

They passed around the official telegram. No matter how often I looked at the words, I couldn't retain them. DEEPLY REGRET TO INFORM YOU THAT 10557 2ND LT CRILLY ROYAL DUBLIN FUSILIERS DIED OF WOUNDS LETTER FOLLOWS RECORDS OFFICE

It was dated 24 April. Two days ago. What was I doing, where was I when it happened, and why didn't I feel it?

When Mother went up to bed that night, she had the look of someone setting out on a long journey, someone we wouldn't see again for a good long while. Dad said we should all get some sleep if we could, and went after her. Then Florrie went up, and Matt. I sat on, downstairs, unable to face Liam's room with my things in it.

Eva said she'd stay as long as I wanted, but her skin was grey and her eyes looked bruised, and finally Bartley insisted she go home.

I put on Liam's gabardine and went out into the darkness. There was no one about to see me walk to Con's boarding house through the rain that had eased a little, but still seeped and spread through the city. The pavements gleamed wet, as though the old rivers were rising to reclaim their rightful place and banish us. Hundreds of years ago there was just such a flood; people drowned in their own basements. Why would it not come again? I'd welcome the rising water. I'd let it take me.

I'd been to Con's street just once before, with Liam, but I had a clear memory of the exterior of the house, at the end of a cramped terrace, its brickwork stained and damp, fronted by small, barren gardens. The gate creaked when I pushed it open.

The pocked and pimpled unfortunate who opened the hall door leered when I said Con's name. 'Late, aren't ya?' She pursed her freckled lips and looked me up and down, lingering on the damp ends of my skirt, the overlarge coat held tight around me by my folded arms. 'Wait, so.'

I stood under a sputtering lamp in the hall, my mind as hollow as a drum. The place smelled stale, of fried food. My teeth clacked off each other, and I could hear the girl's rough drawl above. 'There's a wan downstairs for ya. In a right state, she is. What've ya done now?'

Con took forever to come to the landing. When he saw me, he hurried down the rest of the stairs and pulled me into his arms. 'I heard.'

I cried then, my mouth open against his neck, howling into the warmth of his skin.

'Stop gawking and bring hot water, Annie,' he said. 'Shush, Katie. We'll have you warm and dry in no time.' The girl went off to where the kitchen must have been.

Con kept an arm around my waist, drew me up the stairs to his room. 'It's not much,' he said. 'I won't be here long.' Then the girl was back with a kettle of steaming water, the handle wrapped in a towel. He took it from her. 'Off with

48

you now, Annie, back to that man of yours. I know you have him hidden in the kitchen.'

She laughed, a gust of onions, and went away.

He eased off my coat, moved an open book from a buttoned leather chair by the fire and settled me into it. My cold, damp clothes clung to my skin.

'Your lips are blue,' he said. 'You should get out of those wet things.'

My teeth chattered, louder than before.

'At least take off your shoes and stockings.'

He lifted the lime-green bedspread and held it up in front of him, a screen, while I rolled my stockings down with clumsy fingers. I took the towel he gave me next and dried my legs with it, spread it over my hair like a veil, let him drape the lurid bedspread around my shoulders. I'd have done anything he said. The one thing I couldn't do was think.

He spread my stockings over the fireguard to dry and poured some of the water into a beaker, added whiskey. He poured the rest of the water into a white ceramic shaving bowl, dipped a flannel in the hot water, squeezed it out and wrapped it around my feet. Then he dried my feet and held them in his two warm hands. All the while, Liam's voice spoke into my mind, retelling a scene from a letter he wrote after his first return from the line: *I feel human again, after a bath. The water was ice-cold. It shocked the breath out of me, but when I got out I felt as though I'd been set alight. When we go up to the trenches again it'll be days before we change our clothes or even get our boots off, although our feet are sodden. Can you imagine that, Miss Hog-the-bath? If there wasn't so much loose metal and other noisome articles lying about, things I couldn't bring myself to mention, not even to you, we might be better off with no boots at all.*

The idea of Liam out there in wet mud with no boots on him made me weep in a dry, shuddering way, as though the rain had found its way inside me and couldn't get out.

My head sank to Con's shoulder. His arms came up around me. He smelled of wood smoke and tobacco. He was warm and solid. I burrowed into him.

'Katie,' he said. 'You don't know what you're doing.'

But I did. I was maybe a little delirious, deranged even – but I knew. I wanted to burn, to hurt, to shatter into a million tiny pieces riding violent winds of flame and ruin.

Then it was a fist, banging the door, that shook the room. Con swore.

'Dr Buckley, you have a woman in there. I won't have it!' The door handle turned, but it didn't open. When did he lock it? 'I want her out.'

'She's just leaving, Mrs O'Reilly.'

'Be sure she does. I'm waiting.'

He ran his finger along the length of my arm, raising the small hairs. 'Maybe it's as well. You're not yourself.' But he was the one who was changed, with a cast to his face I hadn't seen before.

I gathered up my stockings. He leaned back and watched me struggle to pull the damp silk apart with clumsy fingers, so I could put them back on. The door rattled. I rolled the stockings into a ball and put them in the pocket of Liam's coat. My boots resisted my bare feet, but I forced them on, stiff and strange as they felt. I was stiff and strange myself, as though I found myself suddenly in charge of a large doll made of wood, with no notion of how to direct it.

'I'll see you home. They'll be worried.'

'They don't know I've gone.'

Damp and all as it still was, I pulled the gabardine tight around me. My fingers flailed, useless, at the belt. Con leaned in and tied it in a knot. 'Ready?' He opened the door. I made myself blind to the landlady's contempt, stalked past her without a word.

*

We walked the streets in silence, not touching. It was an effort to put one foot in front of the other. I wished him gone, but couldn't say so. I'd forgotten how to speak.

We parted awkwardly, a few doors from home. Instinct sent me through the half-gate and down the puddled steps to the area door, away from the street. Lockie opened the door, sat me at the kitchen table, boiled a pan of milk and gave it to me in a cup, laced with whiskey. I drained it, shuddering at the taste, and then let her lead me up to bed by the hand. In Liam's room, I got sense and sent her away. I fancied I was marked in some way that she'd see. When she was gone, I pulled off the sodden gabardine, the reluctant dress beneath it. I climbed on to Liam's high bed and pulled his covers over my head, wanting darkness. No matter how cold or how dark, I would never, ever, be dark or cold enough.

June 1915

Two months later, on the day that should have been our birthday, the longest day of the year, I spread Liam's letters out on the bed and reread them in the order they'd been written. I knew them off by heart.

In January, not long after he went to the Front, he'd sent a letter to Mother, full of certainty that he would come through the war unscathed.

Half an hour ago, Jerry sent a storm of shells over. I thought I was a goner. I heard a Rumbling Mary come my way – that's a 17-inch shell, in case you don't know – but could I run, or throw myself clear? No, I couldn't budge. You'll think I was afraid, but no. I was up to my knees in mud, gripped as tight as though someone poured a ton of cement on me. I stood there, braced for the worst – and the sound roared right on by. After all that, it was only a field ambulance I heard, straining along a track in high gear. The whole thing over in a flash, longer in the telling than in the happening.

So, you see, my life is charmed. There's no call to worry about me. Our last billet was blown to smithereens not long after we'd left it. That building was hundreds of years old. It's nothing but a mess of old rubble now, yet here I am, still in one ugly piece.

I should have known better than to believe him. He was cheerful for our parents' benefit, knowing his letters to them would be read out loud as soon as they arrived and many times over. They were passed around Mother's sewing circle until the paper wore thin and the ink at the edge of the pages got smudged from too much handling. The letters he wrote to me were darker, meant for my eyes only. A shadow fell on them and deepened as the wet, bitter winter dragged on.

After he died, I went on writing to him in my mind, asking questions that fell like stones into black water and sank out of sight. *What is that silence like, Liam? Is it like knives, or a dark net? What happens there?*

Grief made fools of us all. There was shock in it, but there could hardly be surprise. A young man goes off to war – what do we expect of him? What did we think would happen? For me, belief in a personal, all-knowing, all-seeing God had already become impossible in the face of what was happening on the Continent. There had been shocking casualties in the Dublin regiments alone. Thousands dead. We'd heard that, in the Dardanelles, many of the Dublins were put off their boats into water that was too deep for them. Pulled under by the weight of their packs, they drowned, while Turkish bullets and mortar-fire tore into their comrades and churned the sea red. The gas unleashed at Ypres, around the time that Liam died, was still claiming lives two months later. Every second person on Sackville Street wore a black armband, or a cuff.

Liam had had his own doubts. We'd both read Mr Darwin's book. Now I knew my doubt had been a game I played on the surface of my mind. Liam's death destroyed a deeper faith. It cracked the bedrock of my existence.

His chaplain, Father Fogarty, had written to us to say *Liam was a decent, warm-hearted soul. There's not a man in this company who has not felt the better for a steadying word from him in a dark moment others didn't notice. He'll be missed.*

When I last saw him, earlier that day, he was calm.

We laid him to rest in a small cemetery in N—, with others who fell the same day. A cross marks the spot. I commend his soul to God our Father, who will keep him safe, until that joyful day when we are all reunited. May you find comfort in that certainty. May he rest in peace.

I was struck by the sentence that stood apart. *When I last saw him, earlier that day, he was calm.* As though some truth had crept in behind the lines and waited to be claimed. But then: *fell.*

I'd come to loathe that word; the newspapers were full of it. It masked the raw truth, that men were shot to pieces every day, for no good reason that I could see. In the weeks after Liam was killed, I read the Roll of Honour with a kind of greed, scorning the ordinary 'Deaths' in adjacent columns. Why should some people get more than their share of time, when Liam had had so little? I resented every death that came 'after an illness' or at a person's residence. The Roll droned on, repetitive and numbing: 'Killed in action . . . from wounds received in action . . . from gas poisoning in action . . .' It named regiments and foreign places, words we'd never heard before last year, as familiar to us now as the street names of our own city. Its mournful, murderous pattern drilling us all into a state of numbed submission, along with that sly little word, *fell.* Mother said Liam was one of 'The Fallen', as though it was an honour. She talked about sacrifice. No one had the heart, or the nerve, to challenge her.

Liam had often mentioned Father Fogarty in his own letters. Mother took comfort in their friendship. She imagined that Liam's faith had continued strong. 'It would have helped him,' she said. 'Even in the darkest hours.' That could have been the reason why Liam referred to the priest so often, to console her, but his admiration seemed genuine.

Father Fogarty is as brave as any soldier, he wrote to me. *He's the opposite of the overfed Staffers who strut around and get in our way whenever they come near the Front, which is rare enough. They retreat as fast as they decently can, in their clean uniforms, but Froggy — he's called that not only for his name, but because of his big eyes — will crawl out in the worst fire-storm to pray with a dying man. He has time for everyone, no matter what their persuasion. He's patient with me, with my doubt. Mother would say I've lost my Faith. I think I've discovered*

Reason. Belief in a benevolent God seems a screen, a shield, for children. Whatever you do, don't let her know, it would only hurt her. Time enough for those conversations when I come home.

Froggy says, pray anyway. He says faith might be restored to me. I wish for it every night, going to sleep, wondering if I'll see another morning. Then morning comes and I wish for faith again, wondering will I have safe passage through the light of another day. I wonder, is this wanting a kind of faith in itself? But the gulf between wanting and wishing on the one hand, and belief on the other, is wider than the whole world. To think of it gives me an urge to lay me down, deep in its blackest, most silent depths and sleep, longer than time.

I wrote back to Father Fogarty. If he thought Liam's calm was important enough to mention, there was more to be said. I asked him what he knew.

My letter was returned. I later learned from May that the priest had been killed by a mortar. She showed me a letter from her nephew, Hubie, describing what happened, how grown men wept when his body was carried back.

'Liam loved that priest,' I said. 'It's a shame.'

'You should write to Hubie,' May said. 'He'd appreciate a letter. They all do.'

But it was Captain Hubie Wilson who wrote to us. He told a story about a patrol that went out one night shortly before Liam was killed. *There was a boy with them, Acheson. He'd not been out long. He got separated from the rest, and when they found him he mistook them for Germans and started firing. The rest were furious, as you'd imagine. Liam made a joke of it, saying they should all be grateful the boy was such a rotten shot. He spent some time with him after, giving him sighting and shooting tips. That Acheson is still with us is nothing short of a miracle. He has Liam to thank for it.*

Sometimes I pretended to myself that Liam was still out there, cursing the mud, being kind to new boys, cleaning his rifle. My mind couldn't fit itself around the shape of his absence. I couldn't accept that either of us could outlive the other. We were coterminous, weren't we? Wasn't that what it meant, to be a twin?

As children we often begged Lockie to tell us the story. Liam was born after a stormy few hours, she said, we couldn't imagine the like, the window glass rattling in its frames, a gale moaning down the chimneys and Liam's own noise announcing his arrival – telling it, she made a mewling face and gave a squeaky kitten-cry – and, while the midwife was busy with him, Mother let out a little whimper: *Oof!*

Like the French word for 'egg', Liam said, showing off because his school taught French and mine didn't. I pinched the back of his wrist because I wanted her to keep telling it, and she did.

Your Mammy said, Oh, oh, there's more now, more to come, and the midwife said, That's only the afterbirth, missus, not to worry. She lifted the blankets to take a peek, and there you were, Katie. Like a little cabbage. All curled up tight, you had to be coaxed to open up your very mouth and breathe.

And what did Mother say, when she saw me?

Is that the time? Lockie flicked the question away with a tea-towel and stood up. I'd better shift or there'll be no supper tonight.

Ah, Lockie –

Skedaddle now, the pair of ye. Shoo! She went to the stove and lifted the lid from a bubbling pot. Wreaths of steam rose up around her.

That's French for 'cabbage', Liam crowed. *Choux! Choux!*

I gave him a box.

He roared laughing. She called you a shoe!

What'd that make you, only a big smelly old heel, you toe-rag! I chased him out of the kitchen and caught up with him on the stairs to stamp on his feet. It was all right for him: he was like the invited guest, a place set for him at the table and everyone glad to see him, then realizing that they had to budge up and make space for me too. It wasn't that they were unkind; it was more an unspoken, Oh, yes; there's you as well. Liam brought me along in his wake. My claim to existence was predicated on his.

Since he died, I'd run out many times, in my imagination, to save him. To save the both of us. From his bed, in this very room, I'd woken to a dark so terribly fractured by noise that I sprang from the tangle of sheets, his name ringing in my ears. I'd come back to myself, shivering, my bare feet cold on the wooden floor. Many's the time I turned over in the night to see his silhouette etched against the window, and dived to push him to safety. Sometimes, in a waking dream, I caught the fatal bullet myself, or stumbled from the battlefield, his arm heavy on my neck, his breath hoarse at my ear, begging for water. The ground we crossed in my fantasy changed from the cratered muck he described in his letters to harvest-gold, to green. Sometimes I'd add a farmhouse or two for good measure, Connemara cottages, thatched and white-walled, even though I knew well they were nothing like any he might have seen in France or Flanders. I was trying to get him home, but it was its own kind of betrayal, as bad as any matron spouting guff about the noble fallen, the heroic dead of our generation. I should stop cloaking truth with fantasy and face it. For all the times that, in my mind and in my dreams, I'd run out under fire to snatch him back to safety in the nick of time, for all the fantasy rescues I'd enacted, I'd never change the truth.

I tried to imagine the sounds he would have heard as he died. I tried to see him, along with thousands of other men, 'in action'. Every one of them someone's brother, son, father; loving and loved; trying to kill men just like themselves. Trying even harder not to be killed. I hated to think about what soldiers had to do, the business of bayonets and bombs. I couldn't see Liam in any of it. I tried to call up the smells – cordite, lyddite, dynamite, the lethal gas that entered the war as Liam left it. I knew the words people used to describe them: acrid, bitter, burnt – but how far could words be trusted, when there was so much cant about?

'Katie!' Dad's voice was high and strained. My name cracked and echoed up the stairwell. 'Come down, will you?'

'Just a minute!' I folded the letters back into their envelopes and arranged them in their original order.

'Katie! What's keeping you?'

Some other voice, rougher than my own, answered, 'I'm coming.' My heart thumped. I didn't want him to come looking for me. I'd showed some of my letters from Liam around the family, but there were others I didn't want anyone to see. There were things he'd asked me to be sure to keep to myself.

I put the letters away, under the spare blanket on the floor of Liam's wardrobe.

'Katie!' Dad sounded angry now.

I pulled the door open and made my voice ordinary. 'Here. I'm here.'

The stairwell was cold and quiet, and smelled slightly of damp. The lights in the hall threw fingers of shadow up to meet me. From here, the bald spot on the crown of Dad's head glowed, like the fragile shell of a burnished egg. He threw up his hands when he saw me, and turned back into the parlour, his face a blur.

Despite its tall windows, the parlour was dark. I pressed the light switch on my way in. Colours and furniture sprang up from the gloom. Mother winced, as though the light hurt her.

Mourning suited her. Black flattered her generous figure and complemented her silvery hair and sallow skin. She wore a silver mourning brooch pinned to her bodice. In it, a small knot of flaxen baby hair, incongruous considering how dark and springy Liam's hair later became, was mounted on a folded scrap of paper from his last letter. The paper was the colour of a tea stain, with small squares on it, like a copybook a child might use for arithmetic. The letter had been written in a hurry, it said, on a page torn from his field notebook.

Liam was never one for rushing so much as a cup of tea. He liked to take his time, weigh his options, consider all sides of a question. I was the one who was hurried, impulsive. Careless. In the brooch, she'd preserved two things that appeared to bracket his life, but somehow missed the essence of him entirely.

She sat with her spine clear of her chair, as though there were nails embedded in the midnight-blue upholstery. Her plump hands lay coiled in her lap. She flicked her fingernails off each other, a sure sign that her nerves were in flitters. Her eyes darted towards and away from a squat trunk on the hearthrug.

'It was the one and only thing I asked,' I said, 'that you wouldn't.' Then I saw what it was. Not a birthday present, of course not, but Liam's equipment and personal effects, returned to us.

Dad knelt beside the trunk and fumbled with the latch. When it wouldn't give, he grunted his frustration and punched the side.

'Easy, Bill.' Mother's voice shook.

'Where are the others?' I asked.

She didn't take her eyes off Dad. 'Florrie's at the shops. As for Matt . . .'

Florrie was no great loss, and Matt was most likely hanging

around some stage door or other. It was Eva I wanted, but she was at home, getting over one of her many kidney infections.

The trunk's latch clicked open. Dad lifted the lid. Liam's tunic rose, as though it breathed. A mucky, sickening stench seeped through the room. It coated my tongue, stuck in my throat.

Mother pressed a handkerchief to her face. 'God help us, what *is* that smell?'

Dad lifted a corner of the tunic to look beneath it. 'Let's see, what does he have here? . . . Ah, no. Look, Mildred. The watch is broken.'

I looked over his shoulder. The open face of the pocket watch Dad gave Liam when he went to work for the firm, his own father's gift to him, was smashed, the hands long gone. He groped for it, like a blind man. I knelt beside him and put the watch into his hand, closed his fingers over its face. Then I lifted the khaki tunic and hugged it, never mind the stink. The arms unfolded and hung at an angle, stiff and empty. I let go and the khaki slid to my lap. I pushed it to the floor, rubbed my palms on the rug to get rid of its greasy residue.

With his free hand, Dad took a packet of letters from the box. His knees cracked when he stood and carried them to the chair opposite Mother's. He sat into it heavily, letting out a sound like a groan. He slipped the watch into his waistcoat pocket, where it used to live before he gave it to Liam, and unfolded a sheet of paper from a thick ivory-coloured envelope at the top of the pile. 'Here's one from Isabel.' He might have been going through any morning's post at breakfast, sharing snippets of holiday news.

'*My own darling Liam,*' he began.

Something squeezed my throat. 'Dad! That's private!' Liam's love for Isabel Tierney was the one thing about him

60

that was closed to me, a locked room, but I'd a queer urge to defend it. All the arguments I'd had with myself, fighting the jealousy that Eva warned would turn him against me, crowded into my mind.

Mother was pinching the skin between her eyebrows. 'Privacy's no use to Liam now.'

'*Your letters worry me,*' Dad went on. '*They hardly seem to come from you at all.*'

'Please don't,' I said.

He turned his back on me, holding the paper so as to catch more light. '*We've a lot to talk about when you come home.*'

'What date is on it?' Mother asked.

'March. Here's another.'

I tried to see the envelope in his hand, relieved by a glimpse of ivory What if he found mine? But this was another from Isabel.

'*Why have you not written*' – Dad cleared his throat and went on reading – '*since your leave was cancelled? I feel so cheated. It must be a million times worse for you. Don't let the war change you . . .*' He looked away from the page towards the window.

'What's the date on that one, Bill?'

'15th April.'

'He'd have got it the week before . . . Is there a later one?'

He shuffled through them. 'I don't see one.'

She sagged back into her chair. 'She meant to end their engagement!'

'She doesn't say that,' I said, uneasy.

'She doesn't have to, it's clear as day.'

'No, it's not.' I bundled the tunic back into the trunk, any old way, and stood up.

'Imagine it.' Mother's voice shook. 'And, Bill, she has your mother's ring.'

'They're not our letters,' I appealed to Dad. 'We shouldn't read them.'

He appeared to have aged ten years in as many minutes. 'What should I do with them?'

My mind raced back through letters I'd written, things I'd revealed to Liam that I never would have said to my parents, information about our friends, things I might have said that would reflect back on him – whatever happened, I wanted a chance to see them first, to sift through them and decide what to show and what to hide. It was all wrong, that death had left him so exposed. It wasn't only Isabel I was defending when I said, 'I'll take them.'

'No, give them to me.' Mother's eyes were red. There was a queer little pause, while Dad looked from one of us to the other.

'Don't, Dad. Please. It's not fair.' I held out my hand.

I felt the heat of Mother's glare, but kept my eyes fixed on Dad, willing him to listen. 'People wrote things for his eyes only.' I had to swallow the lump in my throat. 'We all did. You wouldn't read them if he were still alive. You know you wouldn't. Give them here, to me, and I'll get them back to the people who wrote them.' I reached for the bundle of letters. He let them go. I moved away, in case he changed his mind.

'It's none of it Liam. It's a travesty!' Tears stood in Mother's eyes. She dashed them away with the heels of her hands. 'I want rid of it. All of it.' A piece of wood spat a shower of sparks into the grate. She swept something unseen from her lap and got to her feet. 'You may as well burn it.'

'But,' Dad said, looking down into the trunk, 'there are photographs.'

'Does nothing I say matter any more?' She stamped her foot. Everything glass in the room shivered – windows, picture-frames, ornaments, siphons, crystal. 'I said, burn it.' A fierce glance dared me to argue. She rushed out.

'You'd better go after her,' I said.

'But –'

'Go on. I'll deal with this.'

I stretched my arms across the cold breadth of the trunk and tried to lift it, but it was too big, too heavy. My knees knocked off the edges. I took hold of one of the handles and dragged it to the basement stairs. I went down first and pulled it carefully after me, steadying its weight with my body. I'd a sudden flash of Liam, that horrible autumn he went away to school. He bumped his school trunk down the stairs just exactly this way, mimed being knocked from step to step, exaggerated his surprise to make me laugh.

The door to the kitchen was closed. When I opened it, a smell of stock made my stomach even more uneasy. Lockie looked around from the pot she was stirring. 'What is it? You're green as mould.' She looked past me, at the trunk. 'Ah.' She moved the stockpot off the heat and came to help, wiping her hands on a rag. 'Bring it through to the scullery.' She bent to one of the tin handles. I took the other. Between us, the trunk was easy enough to carry through to the workbench.

She made no comment about the row she must have heard, even with the door closed. She said nothing about sacrifice or duty, none of the platitudes I was so sick of hearing. Instead she got to work, quick and efficient. I took the letters and photographs from where they lay on top of the clothes that were so alien, set them aside on a shelf. Then I followed Lockie's lead.

There was muck caked into underclothes, a bloodstained shirt, a pair of stiffened, encrusted socks. Underneath, we found a pile of poorly laundered shirts, a dress-uniform jacket that looked brand new, a stiff leather belt. Lockie brought over a scissors and cut away the badges, the single star from the shoulder and the buttons, the shiny and the tarnished. 'Ye might want mementoes,' she said.

I fingered the shirt. A button was missing, the button hole enlarged and frayed. It told me nothing. Mother was right, none of it felt like Liam. The army could have sent any man's things, one khaki uniform was the same as another. Apart from the letters and the two photographs, we wouldn't know the difference.

He and Isabel had met a commercial photographer one day in the mountains, and had their portrait made as gifts to each other. Liam's slightly prominent teeth were showing, his eyes shadowed by his cap. Isabel's face was alight, as though the sun were shining into it. The other one was of me, with a hand clapped to my mouth. I'd had it made in Lawrence's, with money I'd begged from Eva, and sent it in my first letter after he went to the training camp, last August. I didn't have to turn it over to remember what I wrote on the back, *Little sister, big mouth*. The concession to his supposed seniority was my way of apologizing for the stupid row we'd had before he left.

Not even Liam could claim he was older now. I slipped the photograph into my pocket. I didn't want to explain to Lockie what I'd written. If only I could take back the things I'd said to him as easily.

She put the scissors aside, scooped the buttons and badges from the table to her broad palm, and poured them into an empty tea-tin. The tin was black, decorated with Chinese figures robed in scarlet and gold. A tall woman, the height of a Dublin policeman, she didn't even have to stand on tiptoe to put it on the top shelf, where Mother wouldn't notice it. She stuffed the remaining heap of clothes into an old potato sack while I put the other photograph into a manila envelope.

'It should have been me who died. She'd have preferred it.'

Lockie didn't turn a hair. 'God forgive you, girl.' She slid the envelope into a drawer, as calm as if we were sorting laundry.

The trunk itself looked smaller, an indifferent class of a thing, now that everything remotely personal had been taken away. She edged it into a corner with her foot.

I picked up the letters. 'I'll take these upstairs. Then what?'

'We could bring the clothes around to the nuns, for burning. That way your ma doesn't have to know it's happening.'

'D'you really think we should?'

'If that's what she said. It's fitting. It's no use to him now.'

The sorrow in her voice nearly undid me altogether. 'I'll take them.'

The hessian chafed my arms on the way over to the convent. I was glad of its burn, glad to feel something I could put a name to. Overhead, the clouds were the colour of bone.

A short, elderly nun answered the convent door. 'Of course,' she said, when I explained why I'd come, as if people turned up every day with requests just like it. 'Give it here, I'll take care of it.'

'No. I'll do it.'

The nun tilted her head and considered. 'We'll let Harrison see to it,' she said at last. 'He's outside.'

She led me through dark corridors smelling of beeswax, the walls lined with images of martyrdom and upturned, haloed faces, through a stone-flagged kitchen not unlike ours, and out to the yard, where the hens clucked and scrabbled in their pen. There was a row of sheds at the back, where the man who must have been Harrison sat on an upturned pail. He threw away a cigarette and stood when he saw us coming, a bony man with a weathered, good-natured face under a battered hat.

The nun explained what I wanted.

'Not to worry, miss.' He grinned, revealing dark stumps of teeth. 'There's the makings of a bonfire here already. We'll get a dacent blaze going in no time.' He poured oil on a rag and set it on a pile of kindling. Then he reached for the sack. His hands were grimy, his fingernails black.

I hesitated. 'I'd rather.' Part of me wanted to scream at him to hurry and get this over with, but my hands stuck to the cloth, the way Dad had held on to Liam's letters earlier. The little nun laced her fingers together. Harrison smiled, encouraging.

I gave him the sack. He laid it on the kindling, wiped his hands on the sides of his trousers, struck a match. If we all went up in flames right there and then, that'd put an end to this sham of a birthday for good and all. I fought an urge to howl, loud enough so Liam would hear, all the way across the sea and under foreign fields as he was, his ears full of mud.

The nun pulled a black rosary from her pocket and murmured under her breath, a rolling boil of sounds. The familiar rhythm took over and, despite myself, I gave the responses. When the decade was finished, she kept going, into the Requiescat: *eternal rest . . . perpetual light . . . rest in peace.*

I was melting in a blast of heat, and the whole world with me. Oily blue smoke wavered around my face and filled my lungs. Next, I was sitting on Harrison's pail, my face close to the shifting ground.

'Keep your head between your knees, child,' the nun was saying. 'You nearly fell in the flames. Drink this.' A chipped cup was put into my hand. 'It's water.'

It tasted putrid, as though all the world's filth were in it.

Back in Liam's old room, I put the packet of letters on his desk. This is where I used to sit to write to him, after he left. I'd enjoyed the clear surface, the blank paper waiting to be filled, my pen nestled in its snug wooden groove. It was pure luxury to have space and quiet of my own.

In the room I'd shared with Florrie, and Eva too 'til she

married, there were always pots and jars to push aside if I wanted to use the dressing table, a residue of lotion or powder that would stain the page. Florrie would chat away in the background, no matter that I'd little interest in her latest hatpin, or her friend Glenda's new gloves, or if Eugene thought there might be money to be made from the perfumed creams she spent hours concocting in our room. Such rows we used to have, Florrie and I, about whether we'd have the window wide open or shut tight. She had it all her own way now. Eugene had saved her from the fate of the unpromising spinster daughter – which role now fell to me.

During our college days, Liam's and mine, I used to study at the dining-room table, to get away from her. Liam would come in and distract me with the latest chip of economic or political brilliance from Professor Kettle. Liam and his friends canvassed for him in the election that sent him to Westminster. I posted a few bills myself, I have to admit. He dazzled us all with visions of a fair and prosperous future, a future the best of his followers wouldn't live to see. People said John Redmond was to blame for sending so many off to fight, but it was Tom Kettle who turned Liam's head.

Liam would say no good ever came of blame. The national curse, he called it. Always the pointing finger, the excuse. He'd rather find solutions. It went against reason that men like him should die, while the likes of Florrie's rotund, self-satisfied Eugene were left, to fatten and prosper on piety and platitudes.

Mother was bound to come looking for the letters – my attempts to divert Liam, Isabel's heart laid bare – and I wouldn't be strong enough to stop her a second time. The sooner I got them all out of the house, and told her so, the better. I sat at the desk to sort them.

'Have you read them?' Matt was at the door.

'I thought you were out.'

67

'I'm back. Lockie told me where you went, and why.' He scuffed the rug with his foot. 'So, have you? Read them?'

'Of course not.'

His face relaxed. 'Is there one from me?'

I found an envelope addressed in his backward-slanting hand and held it out to him. He stared at his own handwriting, as if it might tell him something other than what it plainly said: Liam's name, regiment, company. He took it from me slowly. 'He never answered it.' He folded the envelope over, then over again.

I looked at my own hands. There was dirt under the nails, as though grease from the fire had lodged there.

'Before he went, Liam asked me to promise that I'd go into the firm instead of him, if anything happened.'

'And did you?'

'At first. I felt I had to.' He stood free of the door and looked at me quickly. 'He said it was my duty, as fighting was his.' He put the folded envelope into his pocket. 'But then I wrote to tell him I wouldn't. He'd made his decision, I'd make mine.' He let his breath out in a low whistle. 'Mother didn't see it, did she?'

'No.'

'I couldn't do it, Katie. I've no interest in the law, or contracts. It was one thing for Liam – he could keep clauses and sub-clauses and parties-of-the-first-part straight in his head – but I can't. I'd die of boredom.'

'What will you do instead? You've only a year left in college.'

'There's only one thing I'm good at.'

'Ah, Matt. Acting? You can't be serious.'

'Why not?' He glared at me. 'It's all right for you. No one cares what you do in life, you only have to find someone to marry you.'

A great weariness came over me then. I could not have

68

cared less about what the future held, for any of us. 'Was there something else you wanted?'

'So long as you don't bring someone like Eugene into the family, that is.' He was trying to apologize. 'I mean to say . . .' He hooked his thumbs into the armholes of his waistcoat and puffed himself up to twice his normal girth. His cheeks reddened and bulged, and he bounced on the balls of his feet. It was so exact a rendition of Florrie's pompous fiancé that I softened a little. I might even have smiled.

'I mean to say,' he repeated in Eugene's nasal whine, 'Con, now, would be all right.'

I leaned forward and swung the door shut between us. 'Go away now, Matt. I'm busy.'

'What's the matter?' His voice was muffled by the door.

'Go away.'

I listened to his footsteps retreat across the landing and down the stairs.

Con Buckley was the last person I wanted to think about, ever again. I hadn't spoken to him properly since that horrendous night when we got the telegram about Liam. I'd barely even seen him, except for a visit of condolence he paid to the house, and one other time, after the memorial Mass I sat through in a daze. Con was one of the people who came back to the house afterwards, but I barely registered any of them. Their clacking, frightened words washed over me like sounds in the parrot house at the Zoo.

Once, I saw him walking towards me in town, but he turned down a side street before he reached me. I wasn't sure if he had seen me or not. I could hardly blame him if he was afraid I'd launch myself at him, given an opportunity, though the very idea made my toes curl. I never wanted to be alone with him again.

Mother was hurt by his continued absence. Dad said Con

was young, and didn't have the benefit of family to advise him that any awkwardness he felt would pass and that Mother would appreciate a visit. I heard him ask Eva later if Bartley might have a word with Con. She said it was to his credit if he was studying hard for his finals, on top of long, unpredictable working hours; he probably spent every free waking second asleep. But Bartley must have said something, because Con did eventually call on Mother. Whatever was said at that interview, he started to reappear at Sunday lunches.

I picked up the letters and fitted my hands around them, holding them as Liam would have done, cradling them, the fingers just so. The worn paper crinkled and whispered to my palms. I smoothed it with my thumbs. I'd never thought, before, about how a soldier has to carry everything, not just weapons and equipment, but anything he values. Even something as flimsy as a letter might tip the balance, drag him down. But they'd been precious to him. He wrote as much, in his own letters to me. *Keep writing to me, Katie. Letters are the lit windows between our two worlds. They remind me of all I used to be. Hold a place for me – the Liam you know, not the filthy, weary, war-stained wretch I've become – in your mind.*

I dealt the letters out across the desk, like playing-cards. They were easy enough to sort. Eva's curled handwriting flowed out to the borders of her blue envelopes. Mother's were addressed in careful capitals. Isabel used a distinctive, thick, ivory-vellum paper and a broad-nibbed pen. Her envelopes had been sliced open cleanly by a blade, as though to preserve as much of her as possible. All the others had been ripped, as with an impatient finger.

I scraped a brownish blot from an envelope with a fingernail. A shred of paper flaked off and fell to the desk, like a piece of dead skin. I picked it up with the tip of a finger, put it on my tongue, swallowed. It had no taste. When we prepared for our first Holy Communion, Liam and I used tiny pieces of paper to practise receiving the Host, so that when the real moment came we wouldn't pollute it with our teeth, an offence that would banish us to hell, forever and ever, amen.

I looked at Isabel's letters. If I read them, I felt certain, I'd be able to tell Mother how wrong she was. I could set her mind at rest. I was curious about them on my own account too. They'd reveal a side of Liam I didn't know.

And had no business knowing.

A draught chilled my neck. Something stirred in the corner of the room. I looked around. 'Matt? Is that you?'

Nothing. But when I turned back to the letters, I sensed it, not so much a shadow as a density. It came to me, as if I'd heard him say it, that Liam was waiting to see what I'd do with Isabel's letters.

The only actual sound in the room was my own breathing. I stood up, took my black mantilla off its hook, wrapped her letters in it and knotted the corners. There.

I risked another peep into the corner. My vision blurred, conjured a pair of big, callused soldier's feet crammed into my rabbit-fur slippers. They'd be ruined.

The feet withdrew. Several toes had poked holes through the ends of a nasty-looking sock, worse even than the ones I'd burned earlier. The lumpy kind I might have knitted, or inadequately darned, during one of Mother's sewing circles. The toenails could have done with attention.

I blinked and they were gone.

The house stirred. Our parents were moving about. A drawer in their room creaked open, then shut. I knew the one, it was where Mother kept her shawls. My heart beat hard, like someone knocking; someone in pursuit and me not wanting to be found. Get the letters out of here, be quick.

I left the letters from Florrie, Mother and Dad on the desk and put the rest in my satchel. Then I went to the wardrobe and took out my own precious hoard, his letters to me. I put them in my satchel with the others and buckled its worn leather straps. Then I bolted downstairs and out of the house, calling a message to Lockie I knew she wouldn't rightly hear.

It was good to be out in the air again and walking fast, shaking off that queer attack of nerves. But where to go – where would the letters be safe, who could I trust? Isabel was still in Cork with her aunt. I'd no intention of handing her letters over to anyone else at her house, where, for all I knew, they'd make as free with them as Mother would, given a chance. I was sure Eva wouldn't read them, if I asked her not to. But I didn't want to make trouble between her and Mother.

I needed a safe place to store Isabel's letters to Liam, and Liam's to me. I'd a vision of Mother on a rampage, in search of them – dragging the covers off the bed, tearing feathers from the pillows, hurling drawers to the ground. The look in her eyes, earlier, reminded me of how she went on when Eva married Bartley, filling the house with priests and sodality women and endless decades of the Rosary. We had to spend hours on our knees, praying for Eva to see sense and for Bartley's conversion. Then she sneaked Alanna off to be baptized, all of us sworn to such secrecy, you'd swear we were still in Penal times.

The best place for the letters was with Dote and May, in Percy Place. I wished Liam could have known them. They'd mind his letters, just as they'd minded me, coaxing me through the first dull weeks after he was killed, when I was no use to anyone.

A woman in bulky tweed loomed in front of me, jolted me out of my thoughts. She pressed a sheet of green paper into my hands. Littered with emblems and exclamation marks, it urged me not to fraternize with my Nation's enemies.

Furious, I glared at her. She had big yellow horse-teeth on her, with a wide gap in the middle. I tore the handbill in two and gave it back to her. A tall girl with a haughty tilt to her dimpled chin came over. 'Miss Crilly,' she said, in a pleasant enough voice. I knew her. Muriel Cox. She was a friend of Matt's.

'Does my brother know what you get up to, Muriel?'

She flushed scarlet. 'Matthew agrees with us.'

'Does he, now? He doesn't say so at home. You should mind out who you foist your rubbish on!'

The tweedy woman's gappy teeth bit down hard on her lower lip. Muriel's heavy eyebrows made a single black line across her forehead. Her small blue eyes sparked. 'Fay didn't know who you are. She didn't know –'

'How d'you ever know?' If hatred alone could kill, the pair of them would've been flat out on a slab. 'You couldn't throw a stone around here without hitting someone mourning a soldier. What gives you the right?' Self-conscious now, my words rang false in my ears, even as a couple of old ladies jeered their agreement. I pushed past Muriel and her ugly friend, sick to death of people telling other people what to think, what to believe, which side to take. How was a person supposed to make up her own mind with all that getting in the way? They were so convinced, that was it, as though they understood the world and their place in it. I didn't under-stand a thing. Maybe they were right, and the rest of us couldn't be trusted to make up our own minds about any-thing, not even what clothes to wear. If not for Lockie taking mine away and putting out fresh, I'd still be in the same things I'd worn when Liam was killed.

I'd reached the river. It flowed and eddied and reversed, drifted one way, then the other, rose and fell. I was bone-tired of a sudden. The satchel grazed my hip, the strap burned my shoulder, the letters getting heavier with each step. Rest and peace were what I wanted. I'd go to Eva first.

Eva and Bartley lived at the blind end of Ely Place, around the corner from Stephen's Green.

Bartley opened the door. A face like thunder on him changed to surprise. 'Katie!'

I was equally surprised. I'd been braced for Nan, their general servant, who could be spiky as a wire brush when she felt like it.

He stood back to let me in. 'Eva's upstairs, at the front.' They had their house arranged with the bedrooms at street level, and the sitting rooms upstairs to give a better view. He took a closer look at me. 'What's happened?'

I put my hands to my hot cheeks. 'I walked fast.'

He closed the door and gestured for me to go up ahead of him, a doubtful expression on his face.

'Are you expecting company?' I asked. 'If it's not conveni-ent, I'll come again.'

'Not at all, come on up. You're really remarkably flushed, Katie.' He'd be reaching for my pulse next.

'There was a row at home.' I patted my satchel. 'Liam's things came. I'm returning Eva's letters.' I went ahead of him upstairs and into the parlour, with its view across the orchard to the leafy well of the Green, its colours deeper for all that recent rain. The window was open a crack at the top. Rich brassy notes flashed through the afternoon over the solid *parrump!* of a drum. In my mind's eye I saw the bandstand in the park, the women in their brightly coloured dresses sitting on deckchairs, men lounging beside them in dark overcoats, the mossy grass studded with daisies. As if no such thing as war existed.

'What's wrong?' Eva moved to stand up when she saw me,

but I waved her back down and bent to kiss her cheek. She was pale as parchment, doing her sewing, her feet propped on a low stool. A basket of mending was on the floor beside her.

'What's happened, is everyone well?'

How quickly we expect the worst, now. 'Yes, everyone's fine.'

The alarm faded from her face. I dropped my satchel on the floor near the basket and sat into the chair beside hers. 'Liam's things came today. I brought some for you. Letters you wrote him.'

Her eyes went watery. I took her hand and waited for her to get used to the idea. It was only a week or so since I'd seen her, but she looked thinner.

'What else was there?'

'His uniform. Photos. Some books. We saved a few odds and ends.'

Bartley went to the window and looked out. I wished he'd leave us alone so I could talk to Eva properly, tell her all that had happened. She might have been delicate, but she wasn't made of glass. 'You should come round when you're better and see if there's anything else you want,' I said. 'Ask Lockie, if I'm not there. We'd to hide everything, from Mother. She – well, she was upset.'

'How's Dad?'

'He's minding her.' I let go her hand and pulled the satchel over. Sunlight fell on Eva's face and lit her skin so it glowed like the soft wax at the wick of a candle. Her eyes were soft too, at the corners, her face a little blurred. She might have been a figure in a painting. If I'd been asked what name to give it, right there in that moment, I'd have said Love. It was a mystery to me, what she saw in Bartley, but I couldn't doubt that she loved him. Or else it was Eva herself who was Love, and always had been. Something soft and easy went out from our house with her, when she left.

'Mother's on the warpath,' I said. 'She wanted to read them.'

'Surely not.'

'You're in a draught there, Eva.' Bartley pushed the window up and stood with his back to us, looking out. 'Excuse me.' He threw me a look that was practically a wagging finger, warning me not to upset her, and left the room.

Eva sighed, looking after him.

'What's wrong?'

'Con Buckley is in trouble.'

My stomach clenched. 'Is that who Bartley's expecting?'

'He promised Mother he'd keep an eye out for Con during the rest of his training. I wish she hadn't asked.'

'What kind of trouble?'

'Some drama with his landlady. She made a complaint.'

'She's a vile creature.'

Eva turned as still as stone. 'How would you know?'

'He says so.' I lifted one of Alanna's nightdresses out of the basket and examined the smocking, pleating and unpleating the material. My mind raced through the disasters that loomed if Con had got into trouble because of me.

Eva turned her attention back to her needlework. 'She may have had reason.'

'Why don't you like him?' I wasn't sure why I was defending him, unless it was because I knew Liam would.

She tied a careful knot in her thread and cut off the ends, then looked right at me. 'I know things you don't.'

'I know enough!'

'Katie.' Eva leaned over and tugged my sleeve gently. 'What's all this? I know you're friendly with Con, but –'

'He was Liam's friend, Eva. Have you forgotten?'

'Of course not! Why do you think we –'

'Bartley's hard on him. He told me he took his studies seriously this year.'

'I should hope so, for his finals. He'll know all about hard work once he's an intern, come the summer.' She held out her hand for the nightdress. 'It'll be the making of him.'

I gave it to her. 'Why do you do your own sewing?' How anyone would volunteer for such torture was a mystery to me. Stitching on buttons and ribbons was the height of my capability.

'I like it.' She stroked the fabric and smiled. 'I like making things for them. You'll see, when you've a family of your own.'

I stood up and went to the window. A boy on a bicycle wobbled past on the street below. He lost his balance, and the bicycle keeled over at an angle, but the boy thrust his foot to the ground, just in the nick of time to break his fall. He made a few hops, straightened the bicycle, turned it and came back, all elbows and knees. The narrow front wheel jerked from side to side. It looked difficult to master, but think of the freedom it would bring. Mother had forbidden me to try.

'It's good if Con has changed his attitude to work,' Eva was saying. 'But, Katie, a person could waste a lot of time waiting for someone like him to take matters seriously.'

'Lockie likes him.' I turned around.

Eva's wide grey eyes were hard to look at. 'Lockie isn't right about everything.'

'No more are you.' I glanced back at the street, just in time to catch a glimpse of the bicycle boy's back as he sailed along towards the main road, straight as a die. Then he was gone.

Eva knotted a thread and cut it. 'Well, that's that.' She folded the nightdress back into the basket and started to look through the other garments. 'Alanna will be up from her nap any minute, and we'll have tea.'

Quickly, I told her about the trunk, the letters and photographs, Mother's reaction to Isabel's letter. The door opened and Alanna came in. A long, thin child, she glided over to Eva like a little nun. Her fine brown hair was gathered into high bunches that fell to rest on the navy-blue shoulders of her velvet dress. She leaned against Eva's leg and looked at me.

I smiled at her. She leaned further back, into the hollow of her mother's shoulder, and the two of them rocked in unison, side to side. It was mesmerizing, as though they were one person.

Eva sat up straighter. 'Say hello to your auntie Katie.' She kissed the top of Alanna's head. 'Then go down to Nan and tell her we'd like some tea, please.'

When Alanna had gone, I gave Eva her letters. She held them in her two hands for a moment, as though weighing them. Then she chose a piece of green silk from her mending basket to wrap them in, got up and moved stiffly to the corner cabinet, unlocked it and put them inside. 'I'll read them later.'

When she sat back down and lifted her feet to the stool, her skirt slipped up her leg. Her ankles were swollen and puffy. She caught me looking. 'I know, aren't they a fright?' She settled her skirt.

'Why are they like that?'

'Fluid.' She shrugged. 'Don't ask what, because I don't know.'

I was a pig. I'd been so consumed by my own concerns, I'd forgotten to ask anything about hers. 'How are you feeling?'

'Better. Tired, but not exactly ill. You know. The usual.' She lifted her shoulders in a half-shrug and went back to her mending. I watched her darn a cuff. She'd always been delicate, prone to these kidney attacks, and she avoided talking about them, saying that while she was ill she hadn't the energy, and when she was well she didn't want to dwell on them. I'd seen her skin turn translucent, her veins rise to become visible rivers on the map of her arms as she burned and shivered in the bed we'd shared, whimpering with pain. When the attacks began, I'd move to a nest of blankets on the floor. I'd tried to sleep with Florrie once, but she was a violent sleeper, tossing and kicking in the narrow bed. She fought me for the blankets, and in the end she'd shoved me out on to the cold floor.

'I don't know why Mother's turned on Isabel,' I said, to break the uneasy silence. 'She's beautiful.' I counted her virtues on my fingers. 'Her father's a judge, she made Liam happy.' I swallowed a lump in my throat. I'd had trouble with that last item myself, as Eva well knew, being the very one who'd pointed out my own jealousy to me.

It happened the day I got a curt, cold letter from Liam, not long after he went to the Front. *Katie, If you can't behave like a sister to Isabel, leave her alone. I won't forgive you if you cause trouble. You know full well I've my own good reasons for deciding to enlist, whether or not you agree with them. You belittle me if you think I'd put on a British uniform – any uniform – 'just to keep her father happy'. Why would I make Isabel's father happy at the risk of hurting her? She objects to this war just as much as you do, if on different grounds. Put this right, or I'll not speak or write to you again.*

He was so annoyed, he hadn't even signed it. I practically ran the whole way across town to push the horrible page into Eva's hands, demanding that she read it. Her reaction disappointed me. She folded the letter calmly and gave it back to me, reminding me that Liam intended to marry Isabel and I'd be wiser not to make trouble for myself. She advised me to apologize, but, as it happened, Isabel's apology came first, a sweetly flowing note inviting me to tea. *I don't know what got into me, I was afraid there was truth in what you said, don't be angry, can we not be friends?*

We were going to be sisters, after all. And we both wanted the same thing, didn't we? A small, simple thing, for Liam to be safe and happy.

*

Alanna came back with Nan, who carried tea on a tray in her big red hands. She'd a man's shoes on her feet, with no laces. The tray held bite-sized pieces of ginger cake and slivers of apple on a plate for Eva, ham sandwiches and a plain sponge for the rest of us.

'Is that all you're having?' I asked, when Nan had gone out again.

'It's all I can stomach.'

Alanna sat on the floor and played with paper dolls.

'I'll be mother,' I said, pouring tea into cups, adding a sliver of lemon to Eva's, milk to my own. I poured a cup of milk for Alanna.

Eva folded the tabs of a paper ballgown around the flat sides of a doll. On the floor beside her, Alanna sorted through a variety of paper capes. I picked up a different doll, in a Red Cross uniform, with a cape and a starched hat on her head. I opened the tabs and took off the doll's clothes, folded them away. Underneath the uniform, the cardboard doll had her full complement of underclothes: petticoat and stockings, frilled knickers. I took them all off to find a final layer of underclothes painted on, a little chemise, frilled longjohns. The doorbell rang, startling me. When I looked up, Eva was watching me. 'See if it's him,' she said.

I got up and looked out of the window, down on the head and shoulders of a shawled woman. 'It's a beggar.' I heard the front door open, an exchange, and the door shut again. The shawled woman turned and sat on the step. A short while later the door opened and Nan went out and gave her something in a twist of brown paper. The woman folded it away under her shawl and left. I turned back into the room.

'Con is not right for you, Katie, if that's what you're thinking,' Eva said quietly, so as Alanna wouldn't hear.

'Is that a fact?'

'I'm serious. You'll have to take my word for it.'

'Why should I? You did exactly what you wanted, no matter what anyone said.'

'What's all this?' Bartley stood at the door. Alanna tilted her head and slid two fingers into her mouth.

'Never mind,' I said. 'I was just leaving.'

On the way to Dote's house, I shook off my unease about the conversation I'd had with Eva, before she started on about Con. I didn't know why Mother suspected that Isabel had intended to end her engagement to Liam. She could hardly have forgotten the day, not four months ago, when Isabel came to the house in a state and asked if there was any way to have Liam recalled from the Front. I certainly hadn't forgotten it. It was like a scene from a play, with Isabel standing in the centre of the room, pleading, and my parents setting their faces against her.

We were in the parlour with the fire lit, a dismal day. Mother was knitting a sock, on three needles. Her clever fingers flew; she didn't have to watch them. But, as Isabel spoke about a change she detected in Liam's letters, the needles faltered and Mother had to stop to count her stitches. When Isabel asked if Dad would write to Liam's CO, and make a case for having Liam sent home on leave, Mother gave up the attempt at knitting altogether. The abandoned sock was a sorry, shapeless puddle of beige wool, the needles pointing every which way in her lap. She demanded to know what, exactly, Isabel was trying to insinuate.

I wanted to know myself. I was as shocked as Mother by the suggestion, but, at the same time, a small flare of hope sang in the back of my mind. What if Isabel was right, and it was possible to have someone recalled from the Front? Just because I'd never heard of such a thing didn't mean it never happened.

Isabel spoke slowly, pronouncing each separate word

carefully but in a low, toneless voice, as though afraid of losing them. She said she was worried that Liam was suffering a kind of fear.

Mother reared back at that. 'I've heard enough.' She got to her feet, her assorted needles loose in her hands. 'I'm disappointed in you, Isabel. I thought you were made of stronger stuff.' She gathered up the half-made sock and the ball of wool from its place under the cushion, wound it all up into a lumped and spiky ball and pushed it into her sewing bag.

'It's not possible, my dear.' Dad spoke gently enough, but he looked disappointed too. 'Out of the question.'

'Oh, I'm sure it's not out of the question, for people with influence,' Isabel said bitterly. 'I'm sure my father could arrange it, if I asked him.'

'I forbid it, absolutely!' Mother said. 'My Liam knows his duty; he'll perform it to the utmost. Our duty may seem a lesser one, less clear to some,' the flash of her eyes veered towards me, then away again, to where Liam's face smiled at all of us from its peaceful silver frame on the mantelpiece. 'But it's perfectly plain to me. *Our* duty is to honour his courage with our own. I can't quite believe you think so little of him.'

Isabel cast a desperate glance at me. I spread my hands, palms up. I didn't know what she wanted me to do.

'I should go,' she said.

I followed her out. In the hall I found her struggling with her coat. I took it and held it open for her, guiding her arms into the sleeves.

'Will you say anything to your father?'

'No.' She fixed the collar of her coat and fussed with the buttons, avoiding my eye. 'I wish I could, but I won't. Liam would never forgive me. He'd hate me for it. I'm such a coward. I wanted your parents to do what I'm afraid to do myself.' Tears rose in her eyes. 'You don't understand, Katie. Liam is your twin, you've shared every second of your life with him. Nothing can take it away from you. But *our* life is all in the future. What if – what if it never happens?'

Shocked, I let her go. 'Don't even say it!'

She slipped the latch of the door and went out into the street.

'Isabel, wait!' I went after her, but the fog came down like a murky brown wall between us, and Mother was in the door, calling me back, the light from the hall a blurred yellow radiance around her.

'Such timing,' said Dote in her rich, gravelly voice, as she opened the door to me at Percy Place. 'The kettle's on.'

'Your kettle is always on.' I let the satchel strap fall from my shoulder and put it down. 'Do you mind if I leave this here for a while?'

'Is it heavy, pet?' May was in an apron at the kitchen table, which was spread with newspapers. She'd a row of plant pots in front of her and was spooning soil into them from a small zinc bucket, three clay pots of vivid red and pink flowers on chairs beside her. 'I told you, Dote. It's not right to have the girl lugging reams of notes around.'

I hesitated. 'That's not it. I've Liam's letters in there. My mother is looking for them.' I felt as though I were making my way through a cold incoming tide, up to my chin in water, testing the seabed with each tentative step, expecting it to shelve away any minute. 'I've brought them here for safekeeping.'

Dote and May exchanged a look.

'They're letters he wrote to his fiancée – and to me. He asked me to keep them safe.' My cheeks burned, but every word was true.

'Leave them upstairs in the dining room,' Dote said. 'Along with the notes. They'll be safe there.'

I knew it, and I was grateful. I brought the satchel upstairs and stowed it in a corner, out of the way. It looked perfectly at home there, unremarkable. Relieved, I hurried back down to the kitchen, where Dote was scalding the teapot and May had resumed her peculiar business with the soil and the spoon. I felt a huge wave of affection for them both, and all the differences between their house and ours.

'What are you doing?' I asked May.

'She's repotting her geraniums,' Dote said. 'Really, May, how are we supposed to have tea, with the table smothered in dirt?'

'Cleanest dirt there is. We can go outside to eat.'

'Isn't that just typical,' Dote grumbled. 'The plants get the furniture and we have to fend for ourselves outside.'

'Al fresco! Nothing better.' May stood up and wiped the palms of her hands on a rag, then on her apron, then through her flyaway hair. 'And no time like the present. Come on outside with me, pet. Fresh air – it works wonders.'

Going home that evening, I took a tram as far as the Pillar. I was too tired to walk. I didn't feel like talking to anyone when I got in. I was too tired to eat. I asked Lockie to tell my parents I'd given Liam's letters back to the people who wrote them. Hoping to be left in peace, I brought a mug of cocoa upstairs to bed with me, but before I'd time to drink it I fell asleep.

PART TWO

Easter Monday, 24 April 1916

Liam's anniversary, and the sun came up beaming.

I was to meet Isabel later and bring her to Percy Place for tea with May's nephew, Hubie Wilson, who'd been discharged with wounds and was on his way home to Mullingar from a military hospital in England. But, first, there was the anniversary Mass to get through. I crossed the landing to Florrie's room, looking for company. She was propped up on her pillows, rubbing cream into her neck. The room reeked like a flower shop, worse even than when I'd shared it with her. Something sickly sweet, gardenia or lily, predominated.

'A year today,' I said.

'I know.' Some unease flared in her face. Of course she knew – hadn't she been counting the days until she could marry Eugene Sheehan? They'd settled on the first Friday in June, six weeks away, for a bit of distance from the anniversary, but the presents had already started to arrive: linen, silver, Waterford this, Belleek that.

I went over to the window and looked out. A flaw in the glass, the hint of a curve, suggested water, but it was a good-looking day. Young leaves shone on the trees across the road, amid hints of colour that the sun would tease out later: white, cherry-pink, burnt-orange. They were wasted on me.

Down on the street, two skinny dogs, a whippet and a reddish mongrel missing a tail, fought over some bloody-looking scrap. They lunged at each other, pulled apart, attacked again, their faces mashed up close and snarling. Soon the scrap, whatever it was, split apart. A splinter of bone emerged, white as a moon, and the mongrel loped off with it. The whippet limped in pursuit. What was a well-bred dog like that doing loose on the streets?

I traced the warp in the glass with my finger. Once Florrie was married, the rest of us would pack up in earnest. Dad had finally agreed to move to Kingstown, near the sea, where the air was better and the neighbours would be more to Mother's liking. He said there was nothing to stay for.

There was everything to stay for. We were born in this house. Its traces were in all our memories, as we'd left traces in it. Inflections of our grandparents' voices lingered on the landings, came out at the end of Dad's sentences and were echoed in my own. Our footsteps had smoothed the floors, worn away the centre of each stair. Old slams were stored in the doors.

My reluctance wasn't only sentiment. Suppose there'd been a mistake and Liam came back – how would he find us, if we'd moved? It could happen. Or suppose a final letter had gone astray. Suppose it turned up in a French farmhouse or a Belgian church, months or even years from now. It would be delivered to this address. 'Not known', the new householder would write on the envelope. 'Return to sender'.

'Strange to think we'll all be gone from the house, come the summer.'

I turned around to see Florrie busy with two halves of a lemon, a knife and a bowl, just about balanced on a wooden tray. 'And I'll be in my own brand-new, spanking-clean house. No draughts, imagine!' She'd scooped the pulp from the lemon while I wasn't looking and a dome of yellow rind now cupped both elbows. She held each in place with the opposite hand. 'Be an angel, Katie?' She pointed her chin at the tray, then at the dressing table.

'What's this, now?'

'Bleaching my elbows.'

I pushed a clutter of creams and lotions aside to make

room for the tray in front of the three-sided mirror and caught a glimpse of my hair, flattened on one side where I'd lain on it. I unpinned it, worked my fingers down through the length of it and took up Florrie's hairbrush to give it a good going-over.

'I wish you wouldn't use my brush,' she said.

'I'll clean it when I'm finished.' I let my head fall and the hair with it, nearly to my knees, brushed the underneath with long strokes. It crackled and sparked. I swung it back up again and tamed it with the brush, made an effort to smooth it with my palms.

Florrie watched. 'Have you heard anything about Con lately?'

'I saw him at the Concert Rooms the other night. Why?'

She inspected one of her lemon elbow-caps. 'Glenda saw him there too. She said he had Helen Stacpole on his arm.'

'And?'

'Mother thought that maybe you and he . . .' She let the unfinished sentence hang between us.

'No.'

'I thought so too.' She stopped fussing with the rind and looked at me. 'Did something happen between you?'

Nothing had happened. We'd been awkward with each other when he joined us for Sunday lunches, but before long he led us back to the easy manner we'd had before. He ignored my silences and averted face, made bad jokes, found and met my eye, treated me as a friend. If a person can court friendship, that's what he did throughout that summer. He may not have wanted me, but he liked me, and he let me feel his liking as a kind of balm to my pride. So the shame left me.

Somewhere in the back of my mind I stored away an idea that if he changed his mind and came looking for me, I wouldn't turn him away. I knew what other people saw in him, different and uncomplimentary things, all true enough. But I'd seen something that went beyond his links with Liam, a thing that was equal to something in me.

Helen Stacpole was the shy, only daughter of doting and wealthy parents. I'd met her at some of Eva's charity bazaars. That night in the Concert Rooms I watched them for a while, unnoticed. Con guided her through the crowd, holding her elbow. I couldn't see the attraction. She'd so little to say for herself, she was sure to bore him rigid inside of ten minutes. Good luck to them.

I cleared strands of my hair from Florrie's brush and swept them into the waste basket. 'Will I wash this?'

'I'll do it.' She detached one of her elbows from its yellow cup, then the other, picked bits of fruit from her skin. 'Your turn will come, Katie. You'll find someone, don't worry.'

Liam stirred in my mind. He'd said the same; now his turn would never come. The normal progressions and milestones of family life would always snag on the ugly nail of his absence.

'I don't know that I want to.'

'You will.' She stopped picking at her elbow and wiped her fingers on a piece of flannel. Then she stretched her arms up over her head, rolled her neck, sighed a happy sigh. She was plump and smooth and soft-looking. Mother might have been like this, in her time. Nothing at all like me, or Eva, both of us thin as rails with long necks and pointy chins.

'I hope Eva's better today,' I said. 'I wish we could visit. Bartley's a scourge, saying we can't.'

'She's resting, Katie. Don't go on about it.'

Eva was in a nursing home, convalescing after a serious kidney infection, and here was Florrie giving me filthy looks, all that kittenish contentment and sisterly concern evaporated. She and Mother had a dread that Eugene's people would get wind of a constitutional weakness and call off the wedding. We had ghosts in the family who were never mentioned: Mother's sister, Abigail, who had died in circumstances we weren't allowed to know, and two infant brothers, born after Florrie. Neither lived longer than six months. Eva had had more than her share of miscarriages too, each leaving her more drained and sad than the last.

I lifted the blankets at the end of the bed and sat in under them, facing Florrie top to tail, the way I used to sleep beside Eva in the days when the three of us shared this room. Before Eva got married and left. Before Liam went off to be a soldier and lent his room to me. I nudged Florrie with my toes.

She jerked her legs away. 'Your feet are freezing!'

'It won't be *my* cold feet putting the frighteners on you, in a few weeks.'

'Katie!' Her face and neck flushed scarlet.

'Are you nervous about getting married?'

'Why would I be?'

I nudged her again. 'You know. After.'

She clamped her lips together so hard they all but disappeared. 'I don't want to talk about it. Neither should you.'

I gave her a swift kick and got out of the bed.

Back in Liam's room, I lifted my chemise from the chair, pulled it over my head and stepped into my new charcoal-grey linen skirt, a shade lighter than full mourning-black now that the first year was over. My fingers fumbled the buttons at the narrow waist, my hair fell around my face. I stopped struggling, took a breath to calm myself. For weeks I'd been agitated and restless. I felt as though a stone were caught in my throat. Something hot and sticky, like a child's thumbs, pressed against the backs of my eyes.

Buttons fastened, I stood in front of the mottled rectangle

of mirror, tilted back against the wall at floor level, to inspect myself. Lockie had hauled this mirror out of the box room when Liam went away, but we never got around to fixing it to the wall. At first it didn't seem worth it, since he'd be home any day and wouldn't thank us for the addition. Then there was all the talk of moving house, so what was the point? After that came the paralysis of not wanting to do anything that might remind us that he wouldn't, ever, be coming back.

I looked into the angled recess of glass. A silvered pool at my feet reflected the high corner between wall and ceiling behind me, where Liam's shaving mirror hung. The shadows were suggestive. In a certain light, they wavered. In the way that paired mirrors throw out an infinity of reflections, I thought I might see back through time, if I looked hard enough. I might catch a glimpse of Liam, before he left.

There was the rest of a fractious morning to get through, everyone out of sorts. First, we had Liam's anniversary Mass in the Pro-Cathedral. The congregation was small, nothing like the day before, Easter Sunday, when the church was crammed to bursting, standing room only at the back, half the congregation got up in new finery, the other half wheezing and coughing in clothes they'd got out of hock for the occasion, lucky if there were laces in their shoes. Against the collective smells of so much humanity, Mother and Florrie had worn orange-and-clove sachets on ribbons tied to their wrists. They wore them again today, when there was no need for them.

After Mass we had a queasy breakfast. Dad planned to get the train to Bray and walk the sea path to Greystones and back. I followed him out to the hall and found him belting his walking coat. He pulled a soft cap out of the large pocket and stretched it into shape. I stood behind him while he put it on, looking over his shoulder at his face in the mirror. 'Don't forget Isabel's coming to supper,' I said. 'You'll be home in time, won't you?'

He laughed at my expression. 'Why wouldn't I?'

'I still don't think it was a good idea to ask her.' I looked back at the dining-room door. 'Mother's got such a wasp in her ear.'

'That's rubbish, Katie. We're over all that now.'

I didn't feel sure about that. Isabel had taken up with a peace crowd run by a woman called Louie Bennett. A letter denouncing the war was printed in several newspapers in February, the *Freeman* as well as the *Independent*. It deplored conditions in the trenches for men on all sides, and the hardships of families left fatherless. There were a dozen signatories and Isabel was one of them.

'Mildred has Liam's memorabilia book, to show her,' Dad said. 'There'll be no politics, I won't allow it.' He jammed the cap down around his ears, a parody of the *hear no evil* monkey, and left.

I hoped he was right, but I was afraid it would be difficult for Isabel, in front of all of us, to look through the scrapbook Mother had made. I'd had time to make peace with it. I'd even added some of Liam's safer letters to the collection. Isabel had sent a photograph, along with a transcription of a poem by Mr Yeats, one that Liam had written into her journal the evening they got engaged.

Matt came downstairs, on his way to a friend's house in Rathfarnham to study for his final examinations. The holdall he carried looked heavy.

'Have you got an entire library in there?' I asked.

He'd a shifty expression on his face. 'I've a lot of time to make up for.'

'That you have. Well, don't forget to be here when Isabel comes.'

'I had forgotten. I might not be here, Katie. I'm sorry. Don't wait.'

'Suit yourself. Don't you always?'

I went into the dining room to say goodbye. Mother and Florrie were looking through the wedding presents spread out on the table. There were several unopened brown-paper parcels. Florrie tore into one and a gift label fell out. I picked it up and handed it to her. She put it down among spills of paper. I rescued it, watching her open the parcel. 'You'll want to know who sent it. Do you have a list?'

'We'll remember.' Florrie was flushed and happy-looking. Of a sudden I felt small and mean-spirited. A shadow crossed my memory, but I shrugged it off and caught Florrie's eye. 'You look lovely today, Florrie. All this suits you.'

She laughed that sudden bark of hers and batted my arm. 'Go on out of that. Are you going out?'

What harm would it do if I was to stay and show interest in her spoils? 'In a minute. I'll help if you like. Let me find some paper and a pencil.'

About twenty minutes later – twenty minutes of unwrapping, exclaiming, discussing gift and giver – I entered a pair of silver sauce-boats with matching ladles on the list. I wondered about the hallmarks. If I knew how to read them, we'd know when they were made, where and by whom. I wondered how to say it, but Mother went looking for a box to store everything in and I missed my chance. Florrie held up the last item, a Dun Emer tablecloth, for my inspection.

I fingered the material. 'It's a good design. I like the band of colour.'

Florrie folded it away. 'Not my taste. It's from Mrs Finlay. By the way, Katie, does Isabel still wear Liam's ring?'

Mother had come back in. She stood behind Florrie, listening for my answer.

'She was wearing it when I saw her, a couple of weeks ago. On the other hand.'

'I haven't seen her in months,' Florrie said.

'No more have I.' Mother put an orange crate on the floor and sat beside Florrie at the table. 'It'll be interesting to see how she's changed.' She set about refolding the linen. 'I don't see the fuss about Dun Emer goods. Too obvious for my taste. Give me a piece of fine French lace any day.'

'Why should Isabel have changed?' I said. 'I don't think she has.'

'Well, if she bothered to stay in touch –'

'I'm in touch with her,' I said. 'But, then, I make the effort.' I caught myself. I didn't want to stir up an argument, today of all days. This evening would be Isabel's first time in the house since Liam's Month's Mind. I wondered who dreaded it the most.

'Have we nearly finished here? I said I'd take Alanna for a walk at lunchtime, and – well.' They knew the rest: meeting Isabel; afternoon tea at Percy Place with Hubie Wilson, then back here for supper.

Mother smoothed the last fold of the cloth and slid it back into its packaging. 'Isabel should really give it back, the ring.'

'What?' I looked at Florrie, and she at me.

'It belonged to Bill's mother. Alanna could have it. Should have it, by rights.'

Florrie shook her head in warning but I couldn't stay quiet. 'You can't mean it. Liam gave Isabel that ring.'

Mother's eyes reddened. 'What of it? She won't marry him now.'

I was literally deprived of speech.

'Mother.' Florrie leaned in between us. 'We've finished here. Will you come upstairs and help me sort through my wardrobe?'

Mother pressed her fingertips to her eyes and stood up to

go with her. I watched them, Florrie's confident hand at Mother's back. Regret for my own awkwardness pressed on my ribs.

Out on the sunlit street, a tram hissed by along the east side of the Square. Although it was mild out, I wore Liam's gabardine. Unbelted, it billowed around me like a cloak, made me feel strong and other than I was. I crossed the road, passed the fat tabby curled asleep in the window of the Rotunda lodge, and walked down the slope of the Square. The Parnell monument waited at the bottom, impassive reminder of the day Liam's telegram came, and beyond it the length of Sackville Street leading south to the river, the ring of mountains beyond.

A familiar figure came striding towards me from Parnell Street, my schoolfriend Frieda Leamy, wearing her nurse's uniform under her dark blue cloak, without the hat. Her fair hair was pulled back into a bun. It had been an age since we spent any proper time together.

'I've been called in,' she said. 'Some mystery illness has caused people to miss their shifts this morning.'

I fell into step with her, as if we were off to school again, and we linked arms. 'What kind of illness?'

'Holiday-itis, I'd say.' Frieda had a rich, throaty laugh. 'It's annoying, all the same. My parents have gone to the Fairyhouse Races. I had to leave Maria in charge.' Maria was Frieda's giddy thirteen-year-old sister. I told her I was taking Alanna to feed the ducks in Stephen's Green and asked if she knew anything about the nursing home Eva was in, Nan Moorhead's, which was not far from the hospital where Frieda worked, in Baggot Street.

'I'm sure it's grand. I've heard nothing bad about it, anyway.'

'I've to meet Isabel, after.'

'How is she? I saw her letter in the paper, against the war.'

'Mother was furious.'

'I'm sure.' There was no love lost between Frieda and my mother.

'We're going to meet Captain Wilson, May's nephew. He knew Liam at the Front. Liam said he showed him the ropes when he first arrived.' I didn't tell her it was Hubie Wilson who'd recommended Liam's early transfer. Dad said we couldn't hold that against him. Liam had made up his mind to get out there as fast as they'd have him; he'd more than one person putting words in various ears, and if it hadn't been this posting it would have been another, sooner rather than later. But, if not for me, May wouldn't have told Hubie Wilson about Liam, and Hubie wouldn't have intervened. Liam might still be in a training camp in England – or even here. I couldn't bear to think about it.

'What?'

I'd stopped walking. Frieda was looking back at me. We'd reached the Pillar. I pretended I'd stopped to admire the flower-sellers' wares. Lines of people were waiting on trams to take them to the seaside or out to Poulaphouca. There was a queue at the cab stand.

'Let's walk it,' Frieda said, turning away from the queues. 'I know I should hurry, but – may as well make the most of the sunshine while it lasts.'

I picked up a bunch of purple violets. 'Look at the gloss on those leaves. Suffrage colours.' I held them close to my face and breathed a deep breath.

'Are ya smellin' or buyin'?' the woman asked.

I inhaled their scent again and put them back.

'How's Miss Colclough's book coming on?'

'It's finished.' This was a sore point. For a year I'd moved through each day to the next with no sense of purpose, time dragging me along behind it. Working for Dote made it almost bearable. She pulled me out of myself and towards

97

the house in Percy Place, the libraries, the National Gallery, gave me something to think about that wasn't war, or Liam. And, despite myself, I'd begun to catch my mind stretching and waking, against my will, humming sometimes with something like pleasure. But now all that was over. The book was finished. I was lonelier than ever.

'What'll you do now?'

I hesitated. If anyone would understand that I wanted to work, it was Frieda. 'I was offered a job last week, in Briscoe's.'

'The showrooms, on the Green? What kind of job?'

''Dote asked me to do some typewriting for Mr Briscoe, a catalogue for their next auction. I spent a couple of days there. It was interesting. I liked him. There's a lot to learn. I'd need to do training, possibly in London.'

Mr Briscoe had a gloomy, jowled face, like a bloodhound's. It didn't suit his character one bit. He took the trouble to explain the background of items that I asked about. He showed me an ornate ebony and brass desk with a shallow kneehole, only an indent, really, and eight pillared legs. A Mazarin desk, he said it was. Named for the cardinal. Mr Briscoe showed me how the sort of people for whom the table was designed would have sat, side-on, to accommodate their swords. I couldn't but catch his excitement. Later, he took a necklace of rare black pearls out from the safe and let me try them on. They glowed warm on my neck, sent blood to my cheeks. I'd never seen myself as acquisitive before, but those pearls woke a kind of greed in me. Everything I looked at in the showrooms demanded to be touched, explored, known.

'What does your mother say?' Frieda asked.

'I haven't told her yet.' She wouldn't take kindly to the notion that I'd work in a shop – but I could hardly say so to Frieda, whose father was a draper.

We went on across the bridge. On the far side, I was distracted by the white stone front of the Lafayette Building, its turreted upper storeys like a dream of a castle, woken up in the wrong place and time. All it needed were coloured pennants flying from the buttresses, veiled women at the windows, horses pawing the ground below, impatient to be off.

'If I tell you something,' Frieda said, 'promise you won't tell anyone?'

'Are we back in school now?'

'It's about Con Buckley. Promise.'

'Cross my heart and hope to die.' My heart did, actually, pound.

She didn't smile. 'I know you're friendly with him, Katie, but he's a rat. One of the younger nurses had to leave the hospital on his account.'

I told myself not to listen, that no good had ever come of listening to gossip.

Frieda looked around again, lowered her voice still further. 'She was going to have a baby.'

I looked at the ground, where uneven paving stones lay in wait for some hapless person to trip on them. 'It could have been anyone's, so. Why would you spread such a rumour?'

All trace of expression smoothed out of Frieda's face. 'At least remember, you swore. On your honour.'

I waited for Alanna in Eva and Bartley's freshly painted hall. The walls were a pale shade of blue, the cornices and mouldings gleamed white. Nan said to wait upstairs in the parlour, but I liked the clean smell of paint, and besides the upstairs room would be chilly and stale without Eva in it. I shifted on the seat, an uncomfortable backless bench upholstered in brown and gold. It was part of a brand-new contraption, the other half being a stand for the telephone. Against the opposite wall, the grandfather clock's burnished mahogany casing would put you in mind of a coffin. Its reedy, insistent tick said time was falling away.

I stared at the ugly black mass of the telephone. It was nothing short of a miracle that a word spoken across the sea in England could travel along a length of wire, direct to an ear in Dublin. I picked up the receiver. A strange, disconnected crackle sounded down the line. 'Hello?' I whispered.

Something spat in my ear. 'Hello, yes?' It was a woman's grating voice. 'This is the operator. What number did you want to reach?'

The receiver fell out of my hand. I pushed it back on to the antlered apparatus that cradled it.

'Here we are!' Nan, on the stairs, had Alanna by the hand. 'Was there someone on that yoke?'

'I knocked it, by mistake.'

Alanna's face was pale and still, watchful. Her fine brown hair was gathered into a black velvet ribbon at each side of her head, in two high ponytails that curled to the shoulders of her sky-blue pinafore.

'Hello, Alanna. That's a pretty dress. Isn't it Eva's favourite colour?'

Her face softened a little. 'Yes. Can we go and see her?'

'Ah, no. It's not allowed.' I caught the echo of what Bartley had said to us and frowned. Alanna frowned back at me. Nan looked from one to the other of us and laughed.

'Well, yiz'll have a fine time, at this rate.' She held up a brown paper bag. 'Here's crumbs, for the ducks.' It was impossible to guess her age. Her black hair had silver flecks in it, but her face was unlined. She had the hands and feet of a larger person attached to the narrow, wiry body of a restless boy. She'd looked the same as long as I'd known her, as long as Eva had been married, eight years.

Alanna took the bag of crumbs, with little enthusiasm, and we went out. We passed the Cancer Hospital and turned on to the broad street that encircled the Green. Cabs clipped past in both directions, the horses' hooves striking brisk sparks of sound from the road. Motor-cars made a line in front of the Shelbourne. Beyond them were the sculpted women whose patient arms held up brass lamps. A gleaming, cream-coloured De Dion-Bouton was parked at an angle on the corner. Alanna followed me over to have a closer look. We admired the gleaming bodywork of the car, its round lamps like eyes. 'It's so shiny!' Alanna said.

'It's beautiful. Isabel's father has one just like it, but his is green.'

Alanna wrinkled her nose, puzzled.

'You know Isabel – she's Liam's fiancée.' Was.

'Who's Liam?'

She might as well have kicked me full in the chest. Her eyes were the palest shade of blue, almost colourless. Like Con's. Unnerving. 'Oh, yes,' she said. 'I remember.'

Did Eva never talk about him? I didn't often say his name out loud myself. It felt too dangerous, a bladed hook that could split my chest and drag my heart from its hiding place. If you love someone, and that person dies, all that love becomes a burden, a weight accumulating, pooling inside you, with nowhere to go. What do you do with it? Sometimes I tried to arrange it, stack it up as if on shelves – this aspect of Liam and that. Sometimes it gathered itself into a shape, a shadow, peeled itself off the ground and attached itself to my heel. It followed me and spoke, in Liam's voice, words I'd memorized from his letters. These things were so vivid, for me – yet Alanna might as well never have known him.

I shivered. I'd gone and given myself a proper fright, in broad daylight on a sunny holiday, other people ambling about the streets in no obvious hurry, untroubled by thoughts of remembering and forgetting. And I'd a child brooding beside me, waiting to see what I might offer her by way of a substitute for her mother, my sister, and surely expecting more from me than gloomy thoughts.

The park smelled of cut grass and spun sugar. In the distance, a barrel organ played its tinny song. People strolled among the formal flowerbeds, where pansies grew in vivid blocks of red, purple, yellow. Others lounged on deckchairs around the bandstand. Lovers, groups of friends, students out with their books – as if they could actually study here. They didn't even pretend to look at the pages spread open in front of them, lifted their faces to the high blue sky instead. It was hard to believe that, two years before, Liam and I were among them, our heads full of dates and facts, not worried about anything more urgent than which questions were most likely to come up in our final examinations.

A man with a cart was selling leftover Easter sweets beside the lake. We were walking in his direction when we heard a commotion from the direction of the park's main gate. A nursemaid hurried past, dragging a sulky-looking boy in a sailor suit. He'd a toy sailboat clutched to his chest with his other arm, spreading a dark stain of damp on the blue of his jacket.

A young man came up behind her. Little more than a boy, really. Short and skinny, he wore the dark green coat of the Citizens' Army, with a bandolier slung across his chest. A wide-brimmed hat jammed low on his forehead shadowed his freckled face. I looked again. That really was a gun in his hands, muzzle half raised in our direction.

'Yiz have to quit the park.'

'Are you from the theatre?' I asked him.

He cleared his throat and tried again. 'We're taking the park. In the name of the Republic. Yiz have to leave.'

'Is this real?' I pulled Alanna in behind me and looked around. The deckchairs were empty. A crowd of people filed towards the gate. A couple were arguing with a man dressed like this one. Over by the shrubbery, men were busy digging. A woman in green breeches conferred with two men through the railings. All three of them held guns. Passers-by glanced in, stopped to take a closer look, were told to move on. A group of women carried boxes into the summer house. One wore a Red Cross cuff on her arm.

A week or so earlier there'd been uproar over a document that came out of the Castle, a plan to suppress so many organizations that the whole city would have been affected, directly or not. One story had it that thousands were to be arrested and soldiers were to be billeted on ordinary homes. It was rumoured that conscription would begin any minute. All the while men in makeshift uniforms marched and drilled in public places, getting in people's way, holding up the traffic, as they'd done for months. There were squads of little boys who mocked them, and squads of little boys who copied them.

Dad said it was all a cod, except the conscription. That could happen, right enough. He said the marching and drilling was only posturing and false alarms. They wouldn't dare try anything more. Not with so many Irishmen fighting and dying in the war.

Only yesterday, a notice had appeared in the *Sunday Independent*, saying that all manoeuvres had been cancelled. We admired the bare-faced cheek of it, then forgot all about it.

Now here was this young man with a rifle that looked real enough, *hooshing* us out of the park. I looked straight at him, and he at me. He was close enough to touch. The coarse fabric of his jacket smelled of damp. 'Out with you,' he said.

A curious shivering sound, like a thousand glasses shattering, came from a distance. A kind of fury was thick in my neck: This goes too far. But with Alanna beside me, I had to do as he said. I took her hand and we hurried along the path and out through the gate.

Windows had been broken in the buildings around the

Green. Furniture was being carried out of them and heaped in a pile that blocked the street. Groups of people stood around watching, in the road and on the steps of the hotel, but no one tried to interfere.

I urged Alanna across the road and back along Hume Street. Her steps dragged as she tried to look back over her shoulder. Sudden shouts erupted behind us, then a *rat-a-tat-tat!* followed by a scream. I tightened my grip on Alanna's hand and hurried on.

Nan was waiting at the door when we got back.

'There was a man with a gun!' Alanna said.

'There's windows broken all round the Green,' I said.

Nan's eyebrows disappeared into her thick fringe. Her narrow, freckled face was sly and lively. 'Who's done it?'

'I'm not sure. They'd different uniforms on them, and I saw a Red Cross armband.'

Nan took Alanna's hand. 'Come on down to the kitchen with me, child, and we'll get some food into you. You must be famished, after all that.'

'I'll be after you in a minute.' I took off Liam's coat and folded it on to the stool beside the telephone. The hall door banged open. I jumped, but it was only Bartley.

'I'm glad I caught you,' he said. 'Don't go out, there's trouble on the streets.'

'We've been! We got as far as the Green, but they made us leave.'

He set his black bag on the floor, went to the telephone, picked up the receiver. 'Hello?' He prodded the connection with his fingers. 'Hello?' He took the receiver away from his ear and looked at the earpiece. 'There's no line.'

I shifted my feet, wondering if I'd broken it, but Bartley slammed the receiver down even harder than I had. 'It's useless. They must have taken out the exchange.'

Alanna came flying up the stairs to hug his knees. 'Daddy! A man made us leave the park. I wanted to stay, but *she* wouldn't let me.'

He swung her up and held her suspended for a minute, studying her face as though to learn it by heart. 'Quite right too. What would I do, if anything happened to you?'

'Mam says the park is our garden.'

'So it is, ours and everyone else's.'

'But *she* —'

'Go back downstairs, Alanna.' When she'd gone he said, 'You should go down with them. Stay 'til the fuss is over. Who knows what's going to happen next?' He picked up his black bag.

'But where are you going, if it's so much safer indoors?'

'Back to the hospital, where I can be useful.' He held up the bag. 'They'll see I'm a doctor.'

'I've to meet Isabel,' I said, but he'd gone.

I called goodbye to Nan and Alanna and went out. Doors stood ajar the length of the street. At the corner of Merrion Row people were grouped in small, conversational knots, looking in the one direction. I joined them, where the street opened to a shoulder of the Green. The barricade in the middle of the road had grown.

'I've to meet someone in the Shelbourne,' I said, to no one in particular.

'I wouldn't chance it.' A grey-haired man eyed the fifty yards or so between us and the hotel.

'Aren't they a right shower of eejits, all the same,' another one said. 'I'd a gone for the hotel, myself. Aren't there beds in it, and no end of food. I'd a let the soldiers have the park, and welcome.'

'They got it arseways. They're like rats in a trap, in there.'

A glint of brass in the barricade caught my eye. I edged

forward for a better look. There was something familiar about two black-and-gilt turned table legs, pointing up, a fat armchair upside down on top of them. 'Did they break into Briscoe's?' I asked. The desk was upside down – all that marquetry would be destroyed.

'They did, and hauled the stuff out. Shocking, the waste. Where are you off to?'

I'd half stepped off the pavement. 'Might they let me take something out, if I asked?'

The woman grabbed my arm. 'Don't be a fool, girl. They mean business. They shot a man, a while back, trying to get his cart out of there.'

A car turned on to the Green from Kildare Street, then jerked to a halt in front of a man waving a rifle. Two others with bayonets ran over and leaned on either side of the car. The driver got out, shaking his chauffeur's cap in their faces. He was pushed over to the pavement by one of the gunmen, while the other got into the car and drove it, hard, into a gap in the barricade.

The driver shrieked at the sound of shearing metal. 'I'll get the sack for this,' he shouted.

I put my head down and walked quickly along the short stretch of pavement to the hotel, slipped inside the main doors. The lovely crimson carpet was all but invisible, there were so many people milling around in the hall: tweed suits, elegant dresses, a pair of khaki uniforms on their way upstairs, a scarlet jacket in the bar, the hum of high and low voices. It was a relief to see Isabel's fair hair, her calm, rosy skin. She gave a sad smile when she saw me. 'What's happening out there?'

'I was just going to ask you the same.' The double doors were open to the drawing room. At the sight of snowy-white tablecloths spread under plates of pastries and sandwiches, toast racks, dishes of butter and jam, I felt faint. 'I forgot to eat. I'm starving.'

A strange *zing!* was followed by the sound of breaking glass. People jumped to their feet, knocking over cups and plates, and spilled out into the already crowded hall. A waiter in a starched white apron pulled the main door shut and turned the brass key in the lock.

'They'd never lock us in, would they?'

'I think they just did.'

I looked around. Porters and waiters were urging people towards the back of the building in a pack that got denser by the second. 'We have to get out,' I said.

Isabel looked doubtful. 'With shooting outside?'

I told her there'd been crowds standing around watching the goings-on when I came in, and no one troubling them. There was an air of unreality to it all. Nobody would want to hurt the likes of us, and there'd always be a building to duck into, for safety, if it came to it. I stopped a waiter carrying a tray of dirty dishes to ask about the service entrance. He nodded at an uncarpeted flight of stairs in a corner, going down.

'Do you mind?' Not waiting for an answer, I took an uneaten scone off a plate and told Isabel to come on. I felt giddy as we clattered down the stairs, ignoring looks of disapproval from the lobby. In the basement there were smells of roasting meat from the kitchen that made my stomach churn. And there, beyond the kitchen, was the door. A kitchen porter came out of a cupboard and told us we couldn't go that way, but on we went. I pushed the door, which opened on to a yard, scaring a black cat from an ash-bin. The lid of the bin hit the ground and rolled away, causing a ringing, steely echo. We held on to each other, laughing in fright. The cat jumped the height of the wall and looked down at us, a pink tongue sweeping its face, its tail twitching.

*

Kildare Street was almost empty – no trams, no traffic. Footsteps echoed to our left, as two men in cloth caps and bulky overcoats came out of an alley. One of them held a long, narrow leather case. Isabel nudged me. We drew in closer to each other. The men gave us sidelong looks as they passed. It wasn't 'til I saw the flute case for what it was that I realized I was holding my breath, and let it out in a big gusty sigh.

Avoiding the Green, we passed the museum and the library, and went on down to the corner where Con once kissed my wrist. The grocer's shop was shuttered for the holiday.

On Clare Street, we saw a small file of men go through the Lincoln Gate to Trinity, as orderly as a turnstile at a football match. A tram had stopped in its tracks on the north side of Merrion Square. Mount Street stretched beyond it, to the bridge. Its stillness made me think of the puzzles Alanna liked. What is wrong with this picture? When you looked closely, it was easy to spot the ludicrous features, the umbrella in the tree, the parrot perched on a policeman's head; others were harder to solve.

'Have you met this Captain Wilson yet?' Isabel asked, as we passed the empty tram.

'He only got here on Saturday.' Hubie Wilson was on his way home to Mullingar after months convalescing in an English hospital. He'd lost most of one of his hands, among other wounds. Dote said life was the main thing, after all, and May said yes, but Hubie would take it hard. He was a practical man, good with his hands. Clever when it came to fixing things that were broken. She'd written to him in the hospital, but only stilted letters came back, polite phrases written in a stranger's script. Nothing at all like her Hubie.

I reminded Isabel about the letter I'd shown her the year before, the one Captain Wilson wrote to us after Liam was killed. I wondered if the hapless Acheson was still alive.

'Is he travelling alone?' she asked.

'I think so.'

'It must be a lonely journey, going home injured. After losing so many of his friends.'

'He's staying with May,' I said. 'She's his aunt.'

'Still – if it was Liam –' She turned her unnaturally pale face to mine. 'One of us would have gone to fetch him, surely.'

'There's some trouble at home, I think.' I was reluctant to tell Isabel what May had confided to me, that Hubie's eldest brother Tom had gone and married Hubie's fiancée while he was at the Front. His father had gone to the convalescent hospital to break the news. His parents supported the match, for one of those country reasons to do with land, the eldest son and shared boundaries. It was too much to know about a person we'd never met. Instead, I said, 'Mother didn't want to meet him.'

'Does she blame him, for Liam?'

I could hardly say no, she blames you, but in any case she didn't wait for my answer. 'I do,' she said. 'A little. If not for him, Liam might still be safe in a training camp.'

'Isabel, I – let's go this way, I prefer it.' I steered Isabel up the east side of Merrion Square. Sunlight played off the reveals, making the houses shimmer the length of the street and beyond, as though they were alive. The hills in the distance cast their bluish light our way.

'Sometimes I lie awake all night, wondering,' Isabel went on. 'Could I have stopped him, if I'd tried harder? It goes on forever. If this Hubie Wilson hadn't put in a word for him with the colonel –'

'He'd have got his commission anyway. He'd have gone anyway. Isabel, please. If you challenge Captain Wilson, he won't tell us anything.' I wished I'd stayed with my first instinct and arranged to meet him alone.

She looked away from me, towards the hills. We walked on without speaking, around the corner on to Upper Mount Street and on towards the Pepper Canister Church.

'What will he do now, missing a hand?'

'I don't know.' It hadn't occurred to me to ask. My mind stopped at the door of his safety. The relief his family would feel to have him home was like a lit room glimpsed from a cold dark street, a table spread with food and candles to taunt a beggar.

'War is an evil.' She stopped on the little curved bridge over the canal. We looked down into the still black water. I hoped she'd be tactful and not antagonize Captain Wilson, who knew more of war than we ever would, or May, whose father had been a hero in the Crimea, and in the raising of the Siege of Cawnpore.

A single swan emerged below us, made a stately curve before the lock and came back. Its reflection made a second bird, snowy-white and upside down. Its eyes were as dark and deep as the water. I remembered the bag in my pocket. 'I have crumbs.'

More swans appeared as the bread struck the water, two perfect white and one black, half a dozen cygnets. Only the black bird cast no reflection. We threw crumbs and watched the water ripple, breaking the illusion as the swans' webbed black feet churned the water. They dipped their necks in sudden thrusts that shattered their reflections into blurs of white and grey.

An ancient old man bent double over a cane stopped to watch. 'Mashed potato,' he said. 'That's what you need. Good for swans, a bit of mash.'

Dote let us in, then dragged the heavy bolt across the door. In eighteen months of coming to this house, I'd never seen that bolt in use.

She shook Isabel's hand. 'We've heard all about you, my dear. You're very welcome.' She caught my look at the bolt. 'Hubie said to keep the door locked. He's not here, I'm afraid. We heard such wild stories that he went to investigate. I was worried, but here you are, safe and sound.' She led us into the kitchen.

'There are gunmen in the Green,' I said.

'So it's true.' The silver bangles May wore on each narrow wrist, relics of her childhood, made an eerie sound as she came to shake Isabel's hand. 'Delighted, my dear. How are you, Katie, pet? Are the streets quiet? We didn't know what to believe.'

We sat at the kitchen table. May scalded a teapot. A tray of tea-things stood ready on the dresser. Dote moved the tray to the table in front of us while I told them what we had seen. May sat with us, to listen.

Isabel described the scene in the Shelbourne. People up from the country for the Spring Show. A wedding party. A couple of soldiers on leave. And then the sound of windows breaking outside, people rushing in from the street to say there was trouble, and everyone going to the windows to look out at the unbelievable sight of carts and furniture making a wall in the street, men passing more items out through gaping windows to add to it. A boy who walked past was fired on, from no one knew where. He vaulted the railings and took shelter in the area before someone had the sense to open a basement window and let him in. A woman was handing her hat around to anyone who'd look. A round hole in it came, she said, from a bullet.

May stood up. 'There! I forgot to make the tea. I'll do it now. Will we go upstairs?'

Dote took the tray and asked us to follow her. We were still in the downstairs passage when we heard a brisk knock on the door. Dote worked the bolt and opened it, and a tall man came in, along with shafts of sunlight, a glimpse of open space behind him.

I had to lift my face to meet his eyes. His damaged right hand was encased in leather. Isabel was flustered by the hand, even though I'd warned her. She thrust hers out to shake it, pulled it back, ended up grasping his sleeve instead.

When it was my turn, I took his other hand, his left, in both of mine. His handshake was limp, a disappointment.

'Thank you for writing to us,' I said, 'when Liam was killed.'

For an instant his hand came alive, solidified, in mine. Tiny points of golden light flared in his irises. The skin of his face and neck was pale at the tightly cropped hairline. He must have been to a barber recently. Liam's hair had been just like that when he came home that last time, before going to the Front. It made him look tender, defenceless as a small boy. I wanted to touch it.

'Well?' Dote asked. 'Did you discover anything?'

'There's trouble, all right.' He took his hand back and shut the door, pushing the bolt home. The passage returned to its natural gloom. 'But it's hard to know the extent of it. It's quiet enough for the time being.'

'We'll have tea so, while you tell us all about it,' Dote said. 'We're all parched.' She went up ahead of us.

My eyes had grown used to the dim light in the passage. Hubie Wilson looked haughty and exasperated, not at all what I'd expected from their affectionate accounts of him. May gave me the teapot, snug in its bright red knitted cosy. She took his arm and smiled up at him. 'We'll see more from upstairs,' she coaxed. So up we went.

He went into the parlour, saying he wanted to look out through the front window. I stopped at the door of the dining room. The table had been cleared and dressed with linen, china and silver, and the books were stacked away in boxes against the wall. Under the window, I could see the type-writer sitting in its case beside the rubber plant with its strong oval leaves, a red tongue of new leaf unfurling from its throat. 'Did you do this for the Captain?' I asked Dote.

She shook her head. 'For your friend,' she said in a low voice.

May had brought Isabel to the window. It looked out on a long green swathe of garden with ordered beds and fruit trees coming into flower. New blossoms were burgeoning, white and pink stars on a canopy of palest green. May was naming them, and Isabel exclaiming at their colours.

'Your garden is beautiful, Miss Colclough,' she said, when Dote joined them.

'That's all May's handiwork. I've a black thumb, I'm afraid.'

May took off her spectacles to clean them, put them back on again, while Dote told us where to sit. I was on my usual side, facing the maps, with May beside me, and Dote sat on hers, with Isabel. They'd left the head of the table, where May liked to sit when she came in to chat to us, for the Captain. I hoped he'd appreciate the view.

'Now,' May said when he came back in, 'tell us everything.'

He glanced at Isabel and me as he sat into his place and unfolded his napkin. Dote leaned across Isabel to say, 'These are sturdy young women. They've already resisted confinement in the Shelbourne.' She winked at us.

'It's hard to know exactly what's happening.' His voice had an unusual low pitch, not at all unpleasant, despite the alarming things he was saying: public buildings had been overrun by men with guns; a policeman killed, and the rest of them vanished into thin air. The trams appeared to have stopped running. The most worrying thing was that the neighbours at the back said *their* neighbours had been turned out of their own home.

'Why on earth?'

'Gunmen have installed themselves at the windows. They said they'd do their best to see nothing gets damaged, and shooed the owners away. The owners went to a house with a telephone and tried to ring the police, but the line is down.'

'But that's – that's –' Isabel grasped for a word and failed to find one. None of us could help her.

'I went to speak to the gunmen,' he said.

'Who are they?' Dote asked.

'Some sort of Brotherhood, they say. They've barricaded themselves in. They won't be persuaded out, they mean business. Their colleagues have occupied the GPO.'

We listened out for any untoward sounds, but we heard nothing other than May's breathing. I didn't have to look at her to be aware of the rise and fall of her breast, or that her hand pressed on it, as though trying to contain it. 'Will they come here?' she asked. 'Is it likely that they'd want this house?'

'I don't see why they would,' Dote said. 'Tea, May.'

'There! I nearly forgot again.' She gathered herself together with visible effort. When the tea was poured, and Dote had handed out the scones, and the butter and jam had been passed around to everyone's satisfaction, Hubie Wilson said it might be no harm to pack any valuables away. 'Just in case.'

Dote was firm. 'Let's not talk about it any more, since we can do nothing.'

I, for one, was relieved. I was at that point where hunger threatens to turn on itself, so that it's nearly impossible to eat. I dealt with my own scone quickly and accepted a second. Spooning jam on to my plate, I caught sight of the slow movement of Hubie Wilson's left hand, spreading butter on a slice of soda bread. I was taken by its steady rhythm. My own left hand was so useless, you'd nearly wonder what it was for, other than symmetry. I tried not to stare.

Isabel said, 'How long have you been a soldier, Captain Wilson?'

He finished what he was doing and set his knife down before answering. 'I'm not a soldier now. It's *Mr* Wilson.'

'Ah, Hubie, no need for that.' May patted his injured hand. 'We're all friends here.'

He stiffened. There was a pause it should have been up to him to fill. I'd been predisposed to favour him, not only because he had befriended Liam, but because his name was part of the currency of conversation in this house. I'd felt as if I knew him a little, but I was unprepared for his stiff manner or how prickly he was.

'Liam spoke well of you,' Isabel conceded at last.

He looked at her, expressionless.

'Tell them about the army,' Dote said, with an air of moving things along.

'I got my commission four years ago.' He pushed his plate away. 'It's in the family, soldiering. I thought it would suit me for a while. I'd see a bit of the world. Save my pay,' he laughed, 'for later. An uncle was in the Dublins. I've two cousins in the Irish Rifles, and Great Uncle Richard . . .' His eyes went to the display of May's father's medals in their frame on the wall behind me. 'Why not? But then the war started . . . It was a shock. Wouldn't you think a soldier would know better? I was young. I'd imagined the odd skirmish, life in a fort in a range of snowy mountains – or a desert. I thought it'd be glamorous. And interesting. Policing people with different notions of the world.'

'Like us,' I said.

'I'm as Irish as you are!'

'I never said you weren't.' I looked at Dote.

She didn't let me down. 'Katie helped me with my book, Hubie. She's a walking encyclopedia by now. Ask her anything about the monuments.'

He raised an eyebrow that was pulled askew by a scar. The kink gave him the look of a satyr. 'Which is your favourite?'

He was most likely mocking, but I decided to take the question seriously.

'I think the one to Constable Sheahan. Do you know it?'

'It's near the river, at the end of Hawkins Street.' Dote shuddered. 'Celtic cross, granite, all spirals and shamrocks – you can't mean it, Katie.'

'I'm not mad about the look of it,' I said.

'Who was he?'

'Quite the legend,' Dote said. 'A giant, even for a DMP man.'

'He carried a whole family out of a falling building once,' I said. 'Another time, he wrestled a rampaging bull to the ground.'

'And that's why they built a memorial?'

'No – there was a workman who went down a drain and choked to death on the fumes. The constable went to save him, and he died too. He'd a massive funeral – did you see it, Isabel? Remember the horses, all the black plumes?'

'We love a good funeral in Dublin.' She smoothed the tablecloth with the flat of her hand, her eyes down. 'We've seen more than our share these last few years.'

Hubie Wilson was watching me. 'If you're not mad about the look of that monument,' he asked, 'why is it your favourite?'

'It's the only one I know of, to an ordinary person.'

His smile took years off him. 'Good reason. There's never been a monument to an ordinary soldier.'

Dote stood up. 'That's enough of all that, now. A bit of fresh air'll do us a power of good; we've been cooped up indoors for far too long.' She ushered us outside.

Wooden garden chairs and a bench made of iron were under the apple tree. Before we were settled, Mrs Delaney, the next-door neighbour, came to the low wall between the two gardens and waved. Dote went to see what she wanted. After a minute or two she came back for Hubie. They spoke to the woman while I tugged one of my chair's legs free of the grass it had sunk into, and pushed it to the path. Isabel and May discussed the flowers, and types of soil, the curse of aphids. Colour returned to May's face while they talked and I was glad of Isabel. May would have known my heart wasn't in such a conversation, even if I'd been able to carry it off.

Dote and the Captain came back to tell us that a meeting of men from the terrace had been arranged, down in Mr Hyland's house, at the corner. Dote looked amused. 'Hubie says May or I should go! I've half a mind to do it too.'

Hubie mumbled an excuse and left. He was a sudden sort of a man. I wondered had he always been like that.

'But – we'd so much to ask him,' Isabel said.

Uneasy, I caught her eye. We'd outstayed our welcome. May looked tired, and Dote wanted to get out to that meeting. Mother expected us, and time was moving on. We'd heard no more firing since we arrived, but I was a little anxious about getting home. 'We should leave.'

'Are you sure?' Dote looked doubtful. 'You could stay here.'

'Not at all. We're expected. It's been quiet since we arrived.'

'Well, if you come across anything untoward, come straight back.'

We promised we would and moved inside.

'Come back tomorrow,' May said. 'Hubie's here 'til the day after; there's plenty of time.' She shook herself and her bangles made their eerie, shivery sound. 'Today has been a jittery day. Fresh start tomorrow.'

Isabel went with May to retrieve our coats.

Part of me wanted to stay and try to coax more out of

Hubie Wilson when he came back, but a stronger part urged me home, to make sure everyone was all right. To hear from Dad and Matt, who'd have stories of their own to tell.

Outside, the street glowed in the afternoon light, like a painting. There was no traffic in the road, but people walked along the pavement as usual. A family of mallard swam along the canal across the road, each spreading its own tiny wake, glassy ribbons of clear green water.

'That man is odd,' Isabel said. 'He's infuriating. A waste of an afternoon.'

We followed the towpath beside the gleaming water, under new-leafed trees, all the way to the basin, in the shadow of the ugly mill.

'Isabel, listen. You know the memory-book Mother made for Liam? She wants to show it to you tonight.'

'She asked me for a letter to add to it. I couldn't.'

'Of course not. No one expected you to part with them.'

'Then why did she ask?'

'She has her moments.'

I had to walk faster to keep up with her. When I drew level again, I saw her cheeks were wet.

'I loved Liam.' She turned on me, the very image of misery.

'I know.'

'I mean, really loved him. You don't know – you act as if you owned him, all of you.' She was furious, suddenly. 'I'm sorry, but I felt – I feel – you took him back when he died.'

After Liam was killed, Isabel had stayed in Cork nearly five months. In all that time we saw her just once, when she came up by train for the memorial Mass. Mother might have resented her less if she'd been here to share our grief that summer. But it was true that Mother had done nothing to encourage her tentative overtures when she came back, in September. I could hardly tell her that Mother thought she was unfeeling, that she had wounded Liam somehow, weakened him. Dad said Mother had got over all that, but I wasn't so sure.

I drew her down on to a wayside bench where we were shielded by trees – not that there was anyone to see us. The path was quiet. The dark mass of the mill brooded over the water, and I could see people walking along Great Brunswick Street, maybe twenty yards ahead, but there was no one to disturb us here. She was crying now, and I gave her a handkerchief.

She pulled off her gloves, turning the ring on her finger so that it caught and returned a flash of sunlight. 'We were all but married as it was. Can I tell you something, in absolute confidence?' She wasn't crying now, but her voice still shook.

'Of course.'

'That last time he was home, we lay together.'

Something happened to my ears, something thunderous, getting in the way of hearing. It made no difference whether I listened or not, she was talking to herself. 'In Glendalough. I'd a blanket, from the car. To sit on.' She twisted the ring on her finger, over and back, as though trying to work her finger loose from the bone. 'To lie on. He wore his own clothes that day. I'd asked him to.' She darted a quick look at me, but kept talking. 'I hated that khaki. I hated the smell off the belt.'

I knew exactly what she meant.

'He was all mine that day. He was a husband to me.' She put the gloves away into her bag. 'Well. Shall we go on?' She stood up, smoothed her skirt.

Liam rose in my mind, watching her. I felt a kind of vertigo, as though I stood in a high place, looking down at this path, myself on this bench, the ground giving way beneath me, pitching me back to the last time he was home.

It was a crisp night, All Saints'. Liam was tense. He was leaving the next day, and soon he'd be going to the Front. He'd been different, the three days of his leave; there had been something unreachable in him. He even sounded different, using a new vocabulary of rank and equipment, sappers, the chaps. He'd a way of biting off the ends of his sentences, as if to control what might escape them. He smoked one cigarette after another, laughed too often and a little too loud.

Everyone else had gone up to bed. The sky was clean, peppered with stars. The moon, just off full, poured its light over the garden. We were in the back parlour with the curtains open, beside a low fire of turf and wood. We sat without speaking, listened to the fire crackle and spark, watched shadows leap along the walls. It reminded me of when we were children and used to hide, from Lockie or Mother, inside a wardrobe smelling of moth powder or under a bed, holding on to each other, trying to stifle our giggles, not daring to speak. But we weren't children now, and this, whatever it was that bothered him, was no laughing matter. I wondered, had he had a row with Isabel, or did he dread leaving and all that lay ahead? He glared at the fire, had a go at the embers with the poker, sending up showers of sparks. A cinder fell out on to the rug. He picked it up and tossed it back in one sure movement. Didn't flinch.

Time was when there were no barriers between our two minds, but now I couldn't reach him unless he chose to allow it. At last he began to talk. He'd walked past Trinity on his way home from Isabel's that evening, he said, when two girls came up to him, giggling and nudging each other, their hands hidden in fur muffs. He stood off the pavement to let them pass, raised his hat to them.

'I was grinning like any old eejit,' he said, mocking himself. 'They were pretty girls. I thought they liked the look of me.'

'And?'

'They gave me this.' He reached into his pocket and drew out a fat white feather, broken in two. 'They called me coward. They wanted to know, am I not man enough to fight?' He slid the broken quill between his fingers and plucked at the fibres, to smooth them. 'The coward's feather. Don't tell Isabel. Would you say it's from a goose or a gull?'

'Stop it!' I snatched the feather from his hands and flung it into the fire, where it twisted and snapped on the coals. A sour blue coil of smoke rose as the quill crackled and split. 'Witches! If I'd been there, I'd have pushed them under a tram.'

He laughed a little. 'Dear Katie, I think you would. You're the one should be the soldier.'

I tried to make light of it. 'Sure, you wouldn't know who to listen to. If you paid attention to them all, you'd be wearing ten different uniforms at once.'

'Or none.'

'Or none.' I risked another look at him. 'I know you're only doing this because you think it's right. I admire you for it. But I'm afraid for you too.'

'Don't be,' he said. 'I'm not. I'm more afraid of what the world would be if we don't put up a fight, what it will be if we don't win. And there are so many Irishmen in the thick of it, we'll have a place at the peace conference, for sure, when it ends. They'll all see it differently then.'

He must have had so much on his mind that night. He was the person I was closest to in all the world, and yet I'd barely known him at all. He'd enlisted without telling me, got engaged without warning – and now this. I couldn't take it in. Even lovely, sad Isabel was not the person I'd thought she was.

*

When we turned on to D'Olier Street, we saw a crowd on O'Connell Bridge. Boys sat on the parapets and clung to lamp-posts. People jostled for a view up Sackville Street.

As we crossed the bridge, the crowd swelled around us. It was like entering a fairground. My heart beat faster. Isabel gripped my hand. People thronged in all directions, pushing carts, wheelbarrows, prams piled high with goods. Children staggered past, their mouths stained with confectioners' sugar. A boy had become a jewellery tree, hats stacked on his head like upside-down nests, watches on the branches of his arms. Girls whose shins were mottled and bruised crammed their grubby feet into high heels and jewelled sandals. Feather boas were wound around their bony shoulders. They swaggered and laughed *Lookit me! Giveit here!* My steps quickened. A wrecked tram was skewed across the tracks, where the remnants of a fire smouldered. People slipped through the crowd carrying bundles and bags, looking neither left nor right.

Feathered women sat astride a dead horse, drinking whiskey by the neck and jeering. They swung their bare legs, skirts hoicked around their thighs. The wrecked tram was being used as a changing room for girls trying on camisoles and lacy knickers. A gathering of men at the windows roared approval.

We found anchor in a broad doorway, breathing hard, as though we'd been running. A man's voice spoke from the shadows. 'They've smashed their way into every shop around. See the shoes? They got into Saxone's a while back.'

I looked at my feet. I had bought my boots in Saxone's a fortnight ago, the day Florrie bought her wedding shoes. The manager was a thin, kindly man we'd known since childhood.

'Noblett's is destroyed. There's no stopping them.'

'Has anyone tried?' Isabel sounded as if she were considering it.

'That shower in the GPO. They fired over their heads. It worked for all of five minutes. There were priests here earlier – but the crowd ran them.'

'Where are the police?' Isabel asked.

He spat. 'Vanished, at the first sign of trouble. Useless bowsies.' He stepped out, turned up his coat collar and was swallowed by a heaving sea of people.

'Look.' Isabel tugged my arm. I looked where she was pointing. Upstairs in Wynn's Hotel, people sat in rows at the large plate-glass window, like an audience at a play.

'We can't stay here,' I said. We edged out into the crowd and jostled our way along the street, towards home.

Behind us, someone screamed. 'Fire! The stables!'

The yelling intensified as people realized the horses were trapped, neighing their panic. In front of the Rotunda we fought free, breathed easier.

Suddenly I remembered Frieda, saying her parents were off to the races, leaving her younger sister Maria in charge, her scorn at their lapse of judgement. With the trams out of action, they wouldn't be back yet. Their shop was a couple of hundred yards away, the distance thick with people. The children must be terrified with all the commotion. With fire so close, there was no knowing what might happen. Frieda might still be at the hospital.

Isabel didn't resist when I turned down a side street that led away from the crowds, the noise and the fires, into a labyrinth of shadowed back-alleys and markets, the reek of the slaughterhouse.

There was no one about. The air, fogged and close, smelled of autumn's loamy fires and of beasts.

I found the door I wanted and knocked. No answer. I tried the latch. It lifted, smooth as cream.

'They'd have been wiser to lock it,' Isabel whispered.

'Well for us they didn't.' I nudged her in ahead of me. 'Hello? Is anyone here?'

Inside was dark, all the windows shuttered. A muffled squeal was followed by a clang, then another squeal.

'It's Katie!' I called, into the ringing darkness. 'Katie Crilly. Maria? Are you here?'

Isabel let me go ahead of her. I walked into something dense and dusty, the heavy curtain that separated the shop from the back entry. I felt for an opening with my hands. Isabel sneezed. Upstairs, something fell.

I parted the curtains and stepped into the thinner dark of the shop itself. My heart skipped in fright when I saw the outlines of a crowd. Then I realized the shapes were bolts of cloth. As my eyes adjusted and my pulse slowed, the gloom resolved into shelves, counter, till, the vault of the stairs. I stood on the bottom step and called up, 'Where are you all?'

A small form came barrelling down and bumped into me with a sob of relief.

'Tishy, is that you? Are you on your own? Where is everyone?'

'Mammie and Da went to the Fairyhouse. Frieda left Maria in charge but she went out with John Joe, ages ago. She said not to budge and not let anyone in.'

Isabel sneezed again. The child pulled back. 'Who's that?'

'It's only Isabel.' A silence lengthened, where once I'd have said *Liam's fiancée.* 'Do you have any lamps, Tishy?'

'Maria said not to light 'em.'

'You can't sit in the dark all on your own.' I followed her back through the curtain to the storeroom. She moved with confidence, but we went more cautiously, testing the ground with our feet.

She handed me a box of matches. I struck one. Light bloomed around us and shadows ran up the walls. Tishy was misshapen. Something bulged under her pinafore. I dropped the match and we were in the dark again.

'What on earth –' I struck another match to a candle on the shelf. A small shape separated from Tishy and scampered across the room.

Isabel shrieked. 'What was that?'

Just then the shop door rattled, splintered, crashed open. The candlelight wavered, showing Isabel's distorted face. I caught the handle of the storeroom door and jerked it shut. The sudden draught extinguished the light. I felt for the key I'd seen on its hook, fumbled to get it into the lock and turned it. Out in the shop, it sounded as if hundreds of hobnailed boots were stamping on the counter. My skin crawled, as though insects were making their way along my arms and in under my hair, down my spine. My heart knocked at my ribs, wanting out. I pushed a fist against it, holding it in place. I didn't understand what had happened. How had the seams of the world come undone so fast? What was this hellish place we'd stumbled into?

Tishy wailed. I put a hand over her face, found her mouth and held it, to quiet her. 'Ssh!'

She pushed my hand away. 'It wasn't me.'

The eerie wail was repeated, followed by chatter, from a high shelf.

'What *is* it?' Isabel whispered.

'He's a monkey.' Tishy coaxed the thing off its shelf and folded herself to the floor against the wall, crooning and rocking.

The door was shaken and kicked. I pressed my back to the cold, powdery plaster of the wall. I'd a strange sensation, as though my damp skin were thickening, squeezing me out of myself.

Another vicious kick. Then nothing.

When it had been quiet for a while, we unlocked the door,

pushed it open a crack, waited, then opened it all the way. Tishy turned on the main electric light. The shop was a mess of tumbled rolls of fabric, spills of colour.

My heart was still racing as we tried to restore some kind of order to what was left of the rolls of cloth. The monkey watched, his large black eyes peering out from a greyish-pink face framed by long black hair. Tishy picked him up and hid her face in his fur.

'Where did he come from?' I asked.

'Da gave him to Mammie for Easter.'

'What's his name?'

'Paschal.'

It wasn't really funny, but we laughed.

'Where did he come from?' Isabel asked.

'He was a barrel monkey, but the man was mean. Dada saved him and brought him home.' Tishy set the monkey free and he scurried along the shelves to sit on a high ledge, scratching his head.

I couldn't leave the girl there on her own. Whoever those people were, they could come back, any minute. We found a receipt book in a drawer and I wrote a note, saying Tishy was with me.

She wouldn't leave the monkey, even though I told her it was a bad idea to bring him. He could take fright and run away, I said, though what I was really afraid of was that Mother wouldn't allow him in the house. He wrapped his hairy arms around Tishy's neck and lifted large, sad eyes to mine.

Tishy carried the monkey, like a baby, on her hip. Up the west side of the Square we went. I wasn't superstitious, but I avoided looking in the direction of the Black Church, glad we didn't have to go any closer. There was enough devilry abroad.

We hurried down the steps to our area door and I knocked on the window. The curtain flicked aside. Lockie's ruddy face appeared, creased in a huge smile, vanished. Seconds later, the door creaked open a fraction, just enough to let us slip through. 'Thank heaven you're safe!' Lockie said. 'They're beside themselves in there!'

I went in ahead of the others. Mother and Florrie were at the kitchen table. Mother blessed herself when she saw us. 'It's all right,' I said. 'We're all right. Where's Dad?'

'He's not back yet.'

'No trams,' Florrie said. 'Matt's not here either.'

'I have Isabel with me and – Mother, you'll never guess, we found Frieda Leamy's little sister Tishy all on her own and a mob in the shop. She's only six and –'

Mother looked past me. 'What is that – *creature*?'

Tishy wrapped both arms around the monkey, who bared his big yellow teeth and scolded us all.

'It's the Leamys' monkey.' I stood between them, pleaded with my eyes for Mother to listen. 'She wouldn't leave without him.'

Isabel came in, touching her hair lightly into place. She swept her palms together and held out one hand to Mother. 'Hello, Mrs Crilly. Hello, Florrie.'

My eyes were drawn to the ring, a hint of demure green against the navy-blue of her skirt.

'There you are, Isabel, welcome.' Mother smiled in a fixed sort of way. 'The child is one thing, but as for that yoke, the monkey – it can't stay. It's likely riddled with fleas.'

'He'd a big long bath this morning,' Tishy said. 'He's clean as squeak.'

As if he understood, Paschal combed his hair with his long fingers and preened, as for a mirror. The corners of Mother's mouth twitched.

'Well. We'll see. Where have you been, Katie? We were worried sick! Isabel. I was beginning to think we'd not see you again. Come upstairs. Tell us your news. Your supper's ruined, I'm afraid. We waited, but –'

Lockie waved away our apologies. 'Can't be helped,' she said. 'I'll make a Welsh rarebit, will that do?'

'That would be gorgeous, Lockie, we're starved.'

'Upstairs with you, and wait. I'll be up directly. Missie here can wait with me. Sit down, child. What about your man, the monkey? I suppose he eats bread?'

'He likes it soaked in milk,' said Tishy.

Lockie put her fists on her big hips. 'Does he, now? He'll take what he's given, I presume?' She busied herself with cups, put a beaker of milk in front of Tishy. 'I suppose water is good enough for his Lordship?'

Florrie sniffed. 'He shouldn't be at the table.'

'Ah, leave him,' I said. 'He's not doing any harm – look, he's dozing off.' It was true. Paschal's head rested on Tishy's shoulder. The thick lids of his eyes slid shut.

Mother and Isabel had gone on upstairs, but Florrie held me back in the passage. 'I met Louisa Nolan on the Square,' she said. 'They saw Matt, a week ago, in the March Theatre. In the matinée!'

'And?'

'*In* the matinée. He was up on the stage. During Lent.'

'If they were at the theatre themselves, they can hardly pass remarks about him. What was the play?'

Florrie waved this irrelevance away. 'Louisa said one of the players was ill and Matt –'

'Was it that Scottish company he admires so much?'

'Oh, Katie! How would I know a thing like that?' She gave me a puck in the arm, disgusted. 'You're no use.' She stamped up the stairs ahead of me.

In the breakfast room, Isabel was reciting our adventures. Already it felt like an invention, from too much telling. I wished I could leave them all and go up to Liam's room to sit at the window and think about all I'd seen and heard.

I let Isabel do the talking. The Shelbourne, the barricades, the file of men going into Trinity. 'Then, we went to Miss Colclough's house.'

'Ah. The famous Captain Wilson.'

'What's he like?' Florrie asked.

'Quite rude,' Isabel said.

Mother looked pleased. I got up to help Lockie serve the food from a tray on the sideboard. There was a plate of golden cheese melting into toasted bread for each of us. 'I thought you'd like some yourself, ma'am. The girl is downstairs with a bowl of bread and milk.'

I could just see it, child and monkey side by side with their identical plates of food.

'Did he tell you anything we didn't already know?' Mother asked.

'No – but he was called away to deal with some trouble. We really didn't see him for very long.' Time had passed, all right, but I couldn't account for it. 'He mentioned putting away valuables, just in case.'

'We've locked up the presents, and the silver.' Florrie spread a thick layer of butter on the last piece of bread. 'Eugene went to the Imperial.'

'What on earth for?'

'To watch.' She took a bite. Her small, even teeth left their mark on the butter.

'We saw people watching, from Wynn's.' Isabel rubbed a knot in the wood of the table with a finger. 'Aren't you worried about Eugene?'

'Not at all, why would I be?'

No one said anything. Isabel's silence was the loudest. At

last she said, with obvious effort, 'You must be looking forward to your wedding no end, Florrie.'

At Mother's bidding, Florrie brought the leather-bound memory-book from the credenza. Mother held it open to show Isabel the epigraph inscribed inside the cover. 'Liam liked these lines, from Professor Kettle.' She'd picked the quote about justice and the flaming coals.

I dreaded Isabel's response. She stared at it for a long time, but didn't comment. She took the book from Mother and turned the pages slowly, murmuring at every one. She looked at each of the letters pasted into the book, but I didn't think she was reading them. 'Oh!' She'd stopped at the thick cream-coloured page, with the poem written out in her own graceful handwriting. She blinked and flicked over the page, fast.

I'd loved that poem since I first read it, when I was fifteen or so and easy to thrill. I didn't know how she could bear to look at it here, in front of us, with Mother breathing down her neck. The words rolled, stately and mysterious, through my mind:

> Had I the heavens' embroidered cloths,
> Enwrought with golden and silver light,
> The blue and the dim and the dark cloths
> Of night and light and the half-light,
> I would spread the cloths under your feet:
> But I, being poor, have only my dreams;
> I have spread my dreams under your feet;
> Tread softly because you tread on my dreams.

I heard them not in the poet's high, incantatory voice but in Liam's, warm and rich.

I was relieved when Isabel finally closed the book and Mother put it away. There was a sound of distant gunshots. 'I don't understand, who *are* these people? What do they want?' She said this the way someone repeats a thing they've said many times already, with no expectation of an answer.

Lockie had come up to clear the dishes. 'I heard your man John Connolly from the Abbey was one of them, and he shot dead,' Lockie said.

'Not Sean Connolly?' Isabel said.

'Sean, John, what matter?' That was Mother.

'Matt's friend?' I was as stunned as Isabel looked. Half the young women in Dublin were gone on Connolly, a handsome young actor. I'd seen him myself a fortnight ago, signing programmes at the stage door, shaking hands with people. He winked at me over their heads, mocking himself and his popularity. I'd walked on, smiling, for no better reason than that he'd smiled at me.

'That anyone we know would be involved – although, really, Matthew's artistic friends hardly count.' Mother shook her head.

'Everyone knows everyone in this town,' I said. 'One way or another.'

'They're after a republic,' Lockie said. 'So they say.'

'Pity they had to use bloodshed to get it,' Isabel said.

'And stab our own soldiers in the back while they're at it.' The mourning brooch on Mother's chest rose to catch the light, like some strange fish. 'It's a scandal, a handful of layabouts, taking advantage of the holiday. Do they think they can throw on any old outfit and call it a uniform, make themselves an army, start off their own war in the middle of town?'

Lockie gathered up plates and clattered them on to the sideboard, but that didn't distract Isabel. 'No uniform justifies killing,' she said.

I sucked in a breath. How did she have the nerve to say such things, and to us?

She put down her cup. Her hands were unsteady. 'No cause is worth it.'

'How disloyal you are.' Mother's lips were white.

Colour flushed through Isabel's neck. 'I'm as loyal as anyone,' she said, with dignity. 'But principles need our loyalty too.'

'I meant to Liam. To his memory.'

Air drained from the room. Isabel's hands tore at each other in her lap. Her fingers found the ring and began to twist it.

I was ashamed. Here she was, stranded in our house, the world outside our door gone mad, and everyone except Lockie lined up against her. Liam would be livid with all of us. My instinct was to get her out of there, and fast. 'It's getting late. Your father will be worried, Isabel.'

'She can't go out in that commotion,' Lockie said.

'I'd like to try.'

I said I'd go with her, and in the heel of it Lockie came too, sent by Mother to make sure I came back. It was bad enough that Dad and Matt hadn't come home.

Unseemly and unsavoury didn't even enter into it. We'd only gone a short distance when we knew it would be impossible to go further. The street was lit by bonfires. It boiled with people, a seething cauldron of firelight and oily shadows. If the city were to drink itself insensible, this is how it might dream, like a sleeping dog, twitching and moaning.

Lockie turned us straight around, as though we were children. And, as though we were children, we turned at her bidding and retreated home.

I pitied Isabel, stuck with us, but I was relieved to be back, whole-heartedly on her side. Where Liam would want me to be.

Isabel couldn't take Matt's room, because what if he turned up in the middle of the night? She would sleep in the spare bed in Florrie's room.

Tishy pressed close to my side. I put an arm around her. 'Tishy can squash in with me.'

'But not the monkey,' Mother said. 'Not upstairs. There are limits.'

Lockie poured the remnants from the teapot on to the table to wash it down for the night. 'Where will we put him, so?'

'He sleeps on top of the wardrobe at home,' Tishy said.

Mother looked scandalized. 'Not in my house, missie!'

Someone wandered past outside, singing in a wavering, off-key voice. 'A little of what you fancy does you good . . .' A woman laughed. In the distance, we heard the crack of a rifle.

Tishy started to cry.

'Oh, all right. But just this once.' Mother sighed. 'I wish Bill was here.'

Isabel stopped me on the landing. 'I've something to confess. I suspected you of reading my letters to Liam last year, before you gave them back to me. I'm sorry. I should have known better.'

Guilty, I remembered that horrible afternoon when Dad read out the letters. Mother's reaction. 'How do you know I didn't?'

'I just do – and I'm not sure I'd have been as principled, in your place. You're a good friend.'

No, I was a fraud. I gave her a weak smile and turned away, into Liam's room. It was his privacy I'd been guarding, not hers.

I spread an old jumper on top of Liam's wardrobe, a nest for the monkey. He seemed to understand that he should stay there. He talked himself to sleep, complaining quietly to the hand he used to cover his face, the thumb in his mouth but the fingers, disconcertingly human, spread in a wide fan across the rounded ridge of his nose. Tishy turned on her side and slid her thumb into her mouth too. The house settled, the city was quiet at last.

I took off my clothes. Too tired to hang them up, I folded them over the chair and climbed in beside Tishy, moving her whitish hair off the pillow so I could put my head down.

Tuesday, 25 April 1916

I dreamed a child at a burning window, yelling for a ladder. A cold draught woke me. Tishy had kicked the blankets off the bed. I hauled them back up over me and tried to burrow down towards sleep again, but sleep wouldn't have me. The dull *crrump* of an explosion was followed by a scare of birds, then a throbbing silence, into which crept a braided sound of breathing, deep and regular. A faint whistle drew my eye to the wardrobe. I froze. A dark tail dangled from the cornice. Then I remembered: the monkey. He was snoring.

Beside me, Tishy slept on, sprawled on her back. One small arm was bent under her head, palm upwards. Her thin feet poked out from under the sheets. I got up, settled the covers over her and went to the window. It was another glorious, blue morning. A pale spiral of smoke wafted away from Sackville Street. Disgruntled birds were returning to roost on chimneys and ridges and in the trees across the road.

Still heavy with sleep, I pulled on my clothes and slipped out of the room, carrying my shoes so as not to wake anyone on my way downstairs. I sat on the bottom step to put them on and went into the kitchen. Lockie was at the sink, running water into the kettle. In front of the oven was the empty space where Beck had slept in a basket through his last months of life.

'Did you hear that noise?' I asked.

Lockie leaned sideways on to the window for a better view of the street. 'I can't see anything, only that cat from next door, the yoke. *Shoo!*' She knocked on the glass, seeming to set off another explosion, then turned back to me. 'You're not going out? God only knows what's happening.'

'I've to go round and see if the Leamys got my note, about Tishy. Listen out for her, will you? I won't be long.'

I was tense, hurrying across the top of the Square and down the west side. There was litter strewn everywhere, paper and rags on the street and banked up against the pavement, but few people, as though the earth had opened up and swallowed the revellers as suddenly as it had spewed them out. On Parnell Street the buildings jostled and nudged each other, the better to whisper last night's scandals. A cart had miraculously escaped the destruction and stood at a tilt, its shafts pointing two long arms at the sky, its two big wheels buckled on the cobbles. My shoes bit down on broken glass. Pity the barefoot children now.

The door to the Leamys' shop was still shut, that was something. Loud knocking roused no one. The victualler next door had a covered arch leading back to the lanes. I walked through it. There were people there, recounting last night's events, assessing the damage. The Leamys weren't back yet, they told me. Two of the children, Maria and John Joe, had come in late, sick from sweets and excitement, to find the shop a wreck and Tishy gone. The granny came and brought the pair away for safekeeping in Drumcondra, or was it Phibsborough? No sign of the parents, or of Frieda.

I explained that we had Tishy with us. 'Frieda left before the trouble started,' I said. 'She wasn't to know.'

There was something in the air I couldn't put my finger on. Some of these people could have been among the mob that stormed the shop, for all I knew. 'That was a bad business, here, last night,' I said, testing.

'Shocking.' This man's voice had a smarmy lilt to it I didn't trust. I'd had it in mind to bring Tishy back and leave her here, where her parents would find her, among people she knew. Now I wasn't so sure.

They were all listening to Mrs Clancy, who owned the newsagent's and knew everyone's business. A narrow woman with a beaked nose and pitted skin, she leaned in to talk, stabbing the air for emphasis. The rebels were holed up in buildings the length of the street, she said, and along the quays. The military would roust them out of it, any minute.

A pair of boys wheeled a cart loaded with wood down the bumpy lane.

'There yiz are,' Mrs Clancy said. 'About time too.'

The neighbours set to work unloading the wood.

'What's it for?'

Mrs Clancy took hold of a plank as long as she was, and propped it against a wall. She might have been wiry, but she was strong. 'We're putting up shutters, for to keep the gurriers out.'

'You're expecting them back?'

'Who's to stop them, only ourselves? You'd best get on home and see what's to be done.' She went for another plank.

'Do ye have a gun in the house?' the smarmy man asked, as I moved away.

'Pardon?'

'Only, ye might need one. If things get any more hectic.'

Liam's voice slid into my mind. *Say nothing.*

'I hope ye've a few strong men about the place, anyways,' Mrs Clancy said.

'My father,' I lied. 'My brothers.'

Back at home, I went straight upstairs to the box room. The gun cupboard was locked. The key was kept in the linen cupboard on the landing. I wanted to see if we had bullets, for all the good they might do. I didn't know the first thing about guns. Matt wasn't likely to either, but Dad should be back before long.

The key stuck in the lock. I jiggled it around 'til it bit and the door creaked open. The cupboard was empty. No matter how hard I stared, there wasn't a single gun in there.

There was hardly a point to locking it up again, but I did, and put the key back in its hiding place. Liam must have moved the guns, after all. I couldn't think why, or where he'd have put them.

I went back down to Lockie, in the kitchen. The monkey was sitting on a chair, gripping the table with both hands, staring at her with fierce concentration.

'Lookit this.' Lockie threw a bite-sized piece of bread into the air. He caught it in his mouth. 'He's gas altogether,' she said, patting his head. 'I wonder has he other tricks. Did you find the Leamys?'

'They're not back yet. And there were no newspapers that I could see. Lockie, Liam's guns have gone. Do you know where they might be?'

'I do not.'

'Did he move them? Who else would have taken them?'

'How would I know?' She threw another piece of bread to the monkey, too hard. He scrambled under the table to retrieve it. He sat on his hunkers, down there in the dark vault made by table and chairs, and peered out like a prisoner. 'Go on and get yourself a bite of breakfast. And don't you go saying anything about the guns, upstairs. This carry-on will end soon enough once and the military decide to grace us with their presence.' She dusted her hands together and wiped them on her apron. 'No need to upset your ma over nothing.'

'Tell me, Lockie. You know something. What is it?'

She scraped leftovers from the plates with a bone-handled knife, into the chipped blue bowl we used for scraps. 'Leave it alone.'

'If you don't tell me, I'll go straight to Mother and tell her the guns are missing.'

The knife dropped to the flags, making them ring with a shrill, bouncing echo that nearly covered what she said. 'I don't know anything for sure. But last week I noticed the key was in the lock. I should have checked the cupboard, but I didn't. I tried the door and it was locked, so I put the key away.' She picked up the knife and slid it into the sink. 'Then Matt called me away and I forgot.' At last she met my eye.

'Matt? Lockie, you don't think he's in with that crowd inside the GPO?'

'I swear to God I don't know. I didn't think of it 'til now.' She looked me full in the face, let me see her worry. 'Do you think he'd be one of them?'

'He's not the type.' No more than Sean Connolly, whose name hovered nearby but refused to be spoken.

There was a queer, unpleasant atmosphere in the dining room, as though I'd interrupted something. Mother was folding her napkin into a tight square. Florrie was inspecting her nails. Isabel looked on the verge of tears.

'What's happened?'

No one answered. The knocker sounded, a loud, fast bang on the front door.

'I'll go,' I said.

'I'll go with you,' Mother said.

'We can't all go,' Florrie said. Nevertheless, we all trooped out to the hall to see who it was, Isabel last. In came Eugene, hatless, perspiring in his heavy overcoat. Tight little curls, darkened and damp, clung to his forehead. Florrie beamed and patted his arm, looking thrilled and magnificent, as though she'd made him herself.

While we bombarded him with questions, Eugene pulled a handkerchief from his pocket and pressed it to the back of his neck, then his forehead. 'There's nothing to see. They say there's Germans behind it. I need to go to Cabra to check on Mother. Come with me. You're too close to the trouble here.' A bald spot the size of a shilling gleamed at the crown of his damp head. 'I've a side-car waiting around the corner. Someone else will take it if we don't hurry. How many are you?'

Mother looked around our small crowd. 'We couldn't possibly.' Her voice was faint. 'I shouldn't leave the house. If Bill – there are too many of us – what should I do?'

'I'll stay, ma'am,' Lockie said. 'When they come in, I'll tell them where ye've gone.'

'I'd rather leave a note. I'll need you, Lockie. We don't want to put a strain on Mrs Sheehan's household.'

'I'll go home, in any case,' Isabel said.

Eugene objected, but she stood tall and proud, at an angle where I couldn't see her face, and said she'd find a way, she had money to pay a cabman.

I waited for Mother to say this was nonsense, but in a chilly tone she said, 'Very well, you must do as you please.'

'Must you?' I asked.

'Believe me, I'd rather.' Her voice shook. She shivered, and folded her arms around herself.

'Then I'll go with you.'

Mother objected, which made me more determined to accompany her than I had been. 'What would Liam have to say, if we let her go alone? And I can call in to Baggot Street to leave a message for Frieda about Tishy.'

Eugene said we must shut all the windows and bolt the downstairs doors before leaving. Florrie and I went off to do this, while Lockie was despatched upstairs for Mother's jewellery case. Nothing else, he said.

When we came back down from checking the windows, Isabel was in the hall with her coat and hat. Lockie had

Mother's teak jewellery box, wrapped in a towel. Tishy was there too, the monkey in her arms.

'I won't foist that brute on Eugene's mother.' Mother glared at poor Paschal, as if everything were his fault.

'He's not the worst, ma'am,' Lockie said, flicking a forefinger against the monkey's cheek.

'I wouldn't dream of asking.'

There was a small silence Eugene did nothing to fill. Tishy tugged on my skirt. 'I want to stay with you,' she whispered.

Isabel sent a look of utter loathing Mother's way. She cupped Tishy's white head with her hands, smoothed her fine hair. 'You and your monkey are welcome at my house, lovey.'

'Whoever's coming, we need to leave now.' Eugene ushered us out of the house and on to the pavement. The side-car was at the corner, with the driver talking to two men who climbed on while we watched. Eugene said something I couldn't hear and propelled Florrie along towards them, gesturing for us to follow.

'Really, Katie! How will you get back?' Mother asked, looking from Eugene and Florrie to me, to Isabel, then back towards the corner. 'I'll be worried.'

'I'll be at Isabel's, or Eva's. I'll come straight home when things are back to normal.'

'They're leaving, ma'am.' Lockie pulled the front door shut and tested it, to make sure the latch had caught. She took hold of Mother's elbow and steered her after the others. I watched 'til they were safely ensconced in the side-car. They made a strange-looking group. I'd a pang of regret, seeing them go.

We stopped a man who was hurrying away from Sackville Street to ask if he knew what was happening. He said the gunmen had the hotels; the guests had been told to leave. He was just after helping a pair of elderly sisters up from the country find shelter. Their boarding house was full to bursting and the woman there said they'd run out of supplies before long. There was no sign of the army, but word of German submarines off the coast. 'You ladies'd be better off staying indoors, 'til it's over.' He lifted his hat and strode away.

A pulse thudded in my neck. 'What would it mean,' I asked Isabel, 'if the Germans were here?'

'One army's as bad as another,' Isabel said.

I looked at her with dislike. Mother could have been right about her, after all. 'But if both sides are here . . .' It was too obvious a thought to finish.

Sackville Street was a scene of wreckage. The air still smelled of fire. Children sifted through the rubbish, gathering scraps of wood. Strips of cloth were caught on spikes of barbed wire.

To avoid the guns, we walked east, then south, east again, then south again, discussing every turn, making dogleg tracks through backstreets and lanes where the atmosphere was one of aftermath: stunned, withheld. Doors, where there were doors, were open to the street. Shadowy figures moved around inside, a few people leaned on doorjambs or squatted against sun-warmed walls, talking in low voices. Lines of limp, drab washing stretched across the street overhead, from window to window. The monkey inclined people to be friendly.

Tishy spoke to him in high, bossy tones. 'Look at the state of the place,' she lectured. She hitched him up higher when he threatened to slide down her hip.

'Do you want me to take him for a bit, Tishy?' I asked. 'I promise I'll give him back.'

I took the animal from her. He was lighter than I'd expected, and his hair was stiffer. He held on to my coat, front and back, bunching the material in his fingers. He swayed along, tilting his head this way and that, while Tishy skipped alongside, humming a tuneless song.

On Abbey Street, brand-new bicycles and motor-cycles were tangled together to make a barricade, about eight feet high. Small boys tugged on a bicycle. It made a harsh, screeching sound, but wouldn't budge.

'I wouldn't go that way.' The speaker wasn't much older than us, but her teeth were blackened stumps. She was sweeping glass and debris into mounds, away from the road. 'They say the British has the Customs House, beyond.' She coughed, and spat. 'Bad cess to them.' She went back to her sweeping.

We took a side street to the quays. Butt Bridge looked clear. We edged up to it slowly, our backs to the quay wall. A trade union banner hung, limp, over the door to Liberty Hall, alongside a green one. The building was strangely still for one that was said to be crammed with revolutionaries, armed to the teeth. The windows were blank.

On the far side of the river, a man in a small crowd of bystanders waved a piece of white cloth. I caught Tishy's sleeve to hold her back. She turned and took Paschal. I'd a strange impression of loss when his weight was lifted from me.

'Are they calling us on, or warning us not to try it?'

A woman shook her fist at us, or at the house behind us. I looked back over my shoulder. A shadow moved at an upstairs window in Beresford Place. 'They're watching the bridges.' It was like speaking lines from a book – or one of Liam's earlier letters.

'Who?' Isabel asked. 'I mean, which side are they?'

'Does it matter?' Lengths of metal jutted from the parapet of the railway bridge above us. I nudged her to look.

'We could go back.'

'If they were going to shoot us, they'd have done it by now.' I wasn't at all sure about that, but I didn't want to turn back. Some stubborn nerve had set in me, driving me on.

Tishy decided it, stepping on to the bridge ahead of us. We edged out after her, then picked up our skirts and ran as best we could. 'Go on, segocia!' someone called. There were cheers and applause when we reached the other side. Tishy made a little curtsey to our audience and on we went.

We turned and turned again, passed under the railway bridge at Westland Row without incident. The station entrance was blocked.

We'd been told there'd been trouble there, but we saw no sign of it. Relieved, we planned the rest of our route. All going well, I'd stop in at the hospital and tell Frieda where her sister was, make a detour to enquire about Eva, then follow them to Isabel's house.

At the top of the street, we paused before crossing the road. 'It's eerie, isn't it?' I said. 'So still.'

As if to contradict me, a motor-car came out through the back gate of Trinity and accelerated towards us. We waited for it to pass so we could cross, but it bumped to a stop beside us, a little Vauxhall. A tall man unfolded from the passenger seat. 'Ladies,' he said. 'The streets aren't safe. You should be at home!'

'We're on our way there now,' Isabel said.

He glanced back at the driver. 'And home is . . .'

'Herbert Park.'

'It's on our way. Will you take a lift?' He grasped Isabel's elbow. 'Do. The streets are unpredictable.'

A burst of rapid gunfire came from the direction of the Green.

Isabel hesitated. 'Katie?'

There was no sign of trouble here. There was no traffic, apart from the Vauxhall. It looked very small.

'You go. I'll walk.'

Isabel bundled Tishy and Paschal into the car.

'But where are you going?' The driver looked cross. I was holding them up now.

'Just up to Baggot Street, to the hospital. It's not far. I'm not worried.'

The two young men assessed the distance between here and there, exchanged a look. 'I insist.' The driver's face was grim.

I got in, with little grace. Two minutes later I was struggling out again, outside the hospital, and Isabel was changing our plan. She'd see me at Percy Place, she said, once she'd shown her father she was still in one piece. The men said it might not be easy to move around for much longer; chances were the authorities would close the streets.

'If that happens,' I said to Isabel, 'let's both stay put, wherever we are. Agreed?'

'Agreed.'

The car made off towards Pembroke Road. A sudden *bang!* set my pulse hammering, but it was only their engine backfiring as they picked up speed.

I stood on the pavement and looked up the shallow stone steps to the red and yellow frontage of the hospital, whose proper title was the Royal City of Dublin Hospital. Everyone just called it 'Baggot Street', except Eva and Bartley, who called it 'The Hospital', as if it were the only hospital in town, because Bartley worked there.

When Liam and I were around ten years old, we all went on an excursion to a bazaar in the RDS showgrounds to raise money for this hospital. The Gigas Bazaar was the thrill of that year. Mother kept the catalogue, in a drawer at home, glossy pages with portraits of various bigwigs and a list of stalls and patrons. Florrie was thrilled by the gondolas that glided through deep caverns lit with green and blue and gold. She and her friend Glenda would get to the end of the ride, rise from the scarlet cushions, disembark and go directly around to join the back of the queue. Liam and I were enthralled by Edison's Animated Pictures of the Boer War: raised bayonets presenting a forest of steel. Horses prancing before they fell. How strange it was, we told each other, to think those men and horses were long dead now, but on film, they'd live forever.

The building was a fright. It was four, in places five, storeys over a basement, with a square porch jutting out of it and maybe fifty windows, some arched, some tall and narrow. It might have been planned to look busy, as a hospital should, but, surrounded as it was by plainer buildings, it only looked confused.

No use putting it off any longer. I dreaded seeing Frieda after yesterday's fiasco, but I had to go in and tell her about Tishy.

The hall was busy with people in street clothes and bandages. I went to the porter's desk. 'I've a message for one of the nurses, Frieda Leamy. Could you find out if she's free?'

I waited on a bench. A nurse came over to see was I all right. I told her I was waiting for someone. She eyed the bench. 'There's those who'd be better off sitting,' she said.

I got up, guilty, and moved off into a corner. Not only useless but in the way. A door opened and Con came through it, his dark head bent to an older bald-headed man. Con was talking, and the older man's eyes were cast down, listening.

Frieda appeared on the stairs and hurried down, her face pinched and anxious. 'Is it bad news?'

'No, no, sorry, I should have said. Just that we have Tishy.' I began to tell Frieda what I knew about the other children and the shop, but she stopped me.

'I know! Jim, our porter, arranged a lift across town for me this morning. I just missed you. Mrs Clancy told me Granny

146

has the two little rips that ran off – she said you'd been, you've got Tishy – where is she?'

'Isabel's taken her, to Herbert Park.'

'That Maria! She's useless. She shouldn't have left Tishy on her own.'

'I'd say Tishy wouldn't leave –'

'The monkey. I don't know what Da was thinking when he bought him, but Tishy's fierce attached. Your mother must have been thrilled. Will Tishy be all right with Isabel, d'you think? I had to come back, we're full to bursting with casualties and expecting more.'

'Casualties?'

'People have been shot and killed.' She said it calm and flat; we could have been talking about weather. It wasn't the first time I'd felt the gap between my experience and hers. 'Tishy's no trouble. We'll keep her 'til we can get her home.'

Over by the main door, the bald man shook hands with Con and left. Con turned around and caught my eye. I waved. He started to come over, but a nurse intercepted him.

Frieda was thanking me. 'I owe you a favour. You should hurry on to Herbert Park. You don't want to get caught up in whatever's going to happen. It's the queerest atmosphere I've ever known. I've to get back.' She threw a glance towards Con, but the other nurse was urging him away. I watched them too. I'd half a mind to ask Con if he knew anything about Matt, because they were friendly, but he'd already gone, down a busy corridor.

I watched Frieda's brisk ascent of the stairs. Everyone here was so purposeful. They all had urgent things to do, places to be, people who depended on them. But: casualties? How many and how bad, I wondered. Would the army come in and annihilate the men in the park and in the GPO and in the houses? Surely they'd put their weapons down and come out, as Captain Wilson said they would. Surely to God Matt wasn't one of them.

I left the hospital and considered my options: left, to Herbert Park? Or right, across the canal bridge, towards Miss Moorhead's nursing home, and Eva, just a few hundred yards away?

Miss Moorhead's nursing home was a pinkish terraced house with a brown neighbour on one side, a red on the other. Its door was ajar. Miss Moorhead herself was out on the front step, looking up and down the street. 'Where've you come from, dear? What have you seen?'

I described our journey across town, all we'd seen and heard. She clucked and *tsked* and shook her head at every word. 'Nonsense, the Germans have nothing to do with it, it's the Sinn Féiners. Daftest thing ever. Well. You've come at a good time, we've just finished with the dinners. Go on, up with you to see your sister, the poor lamb, but don't go tiring her with all this carry-on. She's not able for it. And don't stay long, there's a doctor coming.'

'I won't.' I went past her into a tiled hall that smelled of cabbage with a faint underlay of carbolic, despite the open door. It was just on noon, and they'd finished with their dinners already? A vase of yellow silk geraniums stood on a semicircular table before the inner arch. The doors on either side of it stood ajar, giving glimpses of an iron bedstead in each, with a crucifix pinned to the bare white wall behind, a washstand in the corner. The two rooms looked identical, except that one was empty, while a person in a nightcap slept in the other, the face so old and wizened I couldn't make out was it a man or a woman.

Miss Moorhead closed the hall door and directed me upstairs. Eva was in a room on her own, propped against a mountain of pillows, half sitting and half lying, in a high iron bed like the ones downstairs. A fine blue silk shawl draped around her head and shoulders gave her the look of a statue, 'til she saw me and her face came alive. 'Hello, you,' she said, as though it were the most ordinary thing in the world for me to materialize in front of her.

I kissed her clammy forehead. 'Hello, yourself. How are you?'

'Fine. I'm fine.' She didn't look it. Her skin had an unhealthy tinge and her eyes were bloodshot.

'Miss Moorhead said there's a doctor coming.'

She waved this away. 'I'm only tired. Bartley says it's natural.' She took my hand. 'I'm dying with boredom. And curiosity. What's going on out there? Sit. No, not the chair, here. On the bed. Where I can see you properly.'

I took a jar of Florrie's hand lotion off the bureau. 'Want some?' I unscrewed the lid and poured some lotion into her cupped palms, took some myself. The room sweetened with the smell of flowering almonds.

She rubbed her hands together and dipped her face to them. 'She'll be rich before we know it, once she and Eugene start their shop. There'll be no living with her.'

'Just as well we won't have to.' The joke fell flat in my own mind. It was no laughing matter. Once Florrie was married and gone, we'd be moving. I worked the lotion into my own skin, pushing in between the knuckle-bones and pulling on my fingers. 'How are you, really?'

'Tired.' She winced, put her palms against her stomach. 'Sore, today.' A volley of shots from the direction of the Green turned her head to the window. 'What's happening? No one will tell me anything.'

I looked around to make sure Miss Moorhead wasn't in earshot. 'Rebels have taken buildings all over the city. Sackville Street is in bits, between fires and looting.' I hesitated, unsure what to say next. We'd heard so many different things

149

on our way across town this morning, there was no knowing which version of events was true. She looked worn out. Miss Moorhead had said not to tire her. On the other hand, if I was in Eva's place, I'd want to know whatever there was to know. I wouldn't want people to lie to me. 'Listen,' I said. 'This is what I've heard by way of explanation, you take your pick.' I hammed it up, for her, talking up the rumours and counting them on my fingers. 'The Kaiser is beyond in the Gresham, but they can't give him his breakfast because the cook didn't report for work this morning. They say he's getting very cranky, no telling what he might do. Some boys were playing Cowboys and Indians and lost the run of themselves. There's a submarine stuck in the mud at Grand Canal Dock. The Pope has committed suicide in Rome, in sheer despair at the treachery of the Irish. Robbers, armed to the teeth, have taken over every post office in the country, they're after any first-day-of-issues they can find –'

'Stop!' She was laughing, holding her stomach. 'Be serious.'

'Miss Moorhead says it's the Shinners' handiwork.'

'Were you nervous on the way over?'

'No, but there's a strange atmosphere, right enough.'

A spasm of pain twisted her face. She pushed the covers down off her stomach. She caught me looking. 'Peculiar, isn't it? You'd nearly think I was going to have a baby. Look.' She pulled up her nightdress. Her skin was distended, with dark blotches that looked like broken veins. 'Feel it.'

When I touched it, her stomach was taut as a ball. The last – the first, the only – time I'd touched her that way before was when she was expecting Alanna, and had pulled her blouse and skirt apart in just this way, to show me what it was like. I'd felt something like a tiny bubble ripple against my palm, as Alanna turned inside her. There was no movement now. I took my hand away.

'It wasn't this bad last night,' she said. She adjusted her nightdress. 'What other news?'

I told her about Mr Briscoe, the auctioneer, and the offer of a job. 'Can't you just hear Mother? "No daughter of mine!"'

'"A shop?"' Eva intoned.

We laughed, but not for long.

'When can you go home?' I asked.

'It was meant to be tomorrow, but –'

We both looked at the small mound of her belly. Miss Moorhead's voice could be heard down in the hall, recounting some disaster, and a man's voice in response. 'Bartley.' Eva's face relaxed. 'He said he'd come, if he could get away from the hospital.' She sat up straighter and settled the covers over the bulge at her waist.

I had to be quick. 'Eva, remember you once warned me against Con Buckley? You said you knew things I didn't know. What things?'

'Why?'

'I'm curious, that's all.' I didn't believe what Frieda had said, thought less of her for saying it. I wouldn't give it credence by repeating it, especially not to Eva, who could damage his career, even without meaning to.

'I don't remember.' She looked at the door, expectant. 'Money, I think. Gambling, something like that. He runs around with a shower of high-flyers, Katie.'

We heard Bartley's footsteps on the stairs. He came straight to the head of the bed and kissed Eva's forehead, murmured her name. He looked at the shape she made under the bedclothes, then at me. 'Katie. Miss Moorhead says you've been here half an hour. It's too long. You'll tire her out.'

I'd never disliked him quite as much as I did then.

'Don't be hard on her. She's done me a world of good.' Eva squeezed my hand. 'Better than medicine.' Her head sank back into the pillow and her eyes slid shut. They looked bruised.

I was taken aback by the sudden change, as though she'd been making herself bright for my benefit and the effort had cost her. 'I'll go.'

'Wait, I'll see you out.'

I didn't want him to, but, short of saying it straight and causing a row that would do Eva no good, I couldn't stop him. He clearly had the run of the place. I went quickly downstairs, wanting rid of him, but he stopped me in the hall and brought me into the empty front room, shut the door.

'I'm sorry,' he said. 'She's exhausted. You weren't to know.' He rubbed his face with his hand.

'Why is her stomach like that, have you seen it?'

'Ascites. An accumulation of fluid –'

'What fluid? Why?'

'It could be any number of –'

'Please, Bartley. This is *Eva*.'

His pupils were pinpricks in the blue of his eyes. 'Guy Fitzmaurice is on his way over to have a look at her.'

'Tell me the truth, Bartley. What do you think it is?'

'We don't know for sure. What did she say about it?'

I'd the sense that he was keeping something from me. 'She wishes it was a baby.'

'There won't be any more babies.' He went to the window and stood with his back to me. 'You must know that she's not at all well, Katie. These recurring infections over the years – each one weakens her a little more than the last. She doesn't have much strength.'

'How serious is it? Is she in danger?'

He turned around. 'Danger?' The word hung, almost visible, in the air. 'Katie, Eva is as safe as she can be. I'm not sure I can say the same about Alanna. We're too close to the trouble, in Ely Place. I shouldn't really tell you this but – we were briefed, by an army officer, not long ago.'

'What did he say?'

'They think there are hundreds, possibly thousands, of rebels in positions around the Green. They're marshalling a massive force to counter them. They're on the move.'

Everything in me went cold. Thousands of rebels, and a massive force against them. 'Here? That's official? When will they get here?'

'They'd hardly tell us that. But the fighting could be intense, when they arrive.'

'Don't you think the rebels will back down, when it comes to it?'

'Possibly. It depends how many there are. How well armed they are. I suppose – I know nothing about it. Whatever happens, I want Alanna out of the way. I know it's a lot to ask, but I'm needed in the hospital. Nan would be a help to you.'

'I'll bring them to Dote and May in Percy Place,' I said, making up my mind. 'Their house is near enough to walk to, and quiet. If that doesn't suit, we'll go on to Isabel's, in Herbert Park. I'll get word to you somehow, at the hospital.'

A fine drizzle had started when I came out of the nursing home and walked up Baggot Street in the direction of the Green. Starting around Pembroke Street, soldiers lined the side of the road. A single file of soldiers lined Ely Place, and the atmosphere was horribly tense, but they made no attempt to stop me. It was as if they didn't even see me pass. Their faces were hidden by their caps. Rain beaded the shoulders of their uniforms.

I knocked on Eva's door. Nan opened it a crack and then pulled me inside. I told her what Bartley had said. Quickly, she packed two small holdalls.

We were barely on the pavement before we were stopped

by an officer. 'Excuse me, ladies. Would you mind opening those bags?'

Nan turned scarlet as a pair of knickers was lifted out, shaken, and tossed back into the bag. The bag I carried had food in it.

'Where are you going?' the officer asked.

'We're taking the child to a safer place.'

He laughed, with no trace of humour, but let us go.

Nan looked daggers at him as we turned into a side lane leading back to Baggot Street. 'Our fellas are brave, all the same. Good luck to them. I'd have half a mind to join them, only who'd look after her nibs?'

We walked as fast as Alanna's short legs and Nan's odd limp allowed. I looked sideways at her feet, in a man's large shoes that slapped the pavement like boats expecting water, finding stone instead. Despite what she'd said, she was jumpy. Every bang set her looking around. 'Is it far? Only, it's horrible hot out. My clothes are sticking to me.'

'You could take your shawl off.' From the look she gave me, I might as well have suggested she go naked through the streets.

Alanna had a grip on the shawl in any case, and was looking at the ground, watching where she put her feet. I saw what she was doing – avoiding the cracks.

'We'll be all right once we're over the bridge,' I told them.

Dote answered my knock on the basement door. Before I could explain, she opened the door wider. 'Isabel and Tishy are already here! They said you'd be along. We're glad of the company, to tell the truth. Safety in numbers.'

'We won't stay,' Isabel said, from inside the kitchen. We went in to her. Tishy sat at the table beside her. 'My father's car will come for us later. You're all welcome to come back with me to Herbert Park to spend the night. We have plenty of room.'

'You got here quickly,' I said.

'I changed my mind. We came straight here. I sent a note to Herbert Park, to send the car for us later.'

I decided not to ask her why. She was probably afraid her father wouldn't let her leave Herbert Park again, once she was safely home. She'd been dismissive of Hubie, but perhaps she was as anxious as I was for another chance to talk to him about Liam.

Paschal clung to Tishy's front like the bib of an apron. He looked at me with those sad black eyes of his. I held out my arms and he climbed into them. 'Where's May?'

'Having a rest,' Dote said. 'She got no sleep last night.'

Alanna squinted at Tishy, wrinkled her nose at the monkey and slid her hand into Nan's. 'Are they from the circus?'

I put my free hand on Tishy's curled head. 'The whole town's turned into one big circus, if you ask me. The biggest circus there ever was. Hello, May!'

'Who's this fellow?' May came in, wearing a loose house-dress and slippers. She didn't have to bend far to bring her face level with Tishy's. 'Is he your friend?'

'He's my mam's.'

'I wonder do we have nuts. Let's have a look. Come here to me, child.'

Tishy took Paschal from me and went with May into the pantry. After a while they re-emerged, triumphant, with a bag of walnuts and a nutcracker and set us to work prising the meat free from the shells. Paschal clapped his hands and bobbed his head in thanks for every nut we gave him.

'Does he have other tricks?' I asked, remembering Lockie.

'He dances,' Tishy said. 'He was in a show. And when people shout he breaks things. They taught him to do it, then sold him because of it.'

Alanna opened her mouth to yell, but Nan clapped a hand on her shoulder. 'Don't you dare.' Alanna made a face at Tishy instead.

When the fun of feeding nuts to Paschal had subsided, Dote said, 'Nan, the girls should wash their hands, after all that. There's a cloakroom on the return. May will show you.' She held my elbow to stop me going with them. I took Paschal from Tishy as she passed. When they'd gone, Dote told us some men had been killed nearby, soon after we'd left the day before.

'Then there was shooting through the night, we couldn't tell where. We didn't sleep a wink. Have you any word as to what's happening?'

I told them what Bartley had said to me.

'Never!' Dote said. 'Thousands in the Green?'

'We only saw a handful yesterday,' I reminded them.

Isabel got up and went to the window. 'They've had time to gather, though. I wonder how many there are.'

'And where.' Dote was grim. 'Not to mention how long this state of affairs will last.'

'Nan brought food,' I said, changing the subject as the others came back in. The holdall contained a ham wrapped in muslin, a dozen apples, two loaves of day-old bread and a ginger cake. 'A feast,' Dote said. 'Nan, you are a miracle. We'll have ham sandwiches later.'

'Fresh air first,' May said. She picked up a short-handled rake from the kitchen windowsill to show the girls. 'A thing Hubie made. Did I ever show it to you, Katie?' She twisted the handle and it lengthened; turned it the other way and it retracted, like a telescope. 'Ingenious, for hard to reach places. Come with me, girls, and I'll show you.'

But they soon tired of combing the earth in May's flower-beds and left her at it. Nan laid out a game of hopscotch on the flags near the back door. The air was sweet with honeysuckle and jasmine, the hum of bees. Spring continuing, no matter what. Dote watched from the garden bench, a straw hat shading her face. Tits swooped and darted around the bird feeder hanging from the plum tree, unalarmed by occasional shots in the distance.

Paschal darted in and stole the stone. Alanna shrieked in rage. The monkey screeched back at her and bared his teeth before shinning up the tree, scattering the birds.

'But it doesn't *matter*!' Tishy explained. 'Once it's landed, you *know* where not to hop.'

'I don't want to play any more.' Alanna folded her arms across her narrow chest.

Dote laughed. 'She's the image of you,' she told me.

I couldn't see it, myself. Tishy coaxed Paschal down from the tree. He got busy tangling her hair and scolding. His teeth showed like the yellowed keys of an old piano in the pinkish-grey skin of his face. I rescued Tishy's curls from his fingers.

May looked up from the flowerbed, where she was pulling weeds. 'This'll never do.' She got to her feet, groaning at her creaky knees. 'Come here to me, girls. Birds in a nest –' Next thing she had them, monkey and all, inside in the wheelbarrow and was pushing them around the garden in search of frogs. After a while she wheeled them to the back door and tipped them out and they all went inside in search of drinks of water. Dote went after them. I said we'd be in in a minute. I wanted to get Isabel on her own.

'I thought you were in a mad hurry to get home?'

'Not home, specifically.'

'What happened, back at our house? Did my mother say something that upset you?'

'She said she wants her ring back.'

So that's what caused the atmosphere in the breakfast room earlier. 'It's not hers.'

'She says it is.'

'Well, it's not. It belonged to our grandmother. Dad's mother. And Dad gave it to Liam, for you.'

'And I intend to keep it.' She was fierce, as if she thought I was after it too.

'Mother isn't herself, about Liam. I think seeing you, looking at the book – it upset her. Also, Eva's not well, and Matt's – being difficult. We're moving house soon. She has a lot to be dealing with.'

I sat on a garden bench that could have done with repainting. A song-thrush was singing its heart out from the plum tree. Everything here was ordinary, but for the stone Buddha that faced us, cross-legged, with its jewelled wrists, blind eyes and bare, blunt toes. Water for the birds was caught in its lap. The trees were sturdy, the grass perfectly at home in its everyday greens. You could nearly hear things stirring back to life, down in the black soil of the flowerbeds, at the roots of the plum tree. Before Isabel could say anything, we heard the long mellow note of May's dinner gong and Dote was at the door calling us inside. 'Hubie's back, and Nan's made sandwiches.'

Nan had the children settled at one end of the table. Paschal appeared to be dozing, on top of a standard lamp in the corner of the room, his tail curled around him like a cat's. A slender edition of the *Irish Times* was on a chair, folded around an item describing what it called an attempt to overthrow the government.

'It was the only newspaper I could find,' Hubie said, coming in to join us. 'There's not much in it. Nothing about Verdun.'

I picked it up, knocking a sketchpad I hadn't seen underneath it to the floor. I thought it was Dote's, but the style of the drawings was different. These were of struts and angles, and one was a contraption like the control bar of a marionette, with strings coming out of it. I bent to pick it up, but

Hubie got there first, holding it in his good hand and smoothing the crumpled page with his forearm before closing it over. I apologized.

'It's nothing, only rough work and scribbles,' he said, putting the pad aside.

I scanned the newspaper. It gave a long list of places that had been taken by the rebels, but said many had been taken back already, and that the authorities had come out quickly.

The paper asked us to 'trust firmly in the speedy triumph of the forces of law and order. Those loyal citizens of Dublin who cannot actively help their country's cause at this moment may help it indirectly by refusing to give way to panic, and by maintaining in their households a healthy spirit of hope. The ordeal is severe but it will be short.'

Hubie had been to Clanwilliam House, on the corner at Mount Street Bridge, on the town side of the canal. A large, end-of-terrace house, its windows were barricaded with furniture, but he'd managed a word with the gunmen inside. 'They said no harm will come to anyone who stays indoors and minds their own business.'

'But what will they do?' May asked.

Hubie glanced at the girls, who were busy dipping soldiers of toast into soft-boiled eggs.

'Another time, May. Little pitchers!' Dote passed around ham sandwiches, and egg-and-parsley salad for the adults. She said it was the last of the eggs, but we may as well enjoy them, they wouldn't keep in the heat.

After lunch, May showed the children her music table. When the inlaid surface was lifted open, a Viennese waltz began to play. Paschal swayed to the music. He rolled his shoulders and played the air with his hands. May clapped her hands and the girls joined in. Tishy danced in circles and quarter-turns, her arms held up to an imaginary partner.

Hubie fiddled with marbles cupped in his left hand. I asked Dote about it when he went out of the room to get more cigarettes.

'He's practising,' she said. 'He wants to be as able with his left hand as he once was with his right. You watch. He's always using it. He even writes and draws with it, now, almost as well as he used to.'

Nan suggested a nap and took the girls upstairs. At last, the real talk could begin. I sat on the floor, my back against Isabel's chair. I was facing the window, with its orange curtains. We described the morning's journey across town. I couldn't resist talking up the danger, how exposed we'd been on the bridge, the watching crowd.

'They'd have liked it better if you were shot to ribbons,' Hubie said.

'Ah, now, Hubie,' Dote said.

I wondered was he right. The tension and uncertainty of waiting was giving way to a kind of impatience in me. I'd sensed it on the street as well. If something was going to happen, let it happen, and let it happen soon. Liam had written something similar, about wanting to get out to the Front so that he would know what he was facing and how he'd face it. I said as much. 'But then, it seems, being at the Front was more of the same. Waiting. Strain. Boredom, even?'

Hubie dipped his head, but I couldn't tell if he was agreeing with me or simply changing position to ease out a strain in his neck.

Isabel leaned forward. 'Tell us.'

'Tell you what, exactly?'

'What it was like,' I said.

He tilted his teacup and considered its contents. 'Everyone asks. I'm not sure anyone wants to know.'

'I do.'

He looked straight at me. 'Do you? Because I'll tell you.' He drained his cup in one quick swallow, set it on its saucer on the low table in front of him and leaned forward to pitch his voice into the space between us.

Hubie's people were Westmeath farmers, but there were ancestors on his mother's side who'd left with the Wild Geese, made their fortune in France. His paternal uncles were in the Dublins, so he thought why not? He was the second son, there wasn't much for him at home. He wanted to see a bit of the world, took his commission in 1912. Shipped out at the beginning of the war, he fought in the early battles in France, at the Marne, the Aisne, Armentières, the last under the brightest moon he'd ever seen in his life. A killing moon.

When they arrived in Dover, thousands of men were milling around the docks and laying about in the sheds. It would take days to get them all across the water. But Hubie's battalion were leaving on the next tide and he was kept busy, giving out rations and checking kit.

The crossing was smooth. There was little sign of war when they docked, apart from the roads, busy with military vehicles. They passed a group of prisoners sitting on the ground, the first Germans he'd seen, a misfortunate-looking lot in dusty uniforms. He could hear guns popping and booming in the distance. They were about nine miles behind the lines.

They moved up the next day. The sun shone, the fields were green and gold, harvest-ready. It was all fine and good, marching down country lanes, past orchards bursting with fruit, red-roofed houses. Like a painting. The men singing, of all things, 'One Man Went to Mow'. Nights when he couldn't sleep, that bloody song still drilled its heavy boots on his brain: three men, two men, one man and his dog . . . No meadows now, only a new and terrible Dead Sea.

That first day, they stopped in a town square. People brought them coffee. Apples were pressed into their hands, and bread. Children waved and women kissed them. At night he was dog-tired but couldn't sleep, his nerves strung taut as wire. He was on the brink of something huge. The immensity of the Continent stretched ahead, other continents beyond that. He'd had no notion how small Ireland was 'til he left. In France, even the sky seemed wider and higher than at home. And the sky that first night was spectacularly thick and lush, littered with stars, closer than he'd ever seen them. The ground hard as bone. There was a stillness, as though time itself had stopped. He wished it would. He wished the world itself would stop turning and hold them fast, right there, all that was to come held off and made harmless.

The next morning they moved up towards the Front. They passed a stream of people going the other way, the way they'd come. Leaving their homes, all they could carry bundled in carts or strapped to their backs, hanging in baskets from their shoulders. He wondered how long it would be before those people came back, what they'd find when they did. He pitied them.

What was left of their battalion passed through that place again, weeks later, after they'd been well and truly blooded. It was a waste land. Where there had been columns of marching men, now there were lines of dead. The next time Hubie saw people abandon their homes, he felt nothing. Why squander pity on people who were on their way to safety, while soldiers marched up the line to face death on their behalf?

People sometimes asked what it was like, to be in a show. It was impossible to tell. Confusion was the main thing. Confusion and noise. Hard to say what happened first, or next, or when; whether what he saw was real or phantom, smoke or demon. He couldn't always be sure if it was thunder and lightning come to earth he was dealing with, or war. Only the screams were real – metal, men, beasts – everything jumbled. The earth turned inside out, clumps of it thrown around in a hot sour wind, and he just trying to make a way through it. When it was over, first thing he'd do was breathe. He'd take in one single breath. And, if he got away with that, he'd risk another. Then, when he was sure he was alive, he'd find out who else had come through. When the rolls were finished, he'd take himself off somewhere quiet, first chance he got. He'd go over it all in his mind, try to sort it into something like sense. He'd say goodbye to the lost, and let them go.

Another thing people asked was if the two armies had really played a game of football, that first Christmas. Hubie was on leave, but he'd heard the story. He could well believe it. In some places the lines were so close that at night they could hear each other singing. Sometimes, if they knew the songs, they joined in. Or set their own words to the tune, once they had it. Nights like that, you'd forget to be wary.

I told myself to breathe. I knew what was coming.

They knew there was a big push coming. There'd been heavy shelling for days, and rumours of gas. They'd written their letters, checked their kit, reviewed their orders. A corporal came round with the chronometer. Everything was set for the morning. At midnight Liam went around talking to the men and then went towards the latrine. Hubie was at the fire-step. The moon was just off full, the balloons were silver. Flares went up, trailing green and yellow lights. He heard the shots that got Liam. Jonesy saw it happen. He said Liam stood proud of the whole sorry mess, he just stood there. And they got him, twice. Two shots.

Hubie and Jonesy ran to him. He was still alive, asked had he a ticket home. Hubie said not to get ahead of himself. He held Liam's hand 'til the stretcher boys came, and that was the last he saw of him, when they carried him away.

We all stared at his gloved hand.

'Did you keep track of what happened to him?' Isabel asked.

He flinched. 'Later that morning, thousands were wiped out by gas. So many that *we* became the Front. Everything that had stood between us and Fritz was gone. Wiped out. And they came at us. I lost track of everything. So many died.'

He stared past me, fixing on the mirror over my head. 'There was no let-up. We were so far outnumbered – they'd a field gun for every rifle of ours. They flattened us.'

When the gas came, they were blazing away, the guns roasting hot. Then yellow smoke billowed up around them. Someone, one of the Canadians who'd materialized by some miracle to fight beside them, roared at everyone to piss on whatever cloth came to hand – handkerchiefs or caps – to cover their mouths and noses and breathe through the saturated cloth. It worked, for some. And the gas rolled on, over their trench. Hubie was lucky. Some instinct caught him by the scruff of the neck and dragged him up out of the trench into cleaner air, sucking on urine, and the gas rolled on and left him behind. Hubie and a handful of others. Jonesy wasn't so lucky. They listened to him froth and hiss and choke. He drowned, right there beside them on dry land, and there wasn't a damned thing they could do about it. It took twenty minutes. Jonesy tried to speak but retched instead, spilling clots of matter on his chin. Coughing up his own lung. He clawed at his breast pocket and Hubie remembered he'd a locket in there, his wife's picture on one side, three gap-toothed boys grinning on the other. He took it out and wrapped the chain around Jonesy's fingers. His hands stopped flailing then. He clutched that oval of silver 'til he was dead.

When the gas dispersed they could see the wounded, lying out in the open. The lucky ones were dead. Some wriggled around, calling for help. One, both legs gone, was trying to get back to the line on stumps. Hubie took the locket out of

Jonesy's cold grasp and went to help the legless man. Later he sent it back to Jonesy's wife with a letter telling her it had been a comfort to him, when he died. Sparing her the real details. The twenty frantic minutes and the sounds.

There was no respite. They were straight into another show, and then another. They were gassed again a month later, and Colonel Loveband died and that was effectively the end of the Second Dublins. A proud battalion was diluted when the dregs of one unit were combined with the survivors of another, and then new drafts added, Kitchener's Mob, half trained. Months of stalemate and no ground gained in a barren landscape like a nightmare with no ending. The war would drag on 'til there was no one left to fire the rusted empty guns on the last survivor, who would have long forgotten what silence was, what it sounded like.

The sky outside darkened. I got up to help Dote pass around more tea. I was stiff from sitting on the floor so long, not moving. Isabel leaned forward, her eyes fixed on Hubie, her arms folded around her knees. She shook her head at the cup and saucer I offered, kept looking at him. A light rain drummed against the window.

A deep rumbling roar from outside was followed by another that cracked the world open. My cup rattled on its saucer. Someone moaned in the hall. I looked out, and there was Nan, sitting on the bottom stair, in the gloom, with her shawl up over her head and a weird sound coming from her throat. 'Nan! What are you doing there?'

Her pallor was remarkable. 'The childer are gone asleep.'

'Don't be out there on your own.' I hesitated. This was not my house. But Dote was at my elbow, saying, 'For heaven's sake, come in and join us, Nan.'

Nan looked up the stairs. 'That last one might have woken them.'

'I'll go and see.' I ran up to the bedroom Dote had assigned to me and the girls. There they were, top to tail under the eiderdown, their hair strewn around them, fast asleep.

When I came back down, Nan was sitting, stiff and straight, on a hard-backed chair that she offered to me.

'No, stay there – I was on the floor before.'

Dote patted a cushion on the coal box, beside her chair. On her other side, May had taken her glasses off to polish them with her cuff. Her face had a blind cast to it without them. Beads of perspiration were visible on her forehead. The sound of distant shooting was more insistent. 'Be a pet and close the curtains, Katie?'

I did as she asked and went to sit on the coal box, sideways on to the window. The drawn curtains gave the light an orange tinge.

Nan had a queer look on her face. She hunched over her knees, with her big feet planted on the floor. 'Do youse mind, it'll be Bealtaine five days from now?'

'The start of summer,' said Dote.

Mouth-of-fire. The orangey light in the room played havoc with my mind. It touched Hubie's face with amber. One of his ankles lay across the other. I found myself wondering what his legs might look like – would they be amber too? I looked down at my hands, spread my fingers. There were traces of dirt under my nails; they could do with a scrubbing.

'One of the four corners of the year,' May said.

'What do you mean?' Isabel asked.

'The hinges of the world swing open. All manner of strange things creep through.' May pulled her cardigan tight around her narrow shoulders and shivered. 'When souls cross over, either way.'

'It'd give you the collywobbles,' Nan said, knotting her hands.

'The entire flaming door was ajar, in Flanders,' Hubie said. 'Banging on its hinges, all year long. At night we'd see the Red Cross lanterns, as they gathered up their wounded. One morning we watched them carry out a stretcher, draped in a cloth. We held our fire and watched them busy themselves with men we thought were hurt.' A bitter laugh. 'All that time, they were setting up a gun. We lost three men to it that morning.'

'No!' Isabel said.

'You've no notion.' He glared, as though we were to blame. 'You think old rules still apply. I've heard it said out there' – he swung his cup towards the window, then to his mouth, swallowed – '"No war's ever been fought in the streets of a European city."' He put on a false accent to say it. His face was flushed. 'Those men out there think they're safe, surrounded by people like you, and buildings. I've seen whole villages wiped off the face of the earth, pulverized. Churches and farms destroyed. Why should you be immune, here?'

'People think if they say it often enough, it will be true,' Dote said, careful.

He tugged the black leather glove from his damaged hand and slotted a cigarette between the clawed, livid finger that remained and his thumb. With his other hand he took out a lighter and flipped the wheel, lit the cigarette. He stared at me all the while, as though daring me to look away. He sucked in a deep breath, stabbed the glowing cigarette-tip in my direction. 'This'll give you an idea . . . There was a private, not a young man, lost his head one morning. He keened like a woman, for no reason. Slack mouth, drooling, tears streaming down his face. I'd never seen it before.'

He was talking fast, running through the words. 'I tried to shut his mouth for him with a slap to the cheek. Told the colour sergeant to put him in the funk hole, keep an eye on him. He crammed himself into it, face first. Like a child trying to hide in its mother's skirts. As if he wanted the earth to open up and take him.' He glared at us, defiant. Daring us to judge him.

'What happened?' I asked.

'Not long after, a shell fell in on top of him and killed him.' He stood up, paced the length of the room, then back again. Across and back. Across and back. Across and – 'What no one ever says is that one man's decision sets off a whole train of events that ends in the ruination of another. Someone fires the first shot. Someone decides where troops will go. Every little thing you do out there has consequences. One man's whim can be the end of another; a step this way or that can save or kill you. That was one of my own men, and I'm the one who did for him.'

Dote cleared her throat. 'He was a liability. You weren't to blame.'

'Poor soul.' Isabel was pale. 'It's barbaric.'

Hubie's contempt appeared to settle on her. I was glad it wasn't me. 'Don't ask, if you don't want to know. It's easy to have an opinion from a distance. I'd have liked that luxury, myself.' He leaned down and stubbed out his cigarette, chasing the sparks across the bowl of the ashtray and extinguishing each one. The china rattled. He went back to his pacing, hand clasping wrist at his back, shoulders square and lonely.

'You'd want to have seen the rats.' There was a gleam in his eye – he was enjoying making us uncomfortable. He said he told his men not to kill them because they'd stink up the trench and squelch underfoot, in a way that'd sicken the strongest of stomachs. After he was injured, while he was lying on the ground outside the medical post, waiting for his turn, a rat ran past his head, near enough that he felt its feet disturb his hair. The rat had a human finger in its mouth. 'I wondered was it mine.'

There was a queer silence. Dote and Nan began to clear

the dishes. I looked out of the window. 'There's a car stopping.'

Isabel stood and looked out. 'It's Stephenson. You should come back with me. All of you.'

'There are too many of us,' I said.

'You'd be welcome. There's a command post in the park, soldiers everywhere. And sentries. It might be the safest place in Dublin.'

'There wouldn't be room for us all in the car.'

'Stephenson could come back. If the troops are on their way –'

'What do you think, May?' Dote asked.

'Go if you want. I'm staying.'

'I'll stay with you.' Hubie walked over to the window.

'I will too,' Dote said.

'Katie?'

Before I could answer, Hubie spoke. 'There's no particular vantage point here, for either side. The end houses might be at risk, but I'd say we're safe enough.'

'But the children –'

'Should go,' he said. 'It's liable to get – loud.'

'Or, as you said, the gunmen might surrender. In which case, all's well.' I'd a whole string of reasons for not wanting to go to Isabel's. Percy Place was closer to Eva, for one. Besides, I had to admit that a stubborn flame of curiosity had lit on the floor of my mind, about what might happen here – I was no better than Eugene and those others who sat at the hotel window to watch, when it came to it. And I wanted to know what else Hubie Wilson might have to say, given time. I had questions I'd like to ask him, when no one else was around to hear.

I told them I wanted to be near Eva. May said of course I should stay in Percy Place. Nan and the girls could go to Herbert Park with Isabel, they wouldn't need me. Isabel looked put out, but she didn't complain. She only said again that everyone was welcome, any time.

The front door stood open. The pavement smelled of fresh rain. Trees glistened over the replenished water of the canal, which threw up circles and darts of diminishing rain. Isabel's father's car waited at the kerb. Stephenson stood beside it, talking to Hubie about the car. A De Dion-Bouton, but made in Belfast by an outfit called Chambers, had Hubie heard of them? There was a waiting list. The Judge had had to wait two years for it, but it was worth every minute of the wait, it was a beauty.

Hubie was more interested in what De Dion were making now. Aircraft engines and gun parts. They'd devised an anti-aircraft gun, already in use by the French Army, did Stephenson know that? 'I've seen them,' Hubie said. 'A field gun mounted on a lorry-bed, firing into the sky. Loud as a train.'

On the canal, a pair of swans glided past in the direction of the humped bridge, their black faces turned towards each other, unperturbed by the fine rain.

'Are you not worried that the gunmen will commandeer the car?' I asked Stephenson.

'No, miss.' He lifted one edge of his jacket with a finger, showing the grip of a revolver, snug in a leather holster at his side.

There was a commotion on the stairs behind us. Alanna came down first, neat and serene. Behind her, Nan dragged Tishy by the hand, stair by stair. Tishy's other hand flailed for the banister, trying to hold on. 'I won't go without him!'

Dote moved behind Tishy, pressing her forward. 'We don't have time for this, Tishy.'

'What's wrong?' I asked her.

'The monkey's run away.'

'But don't you worry, pet.' May spoke from the return, above them. 'We'll find him. We'll look after him.'

'He'll be safer here than if he's turned loose in a strange place.' Hubie's air of authority seemed to calm Tishy.

'Let me stay too, then,' she pleaded. 'I'll be good.'

Isabel gathered the child's fine hair in her hands and lifted it away from her neck. 'It's not that, my lamb. There might be trouble. We want you to be safe.'

'Please.'

'I'm sorry.'

'Come too!' She grabbed hold of my skirt.

Feeling like a brute, I pulled it free. 'No, Tishy. I'll see you tomorrow. It's for the best.'

Isabel turned for the car. Tishy went with her, feet dragging, shoulders slumped in defeat. Isabel's arm went around her and pulled her in close to her side. In that moment I saw that she'd meet someone, marry, have children. But the children she would have would not be Liam's. It was as though she'd tugged a plug loose in my chest. Everything vital inside me drained away, as if Liam died all over again. This time I knew he wasn't coming back.

The car pulled away. I crossed the road to look at the water, and the swans. When I turned around, Hubie was still standing at the top of the steps. He was watching them too. 'D'you know, they mate for life,' he said. Smoke curled from the cigarette he held between his thumb and the shortened little finger of his damaged hand. He'd dispensed with the glove altogether.

'You were hard on Isabel,' I said.

'No. You people are bog-soft.' He dropped his cigarette and ground it with his heel. 'I suppose you agree with her?'

'I think she's brave. Every time she speaks like that, she goes out under fire in her own way.'

He kicked the butt into the street and started down the steps. I felt a stab of panic, as though I'd never see him again. 'Where are you going?'

'The driver said a meeting was called, to organize ways to stop the looting.' He looked at the face of a watch strapped to his wrist with a leather strap. 'I'm late, but I might catch the end of it. Do you know where Westmoreland Chambers is?'

'I'll show you.' I ran in to tell Dote I was going, grabbed Liam's coat off the stand and ran out again, afraid he'd have gone without me. I hurried down the steps after him, shrugging myself into the coat.

He was waiting. He didn't move out of my way, but stood there, blocking the path, smelling of smoke and something else I couldn't put my finger on. We were so close, I felt a blast of heat and stepped back, uneasy. It was as though the street and the city beyond it had shrunk to the size of a dressing room, and I couldn't find the door. 'What is it?'

'That coat – do you need one? – it's too big for you. I'm sure Aunt May would lend you one, if you asked her.'

I shook my hair free from the collar and stalked past him, pulling the coat tight and belting it, pulling on my hat. 'It's Liam's.'

'It makes you look like a rebel.'

'Good.'

For the second day running, a crowd had gathered on O'Connell Bridge to watch the dramatics on Sackville Street. A gigantic bonfire raged beyond Abbey Street. Even from the back of the crowd I could see items being flung out of the upper windows of a shop. Ambulances thundered up and down the quays, bells jangling. I didn't know if it was me or the world that shook.

I knew we were in a hurry, but I stood up on tiptoe, as if that would let me see through the crowds, beyond Nelson and the overhead cables, all the way north to our house. 'We live up that way,' I said. 'I should go and see if the house is all right.'

'You'll never get through that crowd, Katie.' It was the first time I'd heard my name from his mouth. It felt like a touch, like his hand at my elbow, guiding me in through the door to the building. 'Come on, we're late.'

Upstairs, a clerkish young man and his portly companion were discussing a battle that had been fought in Dame Street, how soldiers and insurgents alike had needed to shout at bystanders to get out of the way. The portly one was not unlike Florrie's Eugene, the way his plump fingers were tucked into the pockets of a straining waistcoat.

'Where's Mr Sheehy-Skeffington?' I asked, when they'd finished talking. 'Did he not call a meeting?'

I admired Mr Sheehy-Skeffington. He was a familiar figure around town, often to be seen taking notes at lectures for his newspaper, having lunch in the vegetarian restaurant on Foster Place or locked in earnest debate with someone on the street – he'd talk to anyone. He'd stroke a tangle of beard, head to one side, eyes on the ground, as though inspiration might be found in a gutter or emerge from a drain. He was a soft touch for guttersnipes. People mocked him, but they smiled when they caught sight of him. He was known as the Peace Man. Some wags called him the Ladies' Man, because of the Votes for Women button he wore on his lapel.

The clerk took a watch out of his pocket. 'Twenty past six. We've been here ten minutes and there's no sign of him.'

'We were later than I thought,' Hubie said to me. 'The meeting was to start at half past five. Maybe we missed him.'

Footsteps on the stairs made us turn to the door expectantly, but it was a scarlet-cheeked woman who came in, breathing heavily. 'Mercy,' she said when she got her breath back. 'Those stairs'll be the death of me. Mr Thompson from downstairs sent me up to tell you, you missed the man.' She took another big breath and sighed it out, fanning her face with her hands. 'He waited a half-hour or so, and no one came. Then he left.'

'Do you know where he went?' Hubie asked.

'Home for his tea, if he'd any sense. Where we all should be. We'll be locking up the doors in a minute.'

'We might as well go on, so,' the clerk said. 'There's not much to be done with just the four of us.'

'We'd best be going too,' Hubie said, when they'd left. 'The streets are quieter, in any case.'

It was true. When we came out, the looters had retreated to the far end of Sackville Street. I stretched my neck to see as far up the street as I could.

Hubie took my arm. 'Come on.' He steered me past the bank and across Dame Street. Further up, we crossed back again to walk in the shelter of Trinity's walls. He said the presence of the soldiers who'd taken over the college might be enough to bring the situation under control.

I found myself telling him everything: Matt's absence, Liam's guns. I tugged the gabardine tighter around me, folded my arms across my waist. Walked faster. Hubie said nothing.

We'd reached the corner of Merrion Square. He paused to read an anti-fraternization handbill posted to a telegraph pole.

'Pay no attention,' I said, walking on. He came too, his face unreadable. I was mortified, and angry on his behalf. 'Every time you turn around, someone's pushing a handbill at you, or dangling a leaflet, or haranguing you from a soap-box. There's always someone telling you what to think, trying to make up your mind for you.'

'Do you agree with them?'

My face burned. 'I might have, once. I've no time for them now.'

'Did Liam change your mind?'

'Not directly.' Not soon enough, was what I meant. 'In some ways.'

'For instance?'

'Well – once he enlisted in the Dublins, I couldn't refer to the Traitors' Gate any more – how could I? Liam was no more a traitor than I am.'

'Traitors' Gate?'

'The Fusiliers' Arch. The main gate into the Green.'

'Ah.'

A fresh outburst of shots came from near the canal. We stood, still as stone. He pulled me into a doorway. The silence that followed was like a dream, all pearled light and gleaming water, black trees mirrored on a silver that verged on blue, the sky come down to slake its thirst at the bridge. He was so close I felt the rise and fall of his breath against my arm. I didn't know how much time passed before he said we should run across the road.

Safely across, we crept up the street to the smaller bridge in the shelter of the houses, my pulse so loud in my ears I was sure it would give us away. At the bridge he went in front, bent double. I copied him. We didn't exchange a word 'til we were at May's door. I'd never been as glad of anything as I was of the shelter of her solid stone steps.

'Well done.' That voice of his seemed to come from behind my own breast-bone. 'You're sure-footed. And you don't talk too much.' Which saved me the need to answer. 'I'll go to Mr Hyland and see if the situation has changed. They have a good vantage point there, on the corner.'

I didn't feel so safe any more. 'Don't go.'

'I'll go by the lane. Bolt the door when you get in.' He looked up and down the road. 'The longer it takes the troops to get here, the fiercer the fighting is likely to be. They must be planning to come in hard.' His eyes came back to me. There was confusion in them. Had he forgotten who I was?

'Keep the shutters closed and the curtains drawn. Don't answer the door. I'll come back by the lane too.'

'I wish you wouldn't.'

He raised the scarred eyebrow. 'Which do you wish I wouldn't do, go or come back?' That teasing look. A silence opened, like a tunnel. He was the one who broke it. 'Don't worry about me.'

'I was hoping to talk to you –'

'Later.'

When I got in, May was feeding scraps to Paschal in the parlour. 'You found him!'

'He was hiding in a tree.'

The monkey blinked at me, mashed his lips on a pellet of bread. Dote was tidying cups and glasses on to a tray. She looked worn out. I took the tray from her and carried it to the kitchen. While we cleared the dishes into the sink, a cup slipped from her hands and shattered on the tiled floor.

'Stupid!' She was shaking and pale.

'It's the strain. Sit down.'

'It was part of a set,' she said. 'It belonged to my mother.' She looked ready to cry.

I collected the shards into a twist of paper. 'We'll find someone who can fix it. You go to bed, I'll wait up for Hubie.'

May carried Paschal upstairs with her. Later, when she was asleep, I heard him scratching at her door, and let him out. She was snoring, loud, in a nightcap like a turban.

Downstairs again, with Paschal's soft weight warming my lap, I rested my head on the back of the chair and listened to sounds like circus whips and firecrackers. The evening light, filtered through the curtains, glowed like a sunset. Paschal caught hold of my chin between his – what would you call them, paws? They were so like hands – and looked into my eyes. Uncomfortable with his study, I turned his head away. 'Go to sleep.'

What if Hubie didn't come back? The room darkened and turned cold while I waited, but some lethargy held me there. At last I heard the latch lifting on the back door. I moved the sleeping monkey to the dog bed and went down to meet him.

He came in quietly and put a finger to his lips when he saw me. I leaned against the dresser and waited while he latched the door, went to the window and looked out. At last he turned around, took off his hat and rubbed his springy hair with the damaged hand. 'It was strange: the schoolhouse was empty. There were men there last night.' He followed me into the back sitting room, took the matches and lit a row of candles on the mantel.

'I wish they'd left the gas supply intact,' I said.

He took the marbles from his pocket, held them in his cupped left palm and rolled them, one over the other and back, over and back. 'Maybe they wanted to prevent an explosion, when the shooting starts.'

'Are you for them, now?'

'I don't envy them. They're brave. Foolish, but brave.'

'So why did those others leave – did they get tired of waiting? Or think better of it all? Maybe that's what the army wants to happen.'

'You mean, that's what you'd like to happen.' The marbles clicked and grated in his hand.

'What do you think, then?'

'Who knows? Maybe they funked it. The waiting would get on anyone's nerves.' He dropped his hat on a stool, put the marbles into it and went to the drinks cabinet, where he studied the bottles. 'I think it's dawned on them that the Germans aren't exactly in a rush to swell their ranks. They're on their own. You'd nearly be sorry for them.' He checked the watch on his wrist, then looked at me. 'Join me for a drink?'

'Just soda water.' What if he couldn't manage the siphon? 'Let me.'

He stepped between me and the siphon. 'No.' There was that bristling in the air again, a raw heat that ran the length of my body. I sat into the nearest chair, not watching him work the siphon, but aware of the sounds it made, the whisper of his leather glove on metal, the click of the handle, followed by the hiss and splash of gas and water. When he brought the glass over to me, I caught sight of the watch again.

'Why do you wear a watch on your wrist?'

He tasted his drink and smiled. 'Do you not approve?'

'It's just – I don't know any other men who do.'

'I used to think it effeminate,' he said. 'But in the trenches, they make more sense on your wrist than buried in your pocket. They're efficient. I think they'll catch on.' Then, more serious, 'I wonder when the army will make their move. What they're waiting for. It's possible that, the longer it takes, the heavier the retribution will be. I wonder if I was wrong, letting you all stay here.'

'Did you say, *letting* us?'

'I meant encouraging. I encouraged you to stay. Is that better?'

'Marginally.'

I wanted to hold back time, force it to a slower pace: the stillness of the canal as opposed to the tidal pull of the river, say. From where I sat, the round mirror on the wall opposite the window became a disc of light, reflecting a perfect circle of paling sky. It could be a hole in the wall, leading to another world.

He followed my gaze. 'It looks like a porthole.'

I was startled by how closely his thought followed mine. 'I've never been on a ship. Not properly.'

'Only troopships, me. What do you mean, not properly?'

'Liam and I stowed away once. Tried to. We nipped up a gangplank when no one was looking.' If I closed my eyes I could hear the mast creak, feel the dipping motion of the boat under us, smell the tar. The crow's nest was dizzy against a sky that moved with the clouds, the deck scrubbed clean as a dance floor.

'How far did you get?'

'Nowhere! They caught us, each by an ear, and marched us off again. We were lucky they didn't do worse.' I had to smile. 'Liam said they made us walk the plank, but it was wasted, we couldn't tell anyone.'

'How old were you?'

'Seven? Thereabouts. It was a time – but you don't want to hear.'

'I do.'

It was a summer when Mother caught a fever. Her hair stuck to her head, her cheeks were like two pots of Egyptian rouge. She plucked at the bedclothes and muttered to herself, and didn't recognize us when we went to the door of her room to say goodnight.

The doctor came every day and the priest was sent for, twice. Dad was haggard, his own cheeks hollow. When the fever broke and she was strong enough, she was sent off to stay with her sister, who lived near the sea. She was gone for weeks.

While she was away, we ran wild. Matt had a nursemaid still, a woman called Ellen, who took us on long walks every afternoon when he was asleep, leaving Lockie to listen out for him. Only, the walks weren't quite what they seemed. Ellen had a fondness for the public houses around the railway stations, and that's where she used to take us. When we got bored with the talk in the dim, malted dark, we'd go out into the lanes, to play jack-stones and kick-the-can with other children. Sometimes we explored the arches; other times we went down to the docks. It was one of those days that we stowed away.

It came out when a DMP man brought the three of us home one day, in the back of a cab. Ellen was singing, waving her skinny arms as though the horse were an orchestra and she its conductor. She didn't want to get out.

The policeman asked Lockie to bring Dad to the door. 'This wan insists she lives here, sir.'

We skipped up the steps, singing into each other's faces.

'Who should I see, but a Spanish la-a-ady . . .'

'*Whack!* for the tooralooralay!'

We gave each other cheerful slaps with every *whack*, but when I tried one on Lockie, she gave me a box that made my head ring. She grabbed a hold of us by the ears, the same exact way the sailor had. 'The plank, Katie!' Liam whispered and we went bravely up the stairs to our doom. She shut us in Liam's room, while she went back to help Dad with Ellen, who we never saw again.

It was a good story and I'd plenty of practice telling it. It made Hubie laugh. But I was overcome with sudden grief for the boy Liam had been. For the closeness we'd had. Matt got a new nurse and we were reined in, but we'd developed a taste for escape, and one way or another we managed it as often as we could. Down to the railway, or the docks. I only had the nerve for it because Liam was with me to share the adventure and the trouble.

The sick weight in my heart made me think of the time we went into the markets. I hated it, the ground slippery with stinking droppings, the air heavy with cries and moans. Eva coaxed me to say what was the matter, when we got home. I cried, telling her about the cow which had looked right at me with a rolling, frantic eye. 'If you'd heard her moan, Eva. I swear she watched me go. Blaming me for leaving her there. Begging me not to. Can we go back, can we save her?'

'That's just the sound they make, pet. It doesn't mean what we'd mean.'

'How do you know?'

'I just know.' Although of course she didn't. They might not know that it's death they face, but why would a brute creature slipping around in the entrails and droppings of its fellows, surrounded by shrieks and death, not feel fear?

'Tell me more about Liam,' Hubie said.

'He was expelled from school, did he tell you that? He skipped out one day, without permission, to go to Eva's wedding.'

'Doesn't sound like Liam, to abandon a post without leave. Why did he not have permission to go to your sister's wedding?'

'She married a Protestant,' I said. 'In a Protestant church. Our mother wasn't happy; she didn't go herself. She didn't want us to go. I think it was her who kept him home, after. She was mortified by all the fuss. The whole school had been out combing the grounds, looking for him.'

I'd ducked school as well that day. I'd heard Mother tell Eva she was bound for hell and I didn't want her to have to go there alone. I was sitting at the back of the church in a state of terror when Liam slunk into the pew beside me, grinning, smelling of straw and warm milk after the lift he'd taken on a milk-lorry. The bonus of it was that after all the fuss died down, Liam went to the day school around the corner. Eva left home that day, but Liam came back.

A shadow threaded a path across the mirror's disc of imaginary sky. Bombers had visited England. I knew that nights at the Front were anything but still, from Liam's letters. The grandfather clock in the hall chimed the quarter hour, reminding me that morning would come. Hubie was due to leave, to go back to his family, as soon as the trains were running. If I wanted to know anything about Liam, now was the time to ask.

'In his letters, Liam said that when he first got out to France, you told him how to get over his nerves. What did you tell him?'

'I don't remember.'

'You must.'

Distant sounds punctured the night, harmless as corks in champagne bottles. It was hard to believe that they had murder in mind.

His good hand worried the skin of his face. 'I can only say what helped me. I don't remember telling anyone else. I went on leave when he arrived – I'd have been asleep on my feet by then. It does happen.'

'I know.' That was in his letters too.

Silence. I was about to ask something else when he began to speak. 'It wasn't the rum we got before a show, or even the hundreds of other men, all bent on the same thing; neither would be enough, although they help. It's simple, really. You have to pretend you're not afraid.'

'Pretend?'

'As hard as if your life depends on it, because it does. If you can hold on to enough of yourself to do that, you're halfway there.'

'I don't understand.'

His expression mocked me. 'I suppose you're a romantic. To thine own self be true, am I right?'

'Why would you say such a thing? You don't know me at all.'

'I apologize.' But he didn't look in the least repentant. He looked angry.

'Go on.'

He pulled the cigarette case from his pocket and fumbled with the catch. At last it sprang open. He held it out to me. One side was empty, the other nearly so.

'Do you have more?'

'I've a box of them upstairs. You should take some with you if you go out. Just go in and help yourself. These times, they're better than money.'

I took two cigarettes from the box and passed him one. I lit my own with a match from the box on the mantel, and extended the match to him.

He leaned down to the flame, sucked in a lungful of smoke as though it were fresh air and he emerging from deep under-water, and breathed it out in a long, satisfied sigh.

Watching me, his eyebrow made a steeper crease. 'You really are a smoker.'

'Con says it's good for us. A shield against disease. Even Mother smokes. Lots of women I know do.'

'Who's Con?'

'A family friend. A schoolfriend of Liam's. He's a doctor.' But so was Bartley, who didn't favour smoking at all. 'You were saying?'

'Where was I?'

'Pretending to be brave.'

He gave a mock-bow. 'So I was. Let's see – pretence can be every bit as good as willpower. Does it matter what you call it? The effect is the same. Your legs feel like jelly, but you pretend they're steady. You impersonate a braver man; speak, as though you're on a stage, as though you believe them, the lines you learned in training. You play the part of the kind of officer you'd like to be. God knows, there are more than enough bad ones.' He soothed his ruined hand with the good one. 'Even with this, I'd go back if I could. I'd stand with those same men and rally them. They deserve that. At least that. What they really deserve, every last man of them, is to be brought home.'

After a while he gathered himself together. 'Tell me something about yourself.'

'There's little to tell. You wouldn't be interested.'

'I'm interested in anything that has nothing to do with war or killing.'

It was surprising how many things this ruled out. 'I'm very dull. I've no particular talents, no special destiny.' I worried a mark on the arm of the chair with my thumb.

'I suppose you'll marry.'

'I might.' I returned his look. Hated myself for blushing.

'What will you do, now that Dote's book is finished? Did you like the work?'

'I loved it.' The words rang through the room with more force than I'd meant. I willed the hateful blush to stay away and rushed on. 'I've been thinking about a job. A real one. To earn my living. My parents want to move out of town. I don't.'

'What sort of work could you do?'

'History was my subject. In school, and in college. I learned to do research, working for Dote. I was thinking about going for a higher degree, but –' There was too much to explain. Sick of the sound of my own voice, I stopped talking.

'You could probably teach.'

'In a school, yes. Maybe. It's not what I want.' I sat back. The notion of wanting something had crept out unbidden. I looked at it, alarmed.

'What do you want?'

I realized how tense I was, every muscle clenched as though to hold myself in check. As though I might spill out of my skin any second. 'I actually can't think, much, about the future.'

He yawned, put his bad hand to his mouth, apologized.

He was stretched out along the sofa now, nearly horizontal. His eyes half shut, and no wonder. He wasn't long out of hospital.

'I'm keeping you up.'

'No, please. Go on.' He settled deeper. His eyes closed all the way.

I took a rug from the blanket box at the window – the black and green and yellow one May and I sat on that day at the Wellington Monument, the very first day I came to this house – and spread it over him. I blew out the candles on the mantel.

I looked back at him from the door. The chill blue light of the moon fell through the window on to his unguarded face. My breath caught. I'd never been alone with a man I wasn't related to for anything like that length of time. In the corner beyond him, Paschal snored on the scarlet cushion where May's Pekingese used to lord it over the house.

'Goodnight,' I whispered, although they were both fast asleep.

Upstairs, I couldn't get comfy on the lumpy mattress. I thought about home. Let Dad and Matt be there, and let them all be safe.

The blankets scratched my bare arms. I pulled them over my head, made a tent to stifle the sounds of sporadic shooting from the streets. The sheets were icy, a cold that made me think of Liam, the February before he died. I drew my aching feet up to my knees, away from the tundra at the end of the bed, curled into myself for warmth and drifted off to sleep, thinking about the cold that Liam had described in his letters.

It's bitter cold. My fingers cramp on the pen. I'm hunched over the brazier, nearly IN the yoke. The pages might scorch. If they did, they'd warm my hands, thaw my frozen (despite two pairs of Mother's best socks) feet. Death could be like this: blood freezing the veins, heart turned to ice. There's frost on our clothes and hair. Men's feet rot in it. The cold spawns icy visions. At night, the flares breed shadows that swarm through the trenches with the rats. The angel of war moves among the sleepers, touching the ones who'll die with chill fingers, men so cold already they don't sense the warning, or care.

I'd a sensation of falling, in my sleep. The bed, the floor beneath it, fell away and I plunged through space, dipping and reeling towards nothingness. How can you move faster into less? That's what it felt like, the hourglass again, time pressing me thin to squeeze me faster through its narrows. I woke in blind panic under unfamiliar weight. It might be like this to lie in a wartime grave, trapped and suffocating, your ears ringing. Not knowing if the noise you heard came from inside your head or out. I fought free of the blankets and came up struggling for air, full of dread.

Wednesday, 26 April 1916

Liam stepped into a column of mud that exploded into fragments of brick and glass. All around him, men and pieces of men writhed, maggots at work in their mouths. Hubie turned his pale face to me, the sockets of his eyes empty. Guilt ground my stomach to powder, something left undone, a thing that might have saved him.

I woke to the sound of gunfire. It was still dark. I rose and went to the window. All I could see was a series of steep black roofs, a hint of mist, the stillness of trees. Clouds scudded across the face of the waning moon. A vixen, or something like it, cried an eerie, lonely screech. Wishing I knew for sure where Matt was, I went back to bed and fell asleep, the spatter of bullets like heavy rain on a corrugated roof.

A confused impression of a giant bell shattering tore me from sleep. The lumps in the mattress were unfamiliar. The bed made a wrong angle with the door and the window, each where the other should have been. A squat wardrobe, nothing like the one in Liam's room, straddled a corner. The harsh echo faded away. The room began to make sense as events came back to me. Percy Place. Hubie. Gunfire, but nothing like the noise I'd just heard, the worst wrong note ever struck. I took a crimson dressing gown from a hook behind the door and went out to the stair, tying the belt. My mouth was dry and tasted of last night's cigarettes.

'What was it?' May was on the return, beside the plantstand, a hand clapped to her mouth. Her eyes had a blind, watery cast to them.

'I'm not sure. Where are your spectacles, May?'

She groped in the pocket of her flannel dressing gown and pulled them out with shaking hands. 'I'm sorry, pet, I'm useless. Would you?'

I opened the stalks of her glasses for her, put them on her face.

'It's my head. It's thumping.'

There was another crash outside, like dust-bins falling, their lids shattering and all the steel shards rolling to rest in separate corners of the world. It sounded as though the entire city would shatter. A chorus of dogs set off a ghastly racket of barks and howls.

Hubie appeared at the top of the stairs, fully dressed. 'They're here.' He scanned the high window and came down to take May's arm. 'We'll go down to the back.'

I had to dress, but first I crossed to the bedroom window and peeked out, on a slant that gave me a view of the still, inky water of the canal, the mirrored trees, a perfect blue sky. Dull thumping sounds came from the direction of the river. Not as loud as before, but more sustained. A dog loped across the road and vanished down a side street. A cyclist rode the length of the street, turned on to the bridge and went on towards town, unchallenged.

Footsteps on the stairs, then on the landing. 'What's keeping you?' Hubie's voice was low, as though someone outside might hear us.

'I'll come in a minute.'

'Can you see anything?' He came into the room and stood behind me, looking out over my shoulder.

I straightened, conscious of his warmth, that he was fully dressed and I was anything but. The fabric of his clothes was all the more substantial for being near the thin crimson dressing gown, the borrowed cotton nightdress, the untidiness of my hair. I moved away, opening a vista of unmade bed, crumpled sheets I hurried to cover with the eiderdown. 'What was that noise?'

'A field gun. They mean business. It won't be long now.' He raised an eyebrow, reached a finger to the gold piping on the dressing-gown's cuff. 'You should always wear these colours.' There was a glint in his eye. Was he mocking me? His rosy mouth was pursed, fleshy, over his tufted beard. I wondered was it as soft as it looked.

'I'll follow you down.'

That crooked eyebrow of his, along with the beard, gave him a wicked look. I held the robe together at my throat.

He clamped his gloved hand to his waistcoat, made a little bow. 'Forgive me,' he said in a low voice as he went out. I shut the door behind him, checked the latch and got dressed in the clothes I wore yesterday. I ran up to Dote's room to drag a brush through my hair, dipped a finger in her tooth-powder to scour my teeth. Her room looked on to the garden, the backs of other houses. Nothing moved out there. There was only a dazzling, unbroken sky, the clean glow of sunshine after rain, thin young leaves on the trees and May's flowers, not yet fully open to the day.

When I got downstairs, the shelling was a steady distant rumbling. No one spoke. The house trembled, but it might have been my heart that shook at the prospect of the hours ahead, hours that had to be crossed, no matter what. I couldn't imagine what all those men must be feeling in the various buildings that concealed them, or the ones coming to roust them out. I tried, and failed, to see Matt among them. But, whoever they were, they had sisters too, and mothers, who would be sick about them now.

I wanted to go home, to see my own house safe and solid. To touch the warped glass of the upstairs window, to sit at the kitchen table with Lockie, shelling peas. I wondered how she and Mother and Florrie were faring, over in Eugene's house. I was glad I wasn't there. Every single thing that happened in that woman's life was a cause for complaint. She'd be making a meal of this – whatever it was.

The milk had turned. It made white clumps in the tea, which glistened, as though there was oil in it. I poured mine into a cup for the monkey. He drained the lot and scooped around the inside with a hooked finger.

Hubie separated the rind from a rasher and passed it to Paschal. The bread was stale, dry as sawdust. I pushed my plate away. 'How can you all eat?' Although in fact May was crumbling her crust with her nails.

An explosion, louder than the others, made the glass shiver in the windows. 'Where do you think the guns are?' I asked.

Hubie tipped his head, listening. 'I'd say that one came from somewhere near the river, maybe on it. The troops inside Trinity College will set some up as well, if they haven't already done it. They'll take the buildings between there and the Post Office, as they can.'

'Take?'

'Shell.' He moved the teapot to the centre of the table. 'Say this is the Post Office. This knife is Sackville Street, running past it, and this one here's the river.' The sugar bowl was Trinity, the milk jug the bank. His black glove ran between them all, describing a tightening circle. He named the likely vantage points and arranged place mats to represent them. 'If I had the running of it.' He sat back and surveyed the ruin of the table. One of his mats was bang in the middle of Rutland Square.

'How will I get home?'

'You won't, 'til it's over.'

I looked at Dote, as if she could solve this. 'They'll be safe in Cabra, won't they?'

'As safe as we are,' said Hubie. Did he even know where Cabra was? Why were we taking his word for everything?

May's cup shook in her hand. Tea slopped over the table.

'I didn't mean to frighten you.' Hubie took her hand and held it in his good palm, smoothing it with the broad, blunt paw of his hurt one. It was mesmerizing to watch, the most substantial thing in the room.

He suggested that we take down the paintings and maps and wrap them in sheets, as though we were moving house. 'Like a spring-clean,' Dote said brightly to May, who took her hand away from Hubie and put it in her lap, under the table, saying they'd done the spring-clean already, she didn't want to do another one. After a small silence she said she'd better go up and lie down for a bit. Dote went with her, saying something about a faulty catch on a window that needed seeing to.

'Do you really think it's necessary to pack everything away?' I asked Hubie, when they'd gone.

'People need something to do.'

I was disappointed to realize that he thought us children, to be managed and directed and distracted.

He insisted on going out, to gather whatever information he could. Before he left, he gave strict instructions that we should stay indoors. 'But, if you must go out, stay away from Mount Street Bridge. Those fellows in the corner house mean business.'

The air of the house hung heavy as a curtain when he'd gone. While May slept, Dote and I took down the paintings and the maps and May's father's medals and commendations, wrapped them up and put them away. The dejected oblongs of darkness they left behind on the walls depressed Dote, so she called a halt to it and we sat in the kitchen, where May's floral prints remained. We tried and abandoned a game of peggity, played a few hands of old maid before agreeing there were few things more tedious than a game of cards when your heart wasn't in it.

Neither of us wanted tea without milk, so we just sat, talking. I was curious about Hubie. Dote told me about his family's sprawling country house, the varying fortunes of the farm, how Hubie's brother Tom wanted to breed horses and Tom's wife, Philippa – who had been Hubie's fiancée – was the daughter of a famous breeder and trainer. 'I hate to say it, but she's more suited to Tom.'

She said Hubie was always making things when he was a boy. Ingenious things, like a contraption for beating carpets; a hinged and folding ladder; a mechanical raft that worked as a ferry across a fast-flowing river at the back of the house. The younger children, his brothers and sisters, used to spend hours on it, playing ferryman. They pulled themselves across the water on the rope he'd rigged between two trees, moving long-suffering animals, dogs and cats and nursling lambs, from one side to the other and then back again.

I found it hard to imagine Hubie as a child, or even in a family. He seemed the sort of person who could have arrived in the world spontaneously, separate and fully formed.

'That ferry of his made a marvellous toy, but it could have been more. I told him he should patent the idea. He said nonsense, it was the sort of solution people had contrived for hundreds of years – why make a fuss about it?' She drummed her fingers on the table. 'It's a pity he wasn't more savvy about money. He could do with ways to earn a living now.'

I told her Mr Briscoe had offered me a job, and that I might need to go to London for training.

'Would you like to go?'

I shifted in my seat, let my gaze stray to the window. 'This is home.' I didn't know if I wanted to live somewhere Liam had never been.

'What do your parents say?'

'I haven't mentioned it.'

The shots outside were more persistent – but distant enough not to be threatening. I found it hard to grasp the appalling truth: that each one had an aim – to extinguish a specific, living target. I had an overwhelming urge to lie down and cry.

Dote patted my hand. 'What did you and Hubie talk about last night? You were late coming up.'

'This and that. Liam.' I felt strangely shy, reluctant to say more.

'Well. I'll go up and check on May.'

When she'd gone, I looked through the bookcase for distraction. There was *The Riddle of the Sands* – how prophetic that had turned out to be! Two books of Mr Stephens's, *The Crock of Gold* and *The Charwoman's Daughter*, both of which I'd loved. Katherine Cecil Thurston's *Fly on the Wheel*. Mother wouldn't have her books in our house; I'd read them here. I took George Moore's *Ave*, hoping to be amused, but couldn't concentrate.

I fiddled with a set of nesting lacquered Burmese boxes. Ovoid, they were inscribed with intricate, swirling patterns, gold and purple and red. Strong colours. I unpacked the smaller boxes and arranged them in a row, six of them, packed them up again. They nestled inside each other sweetly, like Russian dolls, the lids indented just enough to slide home easy as a knife through soft butter. Their weight was smooth in my palm, the lacquer so rich it was almost warm. *Lacquer.* I liked the shape of the word, its silky texture.

Hours passed. I worried about the others, my parents and Florrie and Lockie. I hoped to God Matt was where he'd said he'd be, away over in Rathfarnham, applying himself to his books. A burst of gunfire made me nearly jump out of my skin. Something enormous was happening, and we were trapped inside it, like one of those boxes, waiting to be released into the next event, the next drama. I couldn't begin to see how I might direct my own life, when all my boxes were set out for me, ready-made, made-to-fit.

More gunfire. The window was a magnet. I couldn't resist looking out. Nothing had visibly changed. The canal was like a length of tin, nailed down between two ranks of houses fronted by road, strips of grass. It seemed solid; it was anything but. Things vanished into it, sank quickly out of sight. A coach and horses, once, with a load of passengers, coming home from a ball at the Castle. Like a fairytale, there would have been footmen and diamonds and too-tight shoes; and dreams, no doubt, of princes – but the water swallowed them all. There'd have been commotion and splashing. There would have been screams, but they'd have been brief, the canal would have swallowed them too, quick enough, and smoothed itself down, like brushing crumbs from a skirt. If you thought about it, you'd be afraid of water. It lay there waiting. You'd be tempted to slip inside it. It looked easy. And the swans swam along its surface as though it were a road, as though it could be walked on.

A hairy bluebottle crept up the glass. At the top corner, it buzzed and turned in tight circles, as if it didn't know there was the space of an entire room at its back. I got up and pulled the sash down so it could escape. It sank too, bouncing and buzzing at the corner of the window-frame, a pantomime of frantic rage. With the window open wide, the fly resumed its buzzing circles, not knowing how close it was to freedom. I could see the veins on its wings. *Shoo!* I said, waving my hands. It sprang away, rediscovered flight and soared off into the morning, leaving me alone in the empty room, to wait.

Stories of atrocities on the Continent brought a sour panic to my throat. I pushed it away. This was Ireland. There were

Irishmen in the British Army. Ireland was part of the Empire. There'd be discipline. There would. British soldiers lived here. They used our shops, stayed in our hotels, walked out with Irish women. Many of them were Irish themselves. *I'm as Irish as you are.*

Not only my hands but my feet were clenched, coiled tight. Tension ran its wires through me; my pulse ticked like a clock. I listened to May humming through the ceiling, Dote's low voice steady and calm. Where on earth could Hubie have gone, what was keeping him? I itched to know what was happening outside, couldn't bear to sit on my hands and wait a minute longer. There were people at the mouth of the lane. They might have fresh news, maybe someone had a newspaper. Hubie had left cigarettes in a silver box on the mantel. Telling myself he'd as good as given me permission, I put a handful into my pocket.

I called up to Dote that I was going out for a minute, grabbed Liam's coat and slipped out.

A notice was pasted to the door of the Pepper Canister Church. The word 'Proclamation' in large letters drew me closer. It was a declaration of martial law.

An elderly man materialized beside me. 'Is it over?' His coat was worn so thin it shone. He smelled of dust and mothballs, peered at the notice as though he had difficulty in reading it, although the print was large enough. 'Can't make it out,' he muttered.

'It says there's a curfew. Half seven in the evening 'til half five in the morning.'

'Bit bloody much. Where do they think they are?' He wandered off.

The further I went towards the river, the more my steps faltered. I'd a sense of being lost, familiar streets made strange by a fear that clogged my ears and beat in my throat. There was no one else around. Full of sudden dread – what had I done, coming out alone? – I saw myself stranded in an empty street, caught between two advancing armies and all doors shut against me, lost in my own town.

I turned into a side street off Great Brunswick Street on tiptoe, as though the sound of a single step might draw gunfire my way. A woman leaned out of a window to ask what I could see, her sleeves rolled up to her roughened elbows. I told her I could see nothing. For all of five seconds I wondered could I ask for shelter. Then she asked me did I want to go in and some reserve made me say no thank you, I wanted to cross the river if I could. 'Not a chance,' she said. 'Did you not hear the gunboat earlier?'

A young man in a doorway opposite took a stick he was chewing out of his mouth and leered. 'Come in here with me, darlin'. I'll look after ya.'

Then there was a crashing explosion, the likes of which I'd never heard before. I ducked, arms over my head. When I took them down, slivers of glass sparkled on my sleeves.

The woman stood back from her window, but I still saw that her fat forearms were threaded with blood. Shouts of outrage sounded the length of the street, where every window had blown out and the nets were gone. I could see right into the corner of the room behind the woman. A young man with no legs was propped up on a mattress against the wall. An army coat was thrown over a nearby chair.

I turned back for Percy Place, cutting through backstreets and lanes. I stopped at every corner, hurried across the empty spaces. I might have given up if I hadn't seen others doing the same. It was nearly like a dance we'd all learned the steps of. Pause, peer, dash. Pause, peer, dash. The one time I came across a small company of soldiers, setting up a roadblock, their captain told me to hurry in off the streets, trouble was on its way.

A low stone railway bridge made a deep pool of shadow I was wary of, the bridge so low I could nearly reach up and touch it.

Liam and I used to come to places just like it. We loved to scare ourselves stupid when the trains passed over, so close you could feel the ground shake underfoot. In the glorious days of Ellen, we'd slip out of the pub, find a railway bridge and wait for trains to pass overhead. We'd close our eyes and be caught up in a storm, an earthquake, a shipwreck, whatever we fancied. The scream of the engine and clash of iron as the brakes squeezed the wheels to a halt approaching the station made our hearts race. Our breath came fast and furious, and we'd run, squealing, terrifying ourselves even though we knew exactly what it was, not a monster at all but a train we might take to the seaside in the summertime.

After Liam left for the Front, I went to the Amiens Street arches on my own. Wrapped in his coat, I pressed my back against the stone, closed my eyes and listened to the trains' roar overhead, thinking, is this what it's like out there?

'How much, love?'

I opened my eyes to find a docker watching me, his hands deep in his pockets. I shook my head, tightened Liam's belt and walked away, tripping over my heels on the uneven ground.

There were men up on the track – their caps were visible above the parapet. I looked around to make sure no one was watching and called up to them, cautiously. The heads disappeared. I called again, 'I have cigarettes, if you want them.'

Slowly, a pale, young face rose from the parapet.

I held up a hand full of cigarettes. 'You're not the army?'

He laughed. 'Who's asking?' A thin man in shirtsleeves

197

stood up beside him, leaned over and let down a basket on a rope. I put the cigarettes into it. While he hauled it up, I asked if by any chance they knew Matt Crilly.

'Never heard of him. What's happening up the town?'

I told him where I'd seen the troops and what the Captain had said, 'There's more on the way.'

'About feckin' time. We're sick of waiting. Ah, well, thanks for these.' He winked, and vanished.

A sound like drumming came from the ground or the air or somewhere else entirely – I couldn't place it. My heart knocked harder at my throat. I began to run, past backstreets and tenements, areas of waste ground I barely knew existed, on past the maternity hospital and up the length of Merrion Square to avoid the corner overlooking Mount Street Bridge – where the gunmen were – that exposed stretch of road Hubie had warned us against. A man ran up to a door and in through it. I was tempted to follow, just to get out of harm's way – but I kept going. Past the Pepper Canister Church, the towpath, the small bridge. A spate of shots to the east, machine guns, hard to say where. The water on my left could be trapped light, the light could be water rising to a surface of sky. I couldn't run another step. My lungs were bursting.

Nearly there. May's hall door was open a crack and there was Dote, leaning out of it, waving with big sweeps of her arm, *Come on, come on, hurry!*

We didn't know it then, but a column of Sherwood Foresters was marching straight into a bloodbath. They would be trapped on an exposed stretch of Northumberland Road, just around the corner from Percy Place, with no shelter other than household steps, kerbstones and a few young trees, while bullets tore into them from well-chosen positions in ordinary-looking houses. More than two hundred of them would crawl over their comrades to be killed or severely wounded in the course of one lethal afternoon.

For all the talk and speculation, my imagination about what was to come had been decidedly orderly, shaped by known streets and spaces, the familiar grid of my existence. Long files of uniformed men would march along the streets and halt in formation outside the buildings where the gunmen were. There'd be a challenge issued, shots fired in the air to demonstrate authority. Flags would be lowered and raised, weapons would clatter to the ground and the rebels would come out, looking sheepish. I'd spent more time wondering what would happen next, what the world would say of them, of all of us.

I didn't expect the relentless racket of rifle fire, all the more frightening for being out of sight, or the piercing shrill of whistles that urged the men forward. I didn't expect the screaming.

I raced up the steps and in through the door. Dote bolted it behind me. May sat on the stairs, holding her head. Paschal was on the banister, tail down, sucking his fingers.

My heart beat in all the wrong places: my wrists and neck, my ears. A sudden crash of gunfire erupted from the bridge down at the main road. May groaned and hurried upstairs with Paschal in her arms, his retreating face a pink heart peering over her shoulder.

I went into the parlour and over to the window, parted the drawn curtains with a finger, and moved my face into a gap that reeked of dust and dead fires. I wanted to see what I hadn't dared look at while I was running. On the far side of the canal a group of people seemed to be watching the bridge. When I looked where they were looking, I saw nothing other than empty road, the steel ribbon of the canal, the black lock, the bridge. But I could hear, like distant, irregular drums, an exchange of gunfire more intense than anything we'd heard so far.

Men in khaki began to emerge from the lane to my left. They moved furtively along Percy Place towards the bridge, pressing themselves into railings, crouching at the coping stones of the canal. There was a single pane of glass and a short garden between me and the broad shoulders and stiff cap of an officer. He was waving at other men to come on. One of them stopped suddenly. His knees made separate angles and he pitched, face down, on to the road.

'Come away from there' – Hubie's voice, behind me. I dropped the curtain.

Hubie brought May down from her room and said we should wait it out in the back hall off the kitchen, in the basement, where there were no windows and we'd be out of sight. The sounds of fighting were muffled down there, and May seemed more relaxed.

It was a space like a well, about ten-foot square. A step beside the scullery led down from the kitchen to its stone floor. A door opened to the upper part of the house at ground level. The ceiling followed the slope of the back stairs leading up to the upstairs hall. The plaster was rough, like the rock face of a pale cave. A broad curtained archway led to the kitchen. The curtain was drawn to cut down on draughts in winter. It was the coldest, deepest part of the house, with the faintest whiff of damp.

Dote gathered cushions and blankets, while Hubie and I carried in kitchen chairs. 'We might be here a while, may as well be comfortable.'

When he pulled the heavy red curtain across, it was surprisingly dark and close. May let out a squeak and we decided to leave the curtain half open for the moment, for the light. Paschal played with currants in a dish and ate them, while

Dote and May and I played cards, despite the tremor in May's hands. Her bracelets shivered, 'til I longed to ask her to take them off. Hubie sat off at an angle, on the low step, drawing in his notebook, the one with squared paper. He steadied it with the edge of his right fist, sketching careful lines and angles with his other hand.

'What's that?' I asked.

He looked at his work, then at me. 'A design for a double-hinged digit. Look.' He showed me the page. I didn't know what to make of the sketches. One gadget was shaped like an intricate, short-handled fork, with four hinged tines and an array of wires.

'Can you not guess?' A spate of sudden shooting started up outside. He folded down the cover of the notebook. 'It's a design for a mechanical hand.' He put it aside. 'It needs more work.'

Something stirred in me. It could have been pity, but felt more like pride – although I'd no idea why I should feel such a thing.

May was fretful. 'How long have we been here? Could we not go out to the garden, even?'

'Not yet,' Dote said. 'I'd say we've been here an hour?' She looked at Hubie for confirmation.

He angled his wrist to the light, tapped the face of his watch. 'It's stopped.'

'Will it ever end?' May sneezed. 'Lord!' She sneezed again. 'Dust.' Paschal curled up in her lap like a cat. It was strange he didn't mind the tremor.

Dote said there were lamps in the press if we wanted to read. I went to get one. I felt foolish, creeping across the kitchen in my stockinged feet in daylight, like a game of hide and seek. I found the lamp and matches and turned to go back to the hall when I heard quick heavy footsteps on the gravel, right outside the front window. I stopped, afraid to move and call attention to myself.

'Katie?' Hubie looked out from the hall. I put a finger to my lips.

Something banged against the glass. I turned my head and found myself staring at a battered-looking face, a bull of a man. Dark, bushy brows on dirt-scored skin, a downturned mouth. Eyes narrowed and fierce. Another, smaller man seemed to hang from his neck by one arm, his head down. The dark soldier said something I didn't catch. He let go the other man's wrist and pounded the window with his open palm. It'd be nothing to him to break it.

'He wants in,' I said.

Hubie stepped into view. The soldier's face changed. He stood back from the window, looked over his shoulder as though for help.

'He's hurt,' I said.

'Let me see.' Hubie crossed to the window. He made an impatient sound and went out to the door.

'Don't,' Dote said, her voice so low I barely heard it over Hubie's struggle with the bolt. But she made no move to stop him. I put down the lamp and went to help him. It took both my slipping hands to work it loose. He turned the latch and pulled the door open. A wave of sound and a sulphurous smell washed in from the street, past two soldiers, one sagging against the other. The standing one jutted his chin our way, as though he'd bite us. I flinched.

'Is he safe here?' His accent was strange.

'Safe enough,' Hubie said.

The soldier used an elbow to push the door wider open. Hubie took the hurt man's second arm around his neck and between them they brought him in, feet dragging. I'd never seen anything like the sweat that coated the younger man's face. I fetched a chair, but it was clear he couldn't sit in it.

202

Hubie said to get blankets and I went for them, pausing only for a second to look at Dote. She shrugged and cupped her hands as if to say, *What difference will it make now?*

I made a sort of nest on the floor for the wounded man: the dark tartan rug first, doubled over to cushion him, then two worn, buff-coloured blankets with bronze satin edging. Hubie and the able-bodied soldier laid the injured one down. I slipped the cushion Paschal last slept on under his head. 'Where is he hurt?' I asked.

'He's my brother. It's his leg. He's not strong.' The soldier hesitated, looking from us to his brother, then back out the door. Heavy footsteps ran down the road. 'There's a field dressing in his pack.'

He patted the top of the man's head and left. I didn't understand how he did that, how he walked away from shelter, shrugging his pack into place, adjusting the rifle in his hands, breaking into a run.

'Oh, dear.' Dote looked at the injured soldier moaning in the nest I'd made for him, his arms crossed on his tunic, his legs bent to the side. A dark stain spread above the knee of his trousers. 'What are we to do with him?'

Hubie said, 'Get the scissors, Katie. You'd better do this, your hands are better than mine.' He took the young man's pack and opened it, looking for the dressing. He asked Dote for clean rags and told me to cut the soldier's trouser leg longways, so we'd see the wound. I was afraid I'd cut skin by mistake, but soon a pale, hairy leg was laid bare, a knitted sock gartered at the knee, a jagged wound in the thigh, surprisingly black and mucky, with blood seeping from it. The soldier cursed when Hubie tried to pull out some threads that were stuck to its edges. He was only a boy, I could see now.

'We'll have to get him proper attention.'

'Should we try to clean it?' Dote asked.

'We could do more harm than good.' Hubie's voice changed when he spoke to the boy. 'Are you hurt anywhere else, mate?'

'Bellyache.'

'Right.' Hubie told me to wrap the field dressing around the thigh, as tight as I could. He took a stub of pencil from the young man's pack and had me wind the end of the bandage around and hold it to slow the blood while he sent Dote for pins. When all of that was done, I worked the boy's garter free of his sock and pulled it up over the bandage, to be sure.

'Good idea.' Hubie stood and went towards the door.

'You're not going outside?' Dote said.

'There's an ambulance,' he said. 'And the shooting seems to have stopped.'

'Wait for me,' I said, but he didn't.

I went after him, out to where he stood in the shelter of the steps, craning for a view of Mount Street Bridge.

On the far side of the canal the crowd of spectators had grown. To the right, a soldier sat against a tree, facing away from the fighting. His cap was gone. Blood ran down his face. There was a spill of khaki further up, at the mouth of the bridge: men strewn in the road, as though someone had flung them down from a height. Only their groans could be heard, and then came shouts from across the water. 'They've stopped the fight! There are women on the bridge!'

I stood out from the shadow of the steps for a better view. Men carried forms on stretchers in the direction of Paddy Dun's Hospital. Two girls carried water from man to man.

Hubie pulled me back. 'Careful.'

'They've stopped firing. We could help.'

As we watched, two ambulances began to creep closer to the bridge, and then a third came into view at the bend in the road on our side of the water. It stopped, maybe two hundred yards away, and made a turn, so that its back end faced us.

'Could we carry him up to them? Or as far as the hospital, if they won't take him?' I was calculating the distance in my mind. I wasn't thinking about Hubie 'til I saw the fury in his eyes. Everything stopped. Of course we couldn't carry the boy all that way. I wasn't strong enough. He only had one usable hand.

I stared him down. 'Dote could help.'

Dote told May to stay in the back hall, minding Paschal. We got the soldier ready to carry, twisting the corners of the blanket he lay on and gathering him into a kind of hammock, with Dote at one shoulder. I had the other. Hubie, his good hand bunching the blanket at the man's swaddled feet, directed us out, around the tricky corner at the door, trying not to knock him, across the gravel and on to the road – just as the shooting started again, louder and fiercer than before.

We stopped at the gate, trying to gauge the risk. I could still see one of the water-jug girls and some nurses on the bridge. 'They'll be hurt.'

'Oh!' There was horror on Dote's face at the sight of the carnage. She paused, gathered herself together, and we continued.

Leaving the pavement for the road was like stepping off a quay on to a boat, precarious balance, black depths waiting below. The skin of the canal puckered and sent darts of reflected light into my eyes. We made our awkward way towards the ambulance. The drill of shots had us flinching, even as we moved away from them. The shocking sound of men weeping. A black pit of space opened inside my head, ready for me to fall into it and disappear. I crouched over our bundle and watched the ground pass beneath. My shoes appeared and disappeared down there, as remote as though attached to someone else's feet. My ears were lungs, straining and loud. I told myself to keep going. *As if you're not afraid.*

We came to a woman huddled over the still form of a man

with twisted legs. I was looking at the ruin of a face, a jagged hole where a cheek should be, the flap of a chin sagging down the length of a bloodied neck. The woman knelt on her folded skirt and whispered a prayer where the dead man's ear should have been.

My shoulders and arms burned from the weight of that skinny young soldier. We half lifted, half dragged him along, bumping the ground; we couldn't help it. He screamed at us to *Stopit! Stopitforchristsssake!* We struggled into the scant shelter of a young tree to wait for the ambulance, now reversing towards us. There, in the tufted grass, was a bloody pulp of flesh and white feathers, a crush of webbed orange feet. The ruined white-and-black head of a swan spelled rotten luck for someone.

Just when I couldn't take another step, someone took the weight from me. My knees gave way and I stumbled, but caught myself before I fell. A man in a black St John Ambulance coat had the boy's shoulders. Another one took the feet from Hubie. Dote sat on the grass, panting, ignoring the dead bird. I rubbed the circulation back into my burning palms, my stinging fingers.

The St John's men lowered the injured boy to the ground. 'Here we go, son. You'll be all right, we've got you now,' the first one said. 'I'm Fitz.' His voice was like Dad's, low and steady. A voice I'd trust. 'We'll get you on to a proper stretcher, Christy'll get it, we'll have you in the rig in no time.'

'It's his leg that's hurt.' The boy looked light as a feather, lying there on the ground. Not a day over sixteen.

They lifted the boy, blanket and all, on to the stretcher. He grunted in pain. They carried the stretcher towards the open van. His arm shot out and grabbed mine as he passed. 'Come with me.'

'They're taking you to hospital,' I said. 'You're safe now.'

'Please.'

'It's not allowed,' Christy said.

The boy squeezed my hand so hard the bones cracked. His knees came up, and his shoulders, so that they nearly dropped him. 'Whoa, steady!' Christy glared, as if it was my fault.

The boy shivered. 'Please.' His teeth chattered.

'Well –' Fitz looked at Christy. 'It's all of two minutes away.'

'Get in, so,' Christy said.

'Don't, Katie,' Hubie said.

'Why not?'

He dropped his eyes. 'You might not get back. The fighting might start up again.'

'I'll be all right at the hospital. I know people there.'

Fitz and Christy lifted the boy into the back of the boxy-looking vehicle. I climbed in beside him, awkward in my skirt. They put the stretcher on a rough floor spread with a horse blanket. I hunkered down between the boy and a groaning bulldog of a man who never opened his eyes in the short, rattling journey to Baggot Street.

I took the boy's rough hand in mine. His grip was surprising, his knuckles big on callused fingers. I wondered what work he'd done before soldiering, who was waiting for him at home.

Liam wrote about the enemy being men just like him. *They bleed the same and weep and moan and die in no way different to the way that our own men moan, weep or die. The one sure thing is that it happens. You do your best not to believe the evidence of your own two eyes. It happens whether you believe it or whether you don't. The power of wishing counts for nothing here. I tell you, Katie, the world is not at all what we imagined.*

By the time we got to the hospital, the boy's teeth were clacking off each other.

'Why does he shake like that?' I asked Fitz. 'Is he having a fit?'

He didn't answer. I prised my fingers free. Released, my hand felt naked, unnaturally light. My knees creaked like an old woman's when I clambered out of the ambulance to let the men to do their work. The boy's pink-rimmed eyes followed me. Someone else, a nurse, applied pressure to the blood-soaked bandage at his thigh as the stretcher emerged into the hospital yard. Men in ordinary street clothes came to help carry the whey-faced bulldog of a man, who was still groaning.

Inside was bedlam. People crying. A woman with two children clinging to her skirt held the arm of a nurse and begged for something I couldn't hear. A reek of Jeyes fluid and sour sweat. People in medical clothes moved quickly through the halls, steering clear of reaching hands, their eyes blind to individuals.

Fitz found a chair, so I could sit beside the boy. I took his cool, slippery hand again. 'I'm still here. I'll stay, as long as I'm let.' A slight pressure on my fingers was the only sign that he'd heard, or that he was aware of me at all.

A nurse began to unwrap the bandage. Blood spurted in a small arc, splashing my face. His eyes fluttered and closed. His grip on my hand relaxed. The nurse was joined by another, who cut his tunic with scissors. A doctor came. I was in the way. I'd never felt so useless in my life. How many hundreds of times had I walked past this hospital and never given proper thought to all that happened here, the world of pain and illness that turned in its own path, right next to mine. How careless I'd been.

In the distance, at the far end of a busy corridor, I saw Bartley's familiar gangly figure, the streak of white hair in a thicket of black falling across his forehead. I was surprised by a rush of relief. 'Bartley!'

'Katie?' He went white as paper. 'Has something happened to Alanna?'

'She's in Herbert Park, with Isabel. She's fine. Everyone's fine. How's Eva?'

'She's upstairs.'

'You moved her here? Why?' I looked around the overcrowded hallway. She must be bad, or they'd surely have left her where she was.

'Last night.' He looked uncomfortable. 'We wanted to keep a closer eye on her, and I'm glad we did. She needs paracentesis.'

I thought he'd said 'Paraclete', imagined beating wings, tongues of flame. 'What?'

'It's a minor procedure, to drain the excess fluid. It's putting strain on her kidneys. She's having trouble breathing.' He lifted my sticky hand and held it between us, turning it over and back. 'What's this, blood?'

'I got caught up in fighting. At Mount Street.'

'Were you on the bridge?'

'No. I'm not that brave. I only helped carry someone out.'

'Sounds brave to me. I'm glad you're safe.' He squeezed my fingers gently before releasing them.

We stood back against the wall to make room for a porter who pushed a creaking wheeled chair past us. The patient's eyes were closed. He looked to be in pain. One half of his head had been shaved; his skin was like puffy yellow wax.

A miasma of antiseptic smells and a taste of metal overwhelmed me of a sudden. My knees buckled. Bartley caught my elbow and stopped me falling. 'Come with me.' He brought me to an empty common room, where a tea-urn stood on a scarred trestle table. 'When's the last time you ate?' He made me wash my hands at a sink in the corner and put me in a chair while he fussed with the urn and a cup. 'It's lukewarm, but better than nothing.' He added several spoons of sugar.

'No sugar.'

'You need it.' He watched me drink, refilled my cup.

My mind skittered across the bloody surfaces and blacknesses I'd seen today, insides turned out. The eminent men whose portraits lined the walls loomed, solid and indifferent to all I didn't want to hear. I dropped my head, looked at the shape my knees made under my stained skirt, a stain on my shoe. 'Can I see Eva?'

Bartley led me down a corridor towards a flight of stairs. On the way he stopped to talk to a man who he introduced as Eva's surgeon.

'Why are you not looking after her yourself?' I asked, when we'd moved on.

'It's not allowed.'

'But she'd prefer it.'

He looked back, over his shoulder. The trace of a smile crossed his face. 'I wonder would she.'

'She says you're the best surgeon there is.'

We'd reached a landing. He pushed open a swing door and held it for me.

'She has to say that.' He looked pleased all the same. 'It'd be unethical; my judgement would be compromised. Bad enough we've to do this on the ward, but everywhere's so busy' – he glanced up at the clock on the wall – 'and I've to get back. I'll leave you with her. Don't stay long, Katie. You're not to tire her. And don't get in the way.'

He steered me into a side room, where Eva was, and introduced me to Gwen Townsend, the sister-in-charge. She made the chilliest of bows, folded her hands into the bib of her apron.

I crossed to stand between Eva and the window. I could see her better from here. She was flushed, and her face seemed puffy, but her eyes were bright. She gave me a weak, worried smile. 'You and Bartley will be friends yet.'

'Threat or promise?' I said, sitting into a chair beside her, turning my back on the nurse.

Sister Townsend went out and came back with a steel tray of instruments under a cover. She laid the instruments out with a pair of tongs, where Eva couldn't see them, while we waited for the surgeon. At last he came and busied himself at the sink.

'You'll have to leave now, Miss Crilly,' Sister Townsend said.

The surgeon looked around, his hairy forearms soaped over the wrist, and raised his bushy eyebrows. 'Wait outside.' His voice was gruff but his eyes were kind.

I waited 'til he said I could go back in and sit with her again. She was drowsy. I listened to the low exchange between doctor and nurse at the door: abdominal dropsy, peritoneal cavity and Bartley's word, 'paracentesis'. He left and Sister Townsend came back in to open the window. 'Time's up, Miss Crilly. She's asleep.'

I looked around the room. 'Is there nothing I can do here?'

'She needs rest.'

'I mean – in general.'

She stood by the door, waiting for me to go out in front of her.

'Please, sister. There must be something. Anything. I'd like to be useful.'

Her doubt was obvious. I could have found Bartley, I suppose, and asked him, but I wasn't sure his opinion of my usefulness would be much better than hers. Anything I'd ever learned in my life up to now had been a waste. The Bible story about the wise and the foolish virgins made a new, appalling kind of sense. The nuns in school said it was about guarding the purity of the soul so that we'd die in a state of grace, because you never knew the day or the hour; but it wasn't that at all. It was about being ready to act, so that

211

when a crisis came one knew how to rise to meet it. I had no skills to apply anywhere that mattered, least of all here, with life and death all around me. I could only get in the way. 'There are voluntary aides downstairs.' She looked at my hands. 'It'll be dirty work. Washing and the like.'

I spread them for her inspection, glad of their wholeness, the blunt fingertips and short nails that Florrie shuddered at.

I was put to work where I could do the least harm, gathering soiled linen into a wheeled hamper and bringing it to the laundry.

'But we're overstretched,' said the nurse in the supply room. 'Don't be too quick to change sheets and covers, unless they're obviously stained.' The nurse was flushed, distracted. 'Please God that will change. People are very good, they're bringing bedlinen and towels from their homes.'

'What about dressings?'

'They need a separate basket. Could you manage two?'

'This smaller one, inside the other?'

I was pleased with myself but she just nodded, and left.

I patrolled the corridors, moved in and out of treatment rooms and cubicles, bundling soiled linen into the hamper's separate compartments, delivering it to the laundry to be sorted further. I tried not to get in anyone's way. Tried not to stare too openly at the wounds and injuries I couldn't help seeing as I passed.

I was tired and worried about too many things; it was hard to keep anything clear in my head. It began to feel like a dream, pushing a cart up and down a hospital corridor, listening to cries and whispers, smelling blood. Human skin was a miracle I'd never considered, like nothing so much as a living canvas bag, deceptively taut and smooth, a receptacle for things never meant to be seen, let alone spilled, so much disorder and mess and dear God the smells, and sounds, things I'd never forget no matter how long I lived.

A nurse came out of a room and saw me with my hamper, almost full. 'In here needs clearing,' she said, and hurried on, leaving the door ajar. I pushed it open and backed into the room, pulling the basket. An old man was asleep on a high bed under a sheet, his face turned away from me.

'Hello?' I said.

He didn't answer.

He wasn't breathing.

It was indecent to look at him, so undefended. I glanced at the door, stepped closer.

An argument broke out in my head. I didn't know this man. I'd never seen him before. I'd no right to stare at him now. But he had something to tell me. I stood beside him and looked into his face, his eyes half open. I'd read about the unseeing eyes of the dead, but that was wrong. It wasn't so much that his eyes didn't see, as that there was no one there to look. His colour was like a slab of fat on a skirt of meat, grey and mottled, his mouth an oval of surprise. I touched the wrist with a cautious finger, then laid the back of my hand against the chill, waxy skin. I stared at the face, the thin lips fallen back on yellowed teeth.

The door creaked, let in a woman in a porter's overalls. I stepped away from the body and busied myself lifting clothes from the floor and folding them on to a shelf. She *ts*ked and pulled the sheet up over his face. 'They must have forgotten. They're run off their feet.' Her brisk, matter-of-fact voice broke the spell I'd been under. She looked at me out of a pleasant, matronly face under a cap of white hair. 'Are you a volunteer too?'

I nodded. The stuff of the man's clothes was coarse and strange in my hands. A pair of trousers. A white cotton vest. The most extraordinary things I'd ever touched, not being my brother's, or my father's, but a stranger's. A stranger who was dead.

She bustled about, straightening things I hadn't seen were crooked. 'I haven't seen you before.'

'I only just started.'

'I've been coming in since Monday.' She looked around, taking stock. 'Terrible, isn't it?' Although she looked rather as though she was enjoying herself. 'They'll move him soon, there's ones waiting on a bed.' She lifted a chart from the end of the bed. 'No name.'

'What happened to him?' There wasn't a mark on him, that I could see.

'Heart, it says. Is that his coat?' She held out her hand.

A man's overcoat lay crumpled in the corner. I picked it up. Not thinking, I slid my hand in the pocket. There was grit in the seam, a cold key, two small coins, a wallet.

She gave me a peculiar look. It woke me up to where I was, my hand inside the lining of a stranger's pocket. The intimate, greasy friction on my skin was shocking, but not as bad as my intrusion. I pulled out the wallet and gave it to her. 'His name might be in there.' She rolled the clothes up on top of the chart, put the wallet in plain sight on top of them and left.

I pushed my hamper of linen out after her, wondering. To think of that man leaving his house that morning, putting the necessaries into his pockets. Every day we cross such ordinary thresholds, not paying attention, no notion of what lies in wait.

I didn't feel the hours pass 'til a nurse came and said it was after nine and I should go home if I could. Else I could spend the night in the clinic they'd set aside for helpers to rest in.

I went upstairs to check on Eva. The door to her room was closed. A nurse came to my knock. 'We're sponging her down; I can't let you in.' She didn't quite meet my eye. 'She needs sleep. Come back tomorrow, if you can.'

Behind her I could see the bedclothes, folded over the bottom rail. Another nurse was helping Eva take off her nightdress. When it was lifted over her head and her arms were freed, her hands flopped to her side. When they rubbed her with a flannel, my sister mewed like a kitten.

I'd seen the cramped space that had been set aside for helpers – it was like the worst kind of overcrowded waiting room, with no hope of a train. I didn't want to have to listen to one more word of prediction or opinion. We'd heard the worst of the fighting had calmed, and I wanted to breathe air that had no brine or disinfectant in it, to be outside, alone and quiet.

I went out to the yard. A close, oppressive darkness had fallen while I was trudging up and down the halls pushing linen baskets. Fitz and Christy sat side by side staring straight ahead, not speaking, like Tweedledum and Tweedledee. Each had a mug of tea in one hand and a cigarette in the other. Curls of steam and smoke rose unnoticed from their fists. 'I hope you're not going out again,' I said. 'You look worn out.'

'One or two more go-arounds, then we'll call it a night,' Fitz said. They told me the battle was over at Mount Street Bridge. It was too soon to say how many had died there, how many had been injured. There was still sporadic fighting towards the docks and the river. They were gathering in the last of the afternoon's wounded, the less serious cases, the ones that had been able to wait.

'I'd say you'd be safe enough to go back,' Fitz said.

Christy shook his head. 'There's a curfew.' He drained his mug of tea and dropped the butt of his cigarette into it. 'And snipers.'

'Do you know if things are bad in Cabra?' I asked. 'Or Rutland Square?'

'No news is good news.' Fitz put on his cap and adjusted

it. 'We'll give you a lift back around the corner, if you like. We're headed that way.'

I was glad of it. The thought of crossing even that short, familiar distance alone and in the dark filled me with dread, after the horrors of the day. And I was uneasy about having stayed away so long. I hoped they were all safe and sound, and that they hadn't worried about me. I wondered about my own family, on the other side of the city, but Christy said there wasn't a hope in hell of getting across the river, unless I'd a submarine in my pocket.

There were soldiers at the east end of Percy Place. I asked Christy to let me out at the lane. I'd slip around the back and avoid questions. Fitz said he'd watch 'til I'd got in the back garden door. He walked me to the corner and gave me a black St John's badge stitched to a cuff. 'If you have to go out again – take this. Use it if you run into trouble. Say you've been helping us. It's no more than the truth.'

A large cloud covered most of the half moon. The lane was a narrow well of darkness 'til my eyes adjusted to the inky light. I held my left hand to the wall and felt my way along the cool bumpy brick, an angled corner, the neighbours' garden door, then Dote's. I waved to Fitz, even though I could barely see him, and put my thumb to the smooth metal saddle of the latch, my foot at last to the path. I closed the garden door and rested my forehead on the wood for a second, gathering my strength for the last short stretch of ground I had to cover. I moved as quietly as I could, barely breathing. With nightfall, the garden was treacherous, the path longer than it should be, shadows larger, darker, closer. Ahead of me a square of light came from the kitchen window. A figure crossed it. Hubie. The darkness thinned as I got closer. Giddy with relief, I dodged the hard corner of the bench and knocked on the glass, no need for the key.

He leaned on a broom, an astonishing sight, and gave me

a long look, in no hurry to let me in. One side of his mouth lifted.

'Are the others in bed?' I asked, when he opened the door.

'They went to your friend in Herbert Park. The ambulance men said they'd be safe there. May's nerves were bad. Dote was in quite a state as well.'

'You let them go alone?'

'I did not; I went with them. Then they sent me back again. They were worried about what would happen if you came back and found no one here. Your peace of mind, apparently, matters more than the safety of a crotchety, disposable nephew.'

'Proper order.' To hide the embarrassment I actually felt, I went to the dresser for a cup. 'I'm parched.'

'Mind you, I think it was Paschal they were really concerned about. He hid.'

'Or the house.' I turned back into the dim light from the single lamp he'd left burning on the table.

'Or all three. Have you been at the hospital since?'

'I have.' It was a mistake to come back here. I didn't want to have to explain why my hair was coming loose or why my blouse was crumpled when I took off my coat and folded it over the back of a chair. He made no comment, as if he knew I'd reached my limit. I took the cup to the sink and filled it, looking out. A burst of shots I didn't bother to remark on seemed to drive the last clouds away towards the sea. A sliver of moon hung in a cluster of stars directly overhead. The garden turned silvery-blue. The cold clean water soothed my mouth and dusty throat.

'There were soldiers here, but they left a while back. They couldn't get a clear line of fire. All the windows at the front of the house are broken, as you can see.' He gestured towards the far window, which had a lacy appearance, more hole than stitch. 'I've been sweeping up the glass.'

217

I took the dust-pan out from the curtained shelf under the sink and hunkered down so he could sweep the shards of glass and ordinary dirt on to it. 'How soon do you think Dote and May will come back?'

'Not before morning, with the curfew. I'm surprised you got through. Then again, I'm not. You seem to do what you want.'

I was taken aback. Was that how I appeared to him?

He hooked his damaged hand around the shaft of the broom and took the dust-pan from me, brought it to the door and went outside to empty it. When he came back, a sliver of moonlight spilled into the house around his feet. He shut the door. I didn't know whether to mock or applaud his work. It amazed me, that people would always try to clean up a mess, mend broken furniture, replace shattered glass, as if the wild forces of the world weren't out there waiting to break in again and smash it all to pieces.

He put his hand into one of May's plant pots. 'It's bone-dry.'

I filled the little watering jug and went over to him, my eyes so tired they played tricks on me in the shifting light. His empty knuckles on the soil looked as though the fingers were still there, rooted deep, out of sight. I gave him the jug. He watered the plant, then went around moistening the roots of others, as I'd often seen May do.

When he finished, we sat at the kitchen table in candle-light. I told him about Eva, and my worry. His sympathy made me uneasy. I'd avoided the topic of his family, not knowing how he'd react if his fiancée's name, or his brother's, came up. I gathered my courage and told him I'd heard the story from Dote, and I was sorry.

He shrugged. 'Far worse if I'd married her, and discovered her true colours later. She did me a favour.' He raised his injured arm. 'After this, I'd have gone back and settled into a subordinate position in the family business, something of a

218

charity case and grateful for it. I'd always be the damaged second son.'

A small thrill of recognition went through me.

'But now, I fancy, I'll strike out on my own.'

'What will you do?'

He stretched his legs and stood up, went over to the broken window and looked out. His entire attitude changed. He went very still. 'Fire,' he said.

'Where?'

He hurried to the door under the front steps. I went after him but he told me to stay where I was while he moved cautiously out towards the road, sheltered by the steps. When he got to the end, he straightened. 'Come here,' he said. 'Look.'

Down at the main road, the terrace on the town side of the bridge was on fire. Flames shot out of the window on the gable wall of Clanwilliam House.

'Is there anyone still in there?' I asked, when I could speak.

'Not alive.' There was no emotion in his answer.

'There are people there, watching. Can we go?'

'There's a guard at the end of the road. They wouldn't let us through. If they did, we wouldn't get back.'

'But –'

'Why must you always try to get a closer look at things that are perfectly evident?'

Stung, I backed away from him. I excused myself and went back inside.

Upstairs, I took off my stale blouse, rinsed it and wrung it out. Thinking I might go to bed, I sponged my skirt clean. By the time I'd hung it up to dry over the bath, I already regretted my efforts. I was far too restless for sleep.

In the wardrobe of the room I was sleeping in, I found a summer dress of Dote's, a pale blue lawn that might have been fashionable twenty years ago. It was pleated on the bodice, had a high neck and tiny buttons on the long cuff. A little on the short side, it was loose at the waist and smelled of mothballs, but it was the best I could find. I tied the crimson and gold sash of this morning's robe around it. Hard to imagine Dote filling a dress like this, she was half the size now.

My hands trembled, but I wasn't cold. It must have been a reaction to the day. When I'd managed a knot of sorts, I went to the window and tried to make out what was happening at the corner.

Hubie came in, holding Paschal. 'He was hiding under my bed.'

Paschal came to me and buried his face in my shoulder. He bunched the soft fabric of the dress in his fist and crammed it into his mouth. I stroked his back and looked past him, at Hubie. He'd put on a smoking jacket over a clean white shirt.

'Katie,' he said. 'Come away from the window.'

'What'll happen now?' I gestured at the smouldering ruins of the houses by the bridge. The shadowy figures of sentries on the road. Night deepened. As I watched, the last light dwindled and sank into the earth.

'I'll tell you what I think, but let's have a drink.' He moved back towards the door that was open to the landing. I followed him, as in a dream: down the stairs and around to the back of the house. Paschal breathed into the crook of my neck. Hubie was talking, his voice a thread pulling me along behind him. What we'd seen that afternoon had raised the stakes. They could expect no mercy now. There'd be rage in high command. 'They'll see us all, every man, woman and child, as potential traitors.'

I stared at the floor. Carpet, stair, floorboard, black-and-white tiles, rug, tile, board, rug. Each step weighted. My ears rang.

'What you mean is,' I said, when we'd reached the back parlour and the cabinet where the spirits were kept, 'that the army won't trust our men now, on the Continent. They'll be undermined.'

'Most likely.' He was looking at labels on the bottles in the inadequate light from the lamp he'd brought in from the kitchen. 'There's not much oil left.'

'Have you a match?'

He passed me a box from his pocket. I took one out and fingered the small round tip before striking it. The matchhead scratched and flared, a neat, blue-and-gold teardrop of flame, strangely pure and clean. I dipped it towards each of the candles on the mantel in turn, making a small forest of light.

My eye was drawn to Paschal's reflection in the mirror. He clambered among the bookshelves behind me, as though he'd a particular volume in mind. He stopped to scratch, caught me looking at him and returned my look, as if he knew all about me. More than he should. His teeth chattered. It sounded like a scolding. I turned around, patted the seat of May's chair. 'Come down here and be quiet.' He jumped to my shoulder and I settled him on the chair. 'So, after today, all those other deaths will mean nothing. Liam died for nothing.'

Hubie steadied a bottle of Irish between what was left of his hand and his belt. He pulled off the lid with his left hand and poured generous measures into two glass tumblers.

'I was proud to be a soldier,' he said. 'Proud of our regiment, of the BEF. It'll be a fiasco now, once Kitchener's Mob are let loose, in conditions a professional soldier would have trouble with. Poor sods. It's not their fault.'

I stiffened. 'Kitchener's Mob – do you mean men like Liam, with not enough training?'

'Liam was quick to learn.' He put the lid back on the bottle, meticulous in tightening it with his left hand, holding it steady with his forearm. He put the bottle back in its place but didn't pick up the glasses straight away. 'We were at the Marne, you know. That was a battle worth fighting. We stopped the Germans' march on Paris. That was the last clear victory we had, and it's more than a year and a half ago.' He offered me a glass.

I took it. 'They'll never give us our own parliament now. We were about to get it, when the war started.'

'I disagree. They never meant to give it. All Irishmen are Mick, to them.'

'Liam thought, if we all fell in to fight beside them, they'd see how trustworthy we were. That we could be allies.'

I looked into the glass he'd given me and set it on the mantel. I didn't want it. I'd never liked the taste. Hadn't touched it since the night we heard that Liam was dead. The night I went looking for Con Buckley. My cheeks were hot. I was glad Hubie didn't look at me. All the little tongues of flame from the lamp and the candles caused the air to shimmer, darken, turn to gold, then black again.

'I've had enough of fighting to other people's purpose.' He crossed to the armchair and sat. 'A cause is one thing. Men enlisted to fight this war for their own reasons, but by the time they'd put on a uniform, khaki or grey or blue, they'd surrendered their right to pursue them. Their will bent to the purposes of idiot generals. Incompetent colonels. And whose purpose did those commanders serve? The King? The Kaiser? Parliament? I will never again raise a gun against another man at the whim of some MP from Yorkshire or Leeds or London – or Dublin, come to that. Never.' He brought his voice under control. 'Did I kill men because the bloody Kaiser wanted it? Whose will directed me?' He glared at me.

'I don't know.'

'I won't do it. Those men out there, the rebels – who authorized any one of them to bring about a single death today? What had any of those boys who were slaughtered on the bridge to do with this benighted country? Nothing. Did they ask to come here? No.'

The candles wavered. Their flames swayed across wells of shadow. The mirror blazed, a sheet of white gold. 'I may well kill a man, again. But, if I do, my reasons will be my own. I'll know what they are.' He said this with the force of someone taking a solemn vow, the embodiment of determination. His two fists were knotted, so tight you couldn't see that one was damaged.

I was spellbound. When I'd wanted to go to college, it was at least in part because Liam was going and, if I was completely honest, in part because my mother didn't want me to. Even working for Dote had been a lucky accident. How unconscious I had been of luck, and how very lucky I had been. I'd never consciously chosen a single thing. I'd left all that to Liam, waited to see what life would chance to offer me.

Paschal had fallen asleep in May's chair, curled up on a red velvet cushion. One callused hand covered his eyes. His breath whistled lightly through the black flare of his nose. The sound of his breathing slowed everything down. My mind emptied. The day, and all its angers, ebbed away. The room was calm again, the candle flames were separate tongues, demure and steady.

'Where did you go, this morning?'

'Down by the river.' His tone was lighter. 'Near Merchant's Arch. There was a crowd on the quays looking over. The bombardment lasted hours. They pumped lead into those buildings 'til there couldn't be so much as a rat left alive in them. A fellow beside me said the men were probably long gone; they'd likely knocked holes in the walls and got out that way, into the next building.'

'D'you think he's right?'

'They'd enough time to do it. I can't imagine what kept the army away for so long. The rebels could have knocked holes in all the buildings around, made them into one long escape tunnel the length of the street. And if Joe Soap has arrived at that conclusion, you can be sure the army have as well. They'll pulverize it.'

'The building?'

'The street.'

Sackville Street. An extension of my own street. The heart of my city.

Strange sounds outside brought us up to the front parlour. Hubie looked out through the chink in the shutters, craned to see better, edged them open a little further for a better look. 'They're setting up a field gun,' he said.

'Let me see.'

He stood close while I looked. A group of soldiers surrounded what looked like an old-fashioned cannon, mounted on a type of cart, a couple of doors up from here, towards Northumberland Road.

'That can't be good.' I straightened, and bumped against him. My skin prickled.

'At least we're on the right side of it,' he said, somewhere near my hair.

The room, when I turned back into it, was darker. I dipped a taper to a candle to catch the flame, cupped my hand around it for shelter and carried it from one unlit wick to the next. The skin of my palm glowed, pink and translucent.

It had been a long, strange day, a day that plunged us into war and brought me closer to Liam and all he'd come to know. And here, across the room, was a man who'd been out there with him. It was like sorcery. Maybe he was a ghost, a messenger, and I should play along. We settled in our chairs again. With our drinks, the remains of Nan's ginger cake and the last two apples sliced on two plates, it was nearly like a normal social encounter. But it felt strange, to be so alone with him, and the whole night stretching ahead. Watching him eat, I felt the ghosts of his missing fingers, holding him back.

'Tell me about Liam. Why was he not more careful?'

He said nothing for a while. Then, 'When we got to him he was alive. There was blood under his hair, but it was his stomach he held.'

I played with the fringes of the antimacassar. 'A year ago this week.'

'Yes.'

I was at a window again. Popping sounds came from everywhere, like a fireworks display without light. I checked the sky in the direction of the hospital, where Eva was, and the boy soldier. There was no sign of fire there. 'It's so dark. How do they know what they're shooting? What's the point of it? Maybe they'll run out of bullets, and in the morning we can all go home again.' I looked over my shoulder at his hunched form.

He sucked in a chestful of smoke, examined the tip of his cigarette, blew across it. It flared. 'Things happen you've no control over.'

I came back and sat near him. 'Tell me.'

'Only a few weeks earlier, we'd to watch their infantry bayonet our wounded. They came at us, and we let loose – I don't know how to describe it, we were possessed. When we got up there and had them surrounded, they dropped their guns. *Mercy, mercy.*' He put on the accent, his face grim.

I was afraid to say anything that might break his trance of remembering, of letting things spill out unfiltered. He shook his head, the way a dog clears water from its coat. 'Not bloody likely. Not after that.'

'Liam wrote to me about that,' I said, thinking that, like Hubie, he'd never finished the story. He never said what had happened next.

Yesterday they came at us, the biggest show yet. We started out, but

225

they poured over from their line and we fell back. You should have seen how we fired to hold them off, more than the fifteen shots a minute, but they kept coming. They came with bayonets ready. Any of ours they found wounded, they finished them. They ripped young Michael Slattery open. His screams were terrible. Rage kept us firing. Our guns over-heated. Fat oozed out of them. A captain ran up and down the line pouring oil on the stocks. We overcame them. When they were sur-rounded, they threw their weapons down and begged for their lives. Kamerad!

I'd nothing but murder in my heart. The silence fell on me as though I were dreaming. All you at home can't begin to imagine the extent of the destruction, the laying waste. The human spirit itself is being slaugh-tered, here.

I don't know if it was Hubie that trembled, talking, or me, listening to Liam's words inside his. The whole room was unstable, the walls threatened to tear free from the ceiling, the floorboards wanting to buckle and pitch us out into the horrible night. 'I read in the papers that their bayonets are terrible. Toothed, like a saw you'd take to a plank. That the worst wounds are inflicted on the way out.'

'Ours were little better. They're useless now. Hopelessly outdated. But we still have to use them. You've no notion, the savagery. Do you know what they told us in training? If you strike badly, or too deep, and your bayonet gets stuck inside a man? Load a charge, and fire. The recoil will do the rest.'

'Oh!' I couldn't help the sound that escaped me, or the hand that flew to my mouth too late to catch it. He stared off, blind to me again. He may as well have been alone.

He stubbed out his cigarette, then thought better of it and struggled to light another one. I took a match from the box and struck it, held it steady for him. He cupped the flame with his good hand and drew in the smoke.

'Bless you.' He rested his hand on mine while he sucked in three quick breaths in succession, then let them out. The

226

room filled with a benign, lazy kind of smoke. I watched it curl and spread in soft aromatic layers, trying, failing, to imagine poison in it. 'Their English was yards ahead of our German, I can tell you. Except Liam, he'd a smattering. Those nights creeping around the wires would break anyone. He used to be sent out more than most.'

Phrases from Liam's letters ran through my mind. I didn't want to betray him. 'He wasn't afraid.'

'Did I say he was?'

'Not in so many words.'

'There's a state beyond fear. It's there, but so are you.'

I took a breath, for courage. 'His last letter had only two words in it: "No more." He didn't even sign it. It came when I was alone in the house. I burned it. I didn't want to worry them.'

You'd swear I was the enemy, the way he looked at me. 'They bloody should be worried.'

I got up and paced the room, to escape his anger or my terror, or both. I stopped at the mantel, in front of the candles. 'The one before it said he could have walked into battle with empty hands. He said there were those who made that choice.' I passed the flat of my hand across the flame. It dipped and grew back. I did it again, lower, so that my hand bisected the flame.

Hubie watched. 'But then he'd have been useless. Worse than. There's nothing more dangerous to the living than a man who's decided to die.'

I stopped moving my hand. Pain seared through it and I jerked it away, despising myself. But there was a lesson in it. If you kept moving, the pain didn't reach you. Stop, and it burned like hell. 'I should have seen what he meant. I didn't pay enough attention.'

'There was nothing you could do.'

'And then, once he was dead, it would have done no good,

227

to say it.' My voice wobbled at the edge of some precipice. I snatched it back. 'I sometimes wonder, did he want the censor to read some of the things he wrote, mad things?'

'Did he use the green envelopes, for officers?'

The envelopes had had a green cross on them, and a statement to sign, stating *On my honour* that the contents were personal only and had no bearing on the war. 'What would have happened, if they'd been read?'

'Nothing. They'd have cut out what they didn't like.'

'Was it not odd, to assume that officers had honour and the men had none? It must have been strange to read all they had to say.'

'Plenty of it about us.'

'They must have hated you for it.' I rushed on, before he could take offence. 'Did you know Liam was deafened out there? It happened early on. He said his hearing came and went. If we'd reported it, might he have been sent home?' Could I have saved him, somehow, anyhow?'

'No. That was common. It made no difference.'

I was in control of my voice again. 'I thought I'd always have him. You know, that we'd die at the same time. It was reasonable, wasn't it, to think that?' Even to myself, I sounded like a child. 'He put on a uniform, got on a ship and went away. For ages, after he was killed, I was able to pretend he was just that. Away. That he might, still, come back. If I saw him walk in through that door, right this minute, I'd believe it. It's at least as likely as that he won't. Seeing his grave might help. Will you show me where it is, on a map? I want to go there after the war.'

'I can't.'

'Why? Is it not true, that you buried him?'

'We did, yes. But –'

'But?'

'Then the cemetery was bombed.'

It was this that made me cover my face and cry. I could not think about a bombed graveyard. Why should I have minded about the dead, who couldn't be hurt any more? But I did. I minded a great deal.

A weight landed on my arm. I jumped, thinking something new had entered the room. It was Hubie's damaged hand, trying to comfort me.

'If the Front taught me anything, it's that we should live each day, every single instant, as though it's the last we'll ever have. Look what's happening here. And you all thought you were safe.'

There was the familiar scorn, even when he was trying to be kind. I took my hands away from my face. The candle flame was steady. Small, inky threads of smoke hovered over them. The walls leaned in to listen. The monkey was asleep in May's chair, curled up on his red velvet cushion, snoring. I risked a look at Hubie, drawn to the good hand, now resting on his knee. Its long, graceful fingers set his glass on the floor, returned to his thigh, smoothed a crease from his trousers.

'I should have been on this morning's train,' he said. 'I'd be home by now.'

I should have known he'd be wishing himself away from here. Away from me.

'In any given circumstance, I ask myself, what would I regret not doing?' His face was in shadow. Only his eyes gleamed. 'I mean, if it all ends – when it all ends – what would I be sorry for not having done? What chance would I wish I'd taken?' His eyes fixed on mine with a tense, coiled energy. The air in the room was thick with things unsaid.

I'd a feeling like vertigo – the way a bird might feel when the gaze of the cat lights on it and settles. The shiver of shingle as the wave rises. The chair creaked under him as he leaned forward. Of all the things I might have imagined from

229

that harsh, surprising mouth, I could never have dreamed the delicacy of his lips brushing the skin of my face. My eyes slid shut.

He kissed my right eye, then the left. Each time he lifted his mouth, he paused, long enough for me to protest or move away, but I waited. My skin wanted to know where his mouth would surprise me next. The only other mouth I'd known was Con's, pressed hard against me, as though to fix me in place. This man seemed to be tasting me, savouring every second. My heart thudded, like the slow tongue of a bell.

He kissed the throat I lifted to him. His hand moved my hair from my face, cupped the back of my head and brought it closer, then we were mouth to mouth and urgent. Whiskey, velvet, fire. I was parched earth, touched at last by rain. Softening. Ripening. A seed that thinned and split. Blood rushed to the surface of my skin through channels I never knew existed, my own secret, unguessed-at geography, all threading rivulets and streams running deep, slaking a thirst I'd never recognized.

At some point, he lifted his head to ask, *Are you sure?* For answer, I pulled him closer. I didn't want to think. I'd assented to this long ago, maybe as far back as the night Liam died, when I'd climbed the stairs to Con's room, shaking with a need I couldn't name, to be held and obliterated at the same time. Certainly from the moment when I'd felt this man's hand become solid in mine, the first time I found myself turning around in search of the light in his eyes.

I lay awake, disturbed by the interesting shape of his body beside mine. Its angles and smells. His breath loud in the room. The strangeness of my own damp skin. My legs burned, my nipples stung. I turned away from him. Stared into darkness. Turned back. Let my arm fall across him, cautious.

A slow heat began to build in my legs 'til I thought bits of me would melt away, like candle grease. I breathed in his ear to wake him. He stirred, came closer to me under the whispering, slippery satin bedspread. Then closer. We pressed against each other, straining to break through every barrier, skin, muscle, bone. Pillar of wax, tongue of flame.

'I knew you'd be like this,' he murmured, later.

'Like what?' But he was asleep again. How could he have known anything, when I couldn't believe that this was me?

I was the one who was fallen, now. How could one word mean such different things? Those men, in the afternoon, bleeding on the road. And me, warm in tangled sheets beside – who was this man? Who was I, come to that, and what would the morning bring?

Thursday, 27 April 1916

The different types of gun all crashed together in a violent percussive storm. The house trembled. The skin of the canal puckered, scattering chips of reflected moon. Hubie let me take his damaged hand in mine and hold it. *This is what time is, a river, banks on either side and leaning trees. The past carries you along but you have to travel the full length of it, come to the place where it wavers, undecided, to know what it means. Forward or back, fresh or salt, rise or fall, then it opens all the way, it is the sea, you are the sea, you'd never have guessed unless you'd made the journey; there's so much, too much, you have to choose something, choose now quickly before it's too late.*

'Katie, wake up. You were crying.'

'Tell me how you were hurt.'

'Shrapnel. From one of our own shells.' Tiny scars shone like pale feathers on the smooth skin of his chest. I lay against him, my ear against his shoulder. His words were muffled, far away and underground.

'There were sly fellows out there. Cleaning their guns, they'd lose a finger, a couple of toes. One company was known for a trick of holding their hands up above the ramparts during a barrage, like beggars, for credible wounds.' His body stiff as rock. As impenetrable. 'Theirs cheapen mine.'

It was so different from what Liam wrote to Mother, soon after he arrived in France, a letter she'd added to her memory-book. *Everywhere I look, I see men from all over the world – there's an Indian regiment, their hair bound up in a thick white cloth that makes their skin seem darker than it is. Canadians who don't seem to feel the cold. It's no mean thing, to have such men on our side. No matter where we come from, we're together in this. When I see hundreds upon hundreds of men in khaki, from every corner of the Empire, all massed together and bent on the same task, it makes me proud. Every single man of us faces the chance of death, any hour, any minute. This is the adventure of our time, of our generation. Professor Kettle is right when he says that the absentee Irishman today is the man who stays at home.*

Hubie moved the warm weight of his arm but I caught and held it, moulded myself closer to him. The martial law notice would keep people indoors a few hours yet. We wouldn't be disturbed. I could lie here and listen, skin on skin, match my breathing to the rise and fall of his.

'A sergeant I knew put a pistol in his mouth, held the muzzle against the lining of his cheek and blew a hole in his own face.'

'What happened to him?'

'The wound got infected and he died.'

I pressed my ear to the wall of his chest, listened to the sturdy knocking of his heart. He rolled on to his back. His ribs rose and fell under my spread palm. I traced the ridged skin of his stomach with my fingers, a pattern like barbed wire, dark weals punctuated by knots. He snatched a breath; his ribs stopped moving.

'Does it hurt, when I touch them?'

He reared up and away. His back was wealed as well. I knelt up behind him, put my lips to the edge of his scars and breathed on them. Wrapped my arms around him and pressed my small breasts to the wings of his shoulder blades, rested my chin at his neck.

His good hand ran the length of my arm, encircled my wrist. 'It's hard to come back,' he said.

I closed my eyes and tried to feel his words rise through my body, imagining the path they took through his: thought, nerve, gut, throat.

'Those few days being here – before the fighting started – it was sickening. In France and in Flanders, I thought of little other than this – a bed, with sheets. A fire, a meal, a woman. I thought I'd never ask for more. But, being here, walking about – it disgusted me. People going about their business. Shawlies and their incessant wheedling and whining. Clerks, bankers, shopkeepers – all the men who don't know the hell they've saved themselves from. Hardly anyone even wondering about what's happening in Verdun, right now. Today. Sweet-smelling women like you, a reminder of all the things that will never be easy again.'

Hardly sweet-smelling now. 'Such as?'

'Every single thing. From the first instant of every day. Waking, and knowing.'

Ah, yes. I knew that one.

'Buttons. Shaving. Food. Everything cack-handed. Your mind seething. You turn the corner of an ordinary street and the face of a dead man rises in your mind, a taste of gore, a roll of names, unanswered.'

He pulled away, stood up. 'Even this. It's no use.'

He plunged his feet into the legs of his trousers and tugged them the full length of his handsome legs, not bothering with underwear. He left the room without looking back, holding the trousers bunched at the waist with his good hand, the maimed one out of sight.

I gathered my own clothes and got dressed. Every hook and eye sealed the rich, strange smell of him against my skin.

He was standing in the pearled light of the early-morning garden, under the plum tree, listening to the guns. Ghostly shapes of hedges and trees gave way to the actual – as though they'd gone away for the night, leaving a mere image in their place, and were just now returning, one by one, to resume the business of daily life. A thin line of smoke spiralled up from his cigarette. Something stirred deep and low in me at the sight of his scarred and pitted back, a code that could take a lifetime to learn. I felt porous. I wondered what other surprises lay ahead. The haze lifted and the sun touched me. Shy as I felt, it warmed me through and through.

I walked out to stand in front of him. The hem of my dress was damp, the grass cold on my feet and ankles, as though the sea might rise from underground, the old marshes reassert themselves any minute. 'Will you please look at me?'

His eyes lifted to the level of my waist and stayed there. I took his two hands in mine. 'You must know – your injuries don't matter to me.'

'Ha! They matter to me.' He jerked his hands away, made the hurt one a claw and shook it at me. 'Every time I touch you. This is dead. It feels nothing, except its own pain, a pain it's not supposed to feel, in parts that don't exist.' His bitterness frightened me.

A series of explosions sounded, not far away. His mouth twisted, mocking a smile. 'A part of me was glad when this happened, here. It makes sense to me. There, I've shocked you. It serves you all right! Why in hell's name should you be spared?' He stopped to catch his breath, rushed on. 'Explosions, ruin, inferno . . . make sense to me.' Fury blazed from his eyes.

I let it break on me, tried not to show my fear. It felt like a test. I'd stepped outside a boundary. This was the climate I could expect, the old protections gone. I touched his shoulder. Stepped closer, wary. Then closer still. At last, he put out his good hand and let it rest on my arm. In his own, dear voice, he said, 'Katie. You're not a bit like him, you know.'

'Who?'

'Liam.'

I turned back into the house. 'I'm hungry. Let's see what there is to eat.'

*

I arranged stale biscuits, a bruised tomato and a piece of sweaty cheese on a plate. We set to it without enthusiasm.

'There's that jar of plums, in the pantry,' I said. 'Will we have those instead?'

I pulled damsons, red as old blood, from their jar with a long-handled spoon, ladled them into his mouth, then mine. They tasted meaty: sweet, rich and dark as the sealed past they came from, with a hint of rust. A trail of purple juice ran down his chin. I licked it off. His skin was rough as a cat's tongue, but his breath tasted like wine. Next thing we were entangled, slippery and close.

The sound of voices and an engine straining brought us to the window. A lorry full of soldiers passed. It creaked to a halt and they jumped down, crouched this side of the vehicle. No shots sounded. We moved back, out of sight, and looked at each other. I leaned against the wall and let my eyes take their fill of his face, the crooked eyebrow, the small pock-mark on his chin, the full curve of his lovely mouth. I put the tip of a finger to the dent in his lower lip. He kissed it.

'You still have plum juice, here.' He traced a line down my neck with a knuckle.

I went upstairs to wash, even though part of me wanted to be found as stained and dishevelled as I was.

I was upstairs in the bathroom, drying my face, when the back gate opened. I stood very still. It was Con Buckley. His stride made short work of the path. He moved quickly for such a big man. From this vantage point, I fancied I saw a softening in his shape, a hint that all that muscle was losing its grip and would, sooner or later, run to fat.

I stepped back, out of sight, and called down to Hubie, 'Someone's coming!' I knocked on the window, so Con would know I'd seen him. *Wait a minute*, I mouthed. I hurried downstairs, twisting my hair up, pushing pins into it to keep it in place. By the time I got to the back door and opened it, I was well and truly frightened. A pulse hammered in my neck. 'Is it Eva?'

'Bartley asked me to tell you there's been no change.' He looked past my shoulder. I didn't have to turn to know that Hubie had come in behind me. Con looked from one of us to the other. 'Miss Wilson's nephew?'

I hoped I wasn't fool enough to blush, making the introductions. 'How did you know I was here?'

'Well,' he said. 'Quite. I went to Isabel's. I have Bartley's car.'

'They're allowing traffic?' Hubie asked.

'Military – and ambulances. Some private cars with Red Cross signs. I got a permit; the hospital needs supplies. There's no milk, no eggs or fresh meat to be had anywhere in town.'

'Don't I know it.'

How peculiar it was to stand between the two of them, a man I once thought I wanted and one whose presence acted like a magnet. Even now, with Con here to watch, I felt a pull towards Hubie. I moved the other way, went to sit at the table in case my legs gave me away.

'I said I'd go to Mick Morton's dairy,' Con was saying. 'They know me there. Isabel's house was on the way, and Bartley asked me to look in on Alanna. And you. Imagine my surprise when they told me where I'd find you.' His eyes were pallid. I used to see them full of light, but now they were chill, empty as glass, while Hubie's glowed, warm as fire.

'Are they all right?' I asked. Needing something to do with my hands, I clapped them for Paschal, who jumped into them, climbed to my shoulder and sat breathing into my ear, stroking my hair. In the background, Hubie pulled the ends of his moustache, reminding me of how soft it was. How it felt against my own lip. His good hand gathering my hair off my neck.

The disapproval on Con's face was new to me. 'Fine. The park is full of soldiers. Isabel's turned the house into a refuge.'

'Ah, Con, two women and two little girls hardly amount to a refuge.'

'She's taken in two families from the cottages as well.' He put his hands in his pockets and scuffed the floor with his feet. 'The Judge is none too pleased, I can tell you, at the state of his dining room. There are ten children there, running riot.' Once, he would have laughed at such a vision. 'I'd have thought you'd go to help her out, since two of those children were originally in your charge. They expected you yesterday.'

'I was at the hospital.'

Hubie leaned against the dresser, one ankle crossed over the other, tumbling marbles in his good hand. 'I stayed to mind the house.'

'I wasn't speaking to you.'

'Con! What's got into you?'

'Miss Wilson was in quite a state, about the house, and about the pair of you. The Judge gave me a letter, to allow me to take a detour down here to check on you.' He pulled a folded piece of paper from his pocket, waved it and put it away again. 'It was nice of him, but I didn't need it, since I've a permit from the army. I promised to go back at once, if there was bad news. I didn't think there would be. Mind you, I didn't expect –' He came and stood in front of me with his back to Hubie, blocking my view. It made no difference. Even blindfolded, I'd have known exactly where Hubie was. Every inch of me was conscious of the shape he made, lounging against the dresser. 'Why are you still here, with a field gun out there, right on the doorstep?'

The imprint of Hubie's body lingered on my skin, even in places he hadn't touched. For all I knew, Con would be able

238

to tell. I got up and crossed the room to put Paschal on the straw chair. 'It's not on the doorstep.'

'It's more than close enough.'

As though we'd woken it, a horrible metallic drag rumbled outside.

'They're moving it,' Hubie said from the window.

The sound rolled and grew. The cups rattled on their hooks. I put my fingers in my ears. 'There must be guns near Isabel's too,' I said, when the noise subsided.

'There's a command post nearby. The army are in complete control. It may well be the safest part of town. Yet here you are.'

'Here I am. And the gun's gone.'

'You're being irresponsible, Katie. Come away with me, now.'

'If you're fetching supplies,' Hubie said, sounding so bored he all but yawned at us, 'why would you take an extra passenger? Won't she take up valuable space?'

I was livid with the pair of them, posturing and grinning at each other like a pair of hyenas. The last thing I wanted was to leave Hubie, to drive away with this unpleasant version of Con to God knew where for God knew how long. But his arrival jolted me back to the reality of conventional life. I saw how my behaviour would look to everyone I knew, and my instinct was to suppress any hint of suspicion before it had time to grow. 'I'll go with you,' I said to Con. 'Why not? It'll be an adventure.'

I ran up to splash cologne on my wrists and at my throat. On the way back, I brushed past Hubie at the bottom of the stairs. Something deep inside me turned. My hands missed the spring of his hair. My ribs wanted to press against his.

His face was averted from Con, as though he were looking at the monkey, who sat on the newel post, and whose stomach he was scratching in an absent way. But his eyes burned into mine. Paschal swayed gently, his eyes half shut, loving the attention. I stopped to pet him too. Our hands almost touched.

'Do you want your coat?' he asked.

'It's warm out,' Con said. 'You won't need it.'

We went out the way Con had come in. I followed him through the lanes. Despite the sunshine, I wished I'd worn the coat. Hubie would have held it for me, helped me into it. I could have felt his arms around me, his shape behind me, brief and fleeting as a ghost, but there.

We came out nearly opposite the church on Haddington Road. There was something raw about the morning, as though layers of the city's skin had rubbed off during the night.

Con went in front of me to open the passenger door of Bartley's car. For an instant he hesitated, the open door between us like a Roman's shield. What was he thinking? He let go the door and stood back. I ducked into the front seat, tugged on the strap and pulled the door shut myself. He stamped around the bonnet to the driver's side and got in with a hefty slam.

Bartley's car was the newest kind of Vauxhall, it needed no crank. Con turned the ignition and the engine fired at once. He looked quickly over his shoulder, pushed in the handbrake and we moved off.

I'd made a horrible mistake, agreeing to this expedition. Now I'd be confined in a small space with him for however long the journey lasted. I'd have to go wherever he took me, exposed to his scrutiny, his questions, his hateful opinions.

He drove the short distance to the checkpoint at Baggot Street. A captain broke off a conversation with a private and started towards us; Con leaned forward and showed his face and we were waved on.

People milled around the entrance to the hospital, on the pavement and the steps. Vehicles of all sorts blocked the road – military cars, private cars with sheets hung in the windows displaying the red cross, a side-car, a cart with no horse in the shaft.

'I'd like to see Eva.'

'I don't think you'd be let.'

'I would, if you brought me.'

'Let's get the milk, then we'll see.'

We'll see. A thing you say to a child. 'You sound like my father.'

'If I were your father, you wouldn't be staying out all night with a stranger.'

Something in me shrivelled and shrank away from him. Memories surged through me, the ghost of old desires, an image of myself curled in his armchair, dragging him against me, the woman shrilling at the door. I looked at his clean profile, the tight downward curve of his mouth. I'd teased him once about how a broken nose could improve his looks, he was too perfect. How wrong I was. The lines of his face were dull, uninteresting. One look and you'd seen it all.

As we got further out from town, there were more people about. Men with baskets, out doing the messages. What was the world coming to? Con pulled in to let a military car pass and I saw inside one: a head of cauliflower and stalks of green and purple rhubarb, incongruous against the man's dark sleeves, his bowler hat.

The silence in the car built up to an unbearable tension. Eventually he said, 'You're not to go back to Percy Place.'

'What's it to you where I go?'

'The Tierneys' house is safer.' He glared at me. 'You've no idea, the extent of it. There's not enough coffins to go round.'

He said it the way you'd hit someone, meaning to hurt them. 'They've started to bury the dead in people's gardens.'

I had to remind myself of all he must have seen at the hospital. No wonder he was on edge.

There was a roadblock at Ballsbridge. Soldiers, military vehicles. Horses milled around the showgrounds, visible from the queue on the road. When Con said the hospital needed supplies, we were waved through, although the officer warned us we mightn't be allowed back, if the situation deteriorated.

We were surrounded by soldiers. A gigantic field gun loomed over the crossroads: an ugly hulk of steel, crouched like a beast from the stone age, its sinister bore directed along the road we'd just travelled. A khaki column stood ready to march, rifles on their shoulders.

'Won't the rebels put their guns down and go home, when they see all this?' I thought about waiting, crouched behind walls or sandbags, for a hail of bullets. That boy yesterday, crying for his mother. All the mothers who didn't yet know they'd never see their boys again.

We drove on past the level crossing, the abandoned station. I stared out, across the calm waters of the bay to Howth, the peninsula so purple it was nearly black. The sea's blues were streaked with mauve and green under a high sky, threaded with wisps of cloud. A day full of its own beauty, utterly indifferent to all that was happening within it. It made me ache so hard I was driven to say, 'It's lovely out here.'

'Oh, for Christ's sake, Katie. Let's not have the weather!'

I stiffened. 'What'll we talk about, so?'

'Are you glad to get away from that character, back there?'

'Who, Hubie?' I settled against the hard leather seat, looked straight ahead. There were more soldiers out here, many military vehicles, fewer people walking. 'Why do you ask?'

'Has he inconvenienced you at all?'

Inconvenienced? I nearly laughed out loud. 'I'm glad I got the chance to talk to him. About Liam. About the war.'

'Are you, now.' His voice was flat. I risked a look at his stubborn profile. I'd a giddy sense of power. I could have teased him, but I didn't, out of respect for all that lay below the surface of his words, not to mention mine.

'I don't like him.'

'Aren't you even curious as to what he said?' Not that I'd have wanted to tell him.

'I can imagine it well enough.' His pallid look slid over me and back to the road. 'I don't need embellishments. What will people think of you, staying alone in a house with a man? Even if he is a cripple.'

I turned that word, 'cripple', over in my mind. Like a faulty bomb, it caused more damage to Con in saying it than to Hubie, its target. His hands gripped the steering wheel like a plate he was getting ready to throw across a room. 'You could have gone next door. They'd have taken you in.'

'I could, I suppose.'

'Why didn't you?'

'Why should I? I barely know them. I was in a house that's like home to me. Not to mention, the monkey needs minding.'

'The monkey.' There was such contempt in his voice. 'If you could hear yourself . . .' His face was a mask of disgust.

So that was what it felt like, to turn to stone. I'd thought we were friends, and he despised me. I blurted out the one thing I didn't mean to say. 'You're telling *me* to be careful what people think? That's a good one! There's no shortage of talk about you.'

He stopped the car so abruptly that I pitched forward. My wrist struck the dashboard. Unapologetic, he pierced me with those pale, hateful eyes. 'What's this?'

I rubbed the sore place. 'I've heard rumours.'

'Have you, now. I'd like to hear them too. Enlighten me.'

Up ahead, there was a checkpoint. Soldiers looked through the boot of a car. They lifted a box to the ground and turned their attention back to the interior. The driver stood by and watched.

'Con . . .' I tried to draw his attention to the soldiers. He wouldn't look, but kept his unnerving eyes fixed on me.

'I'm waiting. I didn't know you were the type for gossip. I thought better of you.'

'Con, the checkpoint. They're watching. Shouldn't we drive on?'

'Not 'til you say what you've heard, and who from.'

'But –'

'If you're so anxious to get going, tell me.'

The soldiers waved us on, but Con wasn't looking at them. He was looking at me.

'I heard you got a girl into trouble. That she had to go away.'

'And where did you hear this fascinating yarn?'

'Never mind.' My eyes were on the soldiers. I could have been with Hubie instead of here, digging myself into more trouble with each passing second. 'Con, they've seen us. They're waving you on.'

'Tell me!'

'No! Drive on.'

He wouldn't budge. Three soldiers and an officer strode our way, guns drawn.

'I can guess who it was.' His eyes flicked to the soldiers and back to me. 'But I'd rather you said it. I'd want to be sure, before I act on it.'

I didn't want to make trouble for Frieda, but he had me cornered.

'It's a serious matter,' he went on, 'telling tales outside the hospital. It could be a sacking offence.'

244

He'd given me an opening. I made myself look at him and not at the soldiers as they spread into two pairs, on each side of the car. 'Why are you talking about the hospital? Do you mean there's a *second* girl? There are two of them?'

Doubt flared in his eyes.

Some demon had got hold of my tongue. 'Does Miss Stacpole know?'

The officer knocked on the window with a swagger stick. Con swung around, as if he really hadn't seen the soldiers before now, every bit as good an actor as Matt. He let go my wrist, rolled his window down. 'Good morning, Captain.'

'Everything all right, miss?' the officer asked.

I nodded.

'The lady here' – Con drawled the word 'lady' – 'was giving out to me. You know what they are.'

Unmoved, the officer demanded papers. Con hunted in the glove box for his military permit, talking all the time in his buttery, crowd-pleasing voice. Supplies in the hospital were running low. The farm he was headed for was less than half a mile further. The sooner we got there the better, or the fresh milk would turn, and only fresh will do when people are ill.

'Supplies are being requisitioned for military use,' the officer said. 'You've had a wasted journey.'

While Con made a case for the sick and wounded in Baggot Street – many of whom included the officer's comrades and others, veterans, who were there before all this – the outrage, as Con called it, began. A subaltern walked around the car, studied the tyres, the interior, me. The officer handed back the letter. 'Drive on. But don't bother trying this tomorrow. If matters continue as they are, there'll be no fresh food to spare. We'll need it for our own men.' He waved us on.

Con turned the car inland, in angry silence. A little further on, he veered off the main road on to a bumpy track between a terrace of houses and a church. Then we were in a farmyard where churns of milk and carefully packed boxes of eggs waited. The farmer put the churns on the floor in the back of the car, like maiden aunts settled in a row. He stacked the eggs neatly on the seats.

I stood in the shade of a beech tree while they loaded the car, transfixed by the pure, sweet sound of larks coasting above the meadow, their song striking straight to the core of me, like liquid honey, forgiving – or mocking – the black blot I was on the beauty of the day. I let myself fill with it. What was it Liam wrote about larks? Something wonderful. In panic, I rummaged through my mind for the letter, but couldn't find it. I summoned his face instead. Bit by bit I assembled it, his freckles and his snag tooth, the lick of hair across his forehead. I resisted the photograph framed on the mantelpiece at home, which pressed itself forward in his stead.

'The missus said to give ye this as well,' the farmer said, heaving a sack of flour into the boot. 'It won't last ye long, she says, but ye may as well have it as not.' He straightened, dusted off his hands. 'Better you than them.'

On the way back to town, Con drove down side streets and filtered through lanes to avoid the military. 'How did your parents take Matt's shenanigans?'

I tensed. 'What shenanigans?'

He looked over at me, curious. 'You mean you don't know? He's gone. He left on the Belfast train, on Monday morning, before all this started. If the boats were running, they'd have got the ferry across to Scotland before nightfall. He went with the troupe.'

I heard 'troop' and was speechless, but he went on to say, 'That theatre crowd.'

It took me a few moments to absorb that. 'But – why didn't you tell me sooner?'

246

He looked back through the windscreen at the rutted lane. 'I assumed you knew. He said he'd leave a note.' He shook his head. 'Maybe he lost his nerve.'

My head buzzed like a fly trapped under glass. 'But why would he take the guns?'

'He needed money. I knew someone who'd buy them.'

'*You* helped him sell them? To who, the rebels? And you a doctor.' They were, both of them, every bit as much to blame as if they were out there shooting people themselves.

'Katie, what you were saying about those women – I don't know what you've heard but you mustn't repeat it. Promise me. You could do such harm. Helen – Miss Stacpole – her father would ban me from the house.'

A sudden thrill flashed through me as one last shackle fell from my mind. His hand arrived on my arm and sat there, a dead, oppressive weight. I stared at it, at the fleshy, unblemished pink fingers, the small hairs that grew from his knuckles. His perfectly manicured nails. A hand as alien to me as though he were a complete stranger. I looked into his face. Our eyes locked.

I didn't need to say anything. It was all there in how we looked at each other, as though into a receding past. It was in the deliberate way he lifted his hand from my sleeve and turned his attention back to driving. We jolted along an unpaved lane. 'I'll take you to Isabel's.' Back to his hoity-toity tone.

'No. If there are cordons around the park, they might not let me out again.'

'So?'

'I want to see Eva.' We were near the end of a maze of lanes, Waterloo Road just ahead, only minutes from the hospital. 'I'll make my own way, later.'

'I don't trust you.'

'What on earth makes you think I'm yours, to trust or not? Why does it even matter to you where I go?'

247

'That man is a stranger.'

'Stop the car, Con. Let me out.' I reached for the door handle. We were moving slowly. I'd get out whether he stopped or not. With a sudden *bang!* the car lurched, and stuttered to a halt. My forehead burned. Hot noise and air rushed in on me, as though I'd been encased in ice 'til now. The world burst in on me, sharp and painfully clear. 'What happened?'

Con was already out there, stooping over the car. 'Puncture. The damned tyre's gone.'

I got out too, surprised by the tremor in my legs. 'I thought we'd been shot.'

He looked towards the road, then back at the food. 'So close. We won't be able to carry all this. We can't just leave it.'

He strode off towards the mouth of the lane. I checked the eggs in the back of the car. Most of them had survived intact. A piece of paper had fallen to the floor. *Allow the bearer . . .* it was the Judge's letter. I picked it up and put it in my own pocket as Con came trotting back. 'You're cut,' he said.

'Am I?' The hand I put to my stinging forehead came away sticky and red. 'Is that blood?'

He came back for a closer look. 'Have you a handkerchief?'

I turned my head away. 'I doubt there's a hankie left in the whole entire city.'

Hand on my chin, he turned my face back towards him. 'Let me see that.'

'It's nothing.'

'Let me see.' His blunt fingers pressed the bone around my eye socket. 'Does that hurt?' He prodded again. Pain shot through my scalp and behind my eyes. I winced.

'There's glass in it. It needs cleaning. And stitches.'

I pulled away from him and walked towards the road. 'Someone will stop.'

*

It was a woman who stopped, in a tourer. Vivienne Dockery, she said her name was. A crude red cross was painted on the sides and back of her car. She insisted I sit quietly and wait, holding a square of clean linen to the cut on my forehead, while she bossed a pair of soldiers into helping Con load the milk churns into the deep luggage compartment, and slid the boxes of eggs on to the back seat herself. It was quite a sight: she was one of the shortest, roundest women I'd ever seen. She came from a farm in Kilkenny, she told me as we drove away, up for the Spring Show when the trouble started. Con said he'd follow us on foot. I didn't care if I never saw him again.

Inside the hospital, Miss Dockery settled me on a chair in a crowded corridor. 'Wait there.'

The wall at my back was cold. The tiled floor was stained. People traipsed past, peered into my face, then away. It was clear they were intent on finding relatives or neighbours, hoping the things they'd heard would prove to be wrong.

A skinny boy lay flat on a bed in a small room across the corridor. A sheet covered him from the waist down. A large bloodstained bandage strapped his ribs. His eyes were half open, his breathing rough. A woman sat beside him and watched his bandaged chest rise and fall, rise and fall.

Miss Dockery came back and brought me to a treatment room. Two beds contained silent forms that could have been asleep or dead. The bright eyes of an old man with a bloodied head peered at me from a third. He gave me a smile and a wink.

'I'll find a nurse,' Miss Dockery said, and left again.

'Grand out,' the old man said. 'A great day.'

I didn't see what was so great about it. 'You're hurt.'

'Only a scratch,' he said. 'A proud mark. You'll have one too.' He nodded at my forehead. 'A souvenir. Stirring times.'

'Nonsense.' A nurse came in on brisk feet. 'Don't be

frightening her.' She threw a quick, professional glance over my face. 'You'll be grand, once we get the bits out. Stay still, now.'

She patted my forehead with gauze soaked in a vivid yellow ointment, making me wince. She said to hold a towel under the wound and keep my eyes shut tight while she poured fluid over it. Then she lifted slivers of glass from under the skin with a tweezers. When all the glass was out, she stitched the skin together with a needle and thread. 'Like a hem. You could do it yourself only for where it is.'

Tears I couldn't help rolled down my face.

'What are you crying for? There's plenty worse off than you. You won't be scarred. Not badly.'

'I thought I'd been shot.'

It hadn't been a real question, and she wasn't listening to my answer. She was cleaning up, wiping surfaces and throwing strips of bandage into a steel receptacle. Instruments clattered into a dish and were set aside.

I tugged my hair down to cover the bandage and came out of the treatment room with a throbbing head. Some new disaster had occurred while I'd been in there. The corridor was packed with people weeping. The bed the boy had occupied had a white-faced woman in it now, staring at nothing.

I ran up to visit Eva. There was no one around, so I went into the room and sat beside the high, narrow bed. There was a deep furrow between her eyebrows, her hair greying where it began its sweep across her face. A sweetish whiff on her breath. She opened her eyes.

'Darling Katie. I knew you'd come.' There was silt in her words, gravel in her throat. Her clammy hand found mine. I lifted it to my forehead and held it there so she couldn't see my face or read what I'd seen in her.

'How are you feeling?'

Her eyes dropped. It was a thing she'd always done, broken eye contact to look inward and assess how she felt, to consider the full weight of a question before she answered. Questions like, was it worth it, do you love him, what was it like? Mother used to accuse her of evasion, but it was part of her character. Everything she did was considered, reflective, calm – like her. She and Liam had more in common than Liam and I did, really. Is that why I loved her? No. I loved her calm, good-natured, steady self. If I lost her, what would be left?

'Not well.' She struggled to lift herself. Her shoulders rose from the pillows, but her head lagged behind, too heavy for her neck. I put an arm across her back and lifted her. She weighed nothing. I could support her easily with just one hand while I adjusted the pillows behind her.

'Is that better?'

Her skin looked slack, wrong. I didn't understand how so much could have changed so quickly and without warning. Her hair was lank and dispirited, its colour faded. Her collar-bones loomed sharp at the base of her neck, where the tendons were in stark relief. I held her hand. My mind brimmed with memory. All the words I couldn't say to her, everything I couldn't tell her and never would, tumbled from my mind and skittered across the polished floor.

She drifted in and out of sleep. Nurses came to check on her and change her bedding. I sponged her face and hands, fluffed up her pillows. Stroked the soft skin of her cheek with the back of my own hand – my skin rough next to the papery delicacy of hers. I sat back and watched her breathe.

A woman cried out somewhere on the ward, a single piercing shriek. A rush of feet, soothing voices, then it was quiet again. A little bit later, Gwen Townsend came in. She didn't seem surprised to see me. 'How are we in here?'

She checked Eva's pulse, watched her breathe. 'She's

peaceful, anyway.' She lifted a strand of hair away from Eva's forehead with a tenderness that frightened me. When she said I had to leave, I didn't argue.

I reported to the volunteers' station to see if there was anything I could do. The nurse there asked about the bandage at my forehead. 'It's nothing,' I said, quoting Con. 'A superficial cut.'

'Still and all.'

Vivienne Dockery came over to ask how I was. Then she spoke to the nurse. 'The College of Science have dressings. I've to collect them, but I don't know where it is. They said I should have someone with me in the car, in any case.'

'I'll go,' I said.

'Are you well enough?'

'Yes.'

'Do you know your way around?'

'Of course I do.' At last I'd something to offer. 'It's not far to the college.'

'All right, then.'

We went out the back way, down a corridor where people lay on mattresses on the floor. At the gate a girl aged about twelve was lurking, an eager look to her narrow face. 'Messages, missus?' she asked.

I stopped and sized her up. 'Could you get to Herbert Park?'

She looked hungry. She could easily run off with whatever money I gave her. She stood proud and looked me straight in the face. 'For sure.'

I gave her Isabel's address and asked her to tell them I was helping out at the hospital and intended to stay there. I gave her a thruppenny bit. She fingered its brass edges. 'Anythin' else, miss, you'll find me here later.'

'Enterprising,' Vivienne said, when the child had gone.

'I probably shouldn't have encouraged her. She'd be better off going home.'

'There's a few of us in it, so.'

The light was turning. A breeze made me shiver, but it was welcome after the heat of the last few days. I pulled on the St John's cuff Fitz had given me, tugged it over the sleeve of my blouse, to just above my elbow, and got into the car beside her.

Out on the road, my skin prickled, as though eyes were on me. We were surrounded by houses, with no shortage of parapets and chimneys to conceal gunmen. The air was heavy with smoke and popping sounds. I asked Vivienne what was so special about the dressings we were to collect. She said sphagnum moss was absorbent, and with the shortage of cotton because of the war, the dressings were in demand everywhere.

We pulled up outside the gates of the college and told the porter what we'd come for. He handed us over to a woman with a list who was directing the loading and unloading of boxes into cars and vans. 'That's your lot, I'm afraid,' she said, when the back seat was loaded. 'We have to ration them. Lucky we had them at all.'

On the short journey back to Baggot Street, Vivienne stopped the car. 'What's this?'

A woman sat on a step with her apron over her head, wailing. Vivienne got out to speak to her. When the apron was coaxed away from her face, we saw a black eye and a split nostril trailing coagulated blood.

'Squash into the front with Katie, here,' Vivienne said. 'What happened to you?'

'Bertie, bad cess to him. Why can't they shoot the likes of him?'

I breathed through my mouth. The woman stank of stale drink, and she cursed that waster Bertie the whole way – I was glad we didn't have far to go.

After we'd unloaded our cargo of woman and boxes at the back door of the hospital, Vivienne asked me to direct her to Butt Bridge, where there was a clearing station. I wondered what time it was, but all the clocks we passed had stopped. The light was fading, but whether it was night falling or the pall of smoke dragging a premature blanket up over the city, I couldn't say. There was a lot of military traffic, but Vivienne's painted red crosses got us by.

'I'm going out to France myself,' Vivienne was saying. 'With the ambulance corps. I'm due to leave next week.' She slowed for a last turn. We both said *Oh!* at the same time. In front of us, on the far side of the river – my side of the river – the city was ablaze.

The flames made a weird kind of light, bright and dark at once. A horde of fiery ghosts, thousands of slaughtered soldiers from the Front, come home to vent their fury. They thrashed their limbs about, struggled with the window-frames, strained to break free, fell back and shoved fiery fists across the streets to rattle the roofs with flaming fingers, their breath black with rage. The river was oily and orange, its surface a canvas of wavering, hot colours. My throat burned. My skin and eyes were dry, inflammable as paper.

After getting permission at the checkpoint, we drove along the quays to Butt Bridge. A gunboat was moored on the seaward side, towering over a barge. At the clearing station, people sat or lay on the pavement, waiting to be taken to hospital. A doctor moved among them, deciding who had most need and where best to send them. Eventually he came to inspect the back seat of Vivienne's car. He looked us over too. 'Can you handle this?' he asked, indicating a pallid man in a torn shirt who lay on a plank with his knees bent, a hand cupped over his right eye.

'What's wrong with him?'

'His eye. Move your hand, there, and show them.'

The man lifted his hand. A piece of metal jutted from his eye. There was a dark ooze running down his face. I felt sick.

'Can you take him to the Eye and Ear?'

Vivienne looked at me.

'Yes,' I said, meaning I knew where it was.

'He needs extreme care,' the doctor said. 'You'll have to drive slowly. And keep him calm.' Two privates lifted the plank and stowed the man across Vivienne's back seat. The plank snagged on the leather. It barely fit inside the width of the car.

Aside to us, the doctor said the man would likely lose the eye in any case. I sat in beside Vivienne, but looked back over the seat at the man. Imagine losing an eye. Imagine being sighted one minute, blind the next.

Vivienne leaned over the steering wheel to see her way. A fraction of moon gave occasional light, shifting through cloud or smoke as we drove away from the checkpoint. I had to switch between telling her where to turn and talking any old rubbish to the groaning man. About the weather. About my daft brother running away with a theatre troupe like a twelve-year-old following a circus. I quickly ran out of things to say.

The moon came and went, what there was of one, through drifts of cloud. We made our slow and careful way. No one shot at us. At Adelaide Road, our charge was carried off on his plank.

'Your seat's destroyed,' I said to Vivienne, but she didn't seem to care.

'Come on,' she said. 'There's more where he came from.'

It was easy to talk in the car, both of us looking out of the window at the road. Vivienne told me she had eight younger brothers and sisters, as well as two older brothers.

'Who'll mind your younger brothers and sisters when you're gone to France?'

She laughed. 'My older brothers have wives now. The farm is theirs, and all that goes with it. It's their turn. This is my chance, and I'm taking it.' She rolled her neck, swivelled her head from side to side.

When we got back to the clearing station, we saw hundreds of people moving slowly through Beresford Place on the far side of the river. They emerged from a dense, reddish fog carrying bundles and bags and babies.

'Not that them poor souls ever had much,' a woman said, 'but what there was is gone up in flames. Them boys in the Post Office have a lot to answer for.'

A heavy rumbling, like a train loose on the road, made us look around. The most peculiar vehicle I'd ever seen approached the bridge. A vast metal cylinder was mounted longways on a lorry driven by a soldier. There were slits, like in a pillar box, cut into its sides. We watched it huff and grumble along. The engine strained under the weight, reminding me of the time Liam mistook a lorry for a shell and thought his time had come. 'What on earth –' I said.

Vivienne snorted. 'It's like some class of a siege engine, delivering boiling oil.'

When the strange vehicle had passed, we were directed to a place where we could stop the car. We reported our success with the eye man to the doctor in charge, who was less impressed than he might have been and assigned us to take three women and a man to Paddy Dun's. We installed them in the back of the car, with much wincing and adjustment of injured limbs, a wrist here, an elbow there, and set off again. One of the women had a shattered shoulder. Tears poured down her face with every jolt.

When we got to the hospital, one of the women shook my hand, declared that mine was cold and gave me her cardigan, saying, I'd have more need of it now she was going inside. 'And nothing, not hell nor high water, will get me out again before daylight.'

We made several more journeys that night. I told Vivienne about Liam, and about Eva. She told me she'd had a sweetheart but he was killed in training for the army. His unit was sent to mend a wall on a local estate and the wall fell on him and crushed him. It was pointless, she said. And that, as much as anything, had decided her on going out with the ambulance corps.

I wanted to say something about Hubie, but I was afraid that if I started to talk about him I wouldn't be able to stop. Instead I told her I might go to London to learn about antiques and fine art, come back to work in a shop.

'What's stopping you?'

'Good question.' I was an adult, after all. Thousands of people, millions, made their way through life alone. Why did I need my parents' approval?

Vivienne mistook my silence. 'Are you tired? I am. But let's keep going as long as we can.'

I'd stopped noticing corners and low-hanging railway bridges by then. Anyone could have shot at us, at any time, but no one did. Less was said as the night wore on. Less needed to be said. There was a fog in my mind that matched the smoky, acrid air. I lost track of time, but hours must have passed before the engine stuttered and we coasted to a stop on a side street off Great Brunswick Street.

'That's it,' Vivienne said. 'We've no more petrol.' Some soldiers pushed the car into a yard, said it could take its chances there for the night. They told us to go on up to Holles Street, where there was a waiting room set up for volunteers like us, with blankets on the floor for us to sleep on.

The waning moon took a knife to the sky, spilled a weird

light through the smoky air as we made our way along. Was it my imagination that the walls of the houses we passed were warm, that they breathed sulphur? Ahead of us, at the mouth of a lane, were three soldiers. One of them had a corporal's chevrons on his sleeve. They were looking our way. A fox in a moonlit garden is one thing; in a kitchen seeking eggs it's another. I wished I'd Liam's coat to pull around me.

'Well,' the fat soldier drawled. 'Well, well. What have we here?'

Their eyes were hard and flat. I pulled myself up straight and tried to walk past, but he lowered his rifle and stopped me. Vivienne stood a little behind me. She was so small, almost like a child.

'Let us through.' I hated that my voice was uneven.

The fat soldier planted himself in front of me, so close the buttons of his uniform grazed the front of my dress, his face pushed towards mine. I could smell him. Sweat and the rotten breath of teeth unwashed for days, a stink of tobacco.

Cold stirred in a place so deep inside me I couldn't name it. Everything inside me slowed. I'd a sensation of creepy-crawlies tracking across my skin, through the fine hairs on my neck and down my goose-fleshed arms. This was my city. They'd no business here, telling me where I could or couldn't go.

Fatty bumped himself against me. 'Give me a fucken reason.' His voice slimed into my ear. 'Just one.'

Liam's voice bid me go easy, but words flooded out of me in a low torrent. 'My brother fought and died in your army. If he was here now, he'd soon sort you out. Have you nothing better to do than harass women on the streets?' The strangest thing happened then. I felt Liam leap to surround me, like a cloak, his hand at my mouth. *Say no more.*

The fat soldier bounced his bulk against me again, almost gently. 'And have your lot nothing better to do than stab us in the back?' He stood back and lifted his rifle to my breast. 'If this was a bayonet,' he growled, 'I'd rip your traitorous, bitching guts out and spread them for the dogs.'

I couldn't speak through Liam's restraining fingers, or the hammer of my heart.

'Steady, Phil.' The Corporal gripped his arm and pulled it back. The other soldier shouldered his rifle and slipped away, eyes averted. The Corporal spoke rapidly into Fatty's ear. 'Save your bullets for them that needs 'em.'

Fatty bristled and glared, but he lowered the gun.

'Come on.' The Corporal's voice was clipped. He stamped along beside us, a tense escort, leaving his horrible friend behind. When we reached the back door to the hospital, Vivienne thanked him. I said I'd go on back to Percy Place.

'There's a curfew,' the Corporal said.

'I have a permit.' I showed him the paper I'd taken from Con's car. While he scanned it, I told Vivienne she could come with me if she liked. I wasn't sorry when she said no, she couldn't walk another step, she'd stay in the waiting room. She said she'd keep me a spot, in case I was turned back.

The Corporal sighed. 'Considering what happened to you earlier,' he said, 'I'll walk with you.'

We didn't speak on the way. I moved in a half-dream, as though I flew, towards Hubie.

There was a checkpoint at the bridge. Yesterday's slaughterhouse. No, it was past midnight, that carnage was two days ago. 'Let her pass,' the Corporal said.

'You live here?' the sentry asked. 'One of your neighbours got himself shot this afternoon. Watching. What do you all think this is, sport?'

A chill ran through me. 'Who? Which house?'

'Go on before I change my mind,' the Corporal said. 'Stay off the streets from now on, or you'll get what's coming.'

*

All the young leaves had been blasted from the trees. A hole in the paving showed where the big gun had been. Every window gaped, empty of glass. I craved water. The canal was a black velvet ribbon beside me, a margin I could slip inside and vanish, nestle on the reedy bottom, where the world was cool and silent.

I put the palm of my hand flat on the paint of Dote's front door. It swung open, as though it had been waiting. I stepped over the threshold, straight into Hubie's arms.

'I was so afraid.' His mouth at my ear. His voice coursed through me, flooded me with a rush of feeling I told myself was relief at being indoors, enclosed again in the incurious sheltering darkness of the house.

A piercing, unearthly shriek made me jump.

'He missed you.' Hubie moved away, struck a match and held it to a candle. Paschal leaped from the newel post to my shoulder, tugged my hair, butted his head against mine. He grabbed my collar, jabbering away.

'Hello, yourself,' I said.

'What's this?' Hubie touched the bandage.

'Nothing, only broken glass.'

Paschal patted my hair. I shivered a little. 'It's colder in here than on the street.'

'It's warmer in the kitchen; I've the stove going.'

In the kitchen, two lamps threw amber shadows on the table. I put Paschal down and went to the sink, poured a long cold drink of water, then another.

'You're pale as a ghost,' Hubie said. 'Look, I found a cake of soda-bread, fresh, made by a woman who gave it to me for cigarettes. And these.' He put two smooth eggs into my hands. 'We'll have a feast. Katie? You're shaking.'

He took back the eggs and set them in a bowl. I leaned into him and shut my eyes. He smelled of something like straw in the sun, a smell of summer dust and horses. 'I'm so tired,' I said to his solid chest. 'I can hardly stand.'

'Where were you?' He helped me out of the borrowed cardigan and put it aside. Rested his thumb in my palm.

It was too big a question to answer. Instead I said, 'A soldier said one of the neighbours was killed. Who was it?'

'Mr Hyland.'

'I was afraid it was you.'

He busied himself with a pan on the stove while I eased my sore feet from my shoes and worked the toes, telling him about the fires, which he could smell for himself, and the people streaming into Beresford Place for shelter. 'Hundreds of them. Thousands, maybe.' I was half hallucinating – was it Lockie I heard, banging that skillet on the stove, rattling plates loose from the dresser? What house was I in – everything smelling of peat and fire. Was I in the countryside, somewhere with a bonfire raging, was it autumn? No, I was in Percy Place. There was Hubie, coming with a knife to cut the bread. Behind him a tap dripped into the Belfast sink. If I looked, I'd see the stained, coppery runnel in the enamel.

'There's no butter, but the eggs will help.' Hubie pinched salt on to perfect domes of golden yolk. Pierced, they bled sweetly into the floury bread. The most delicious thing I'd ever tasted. When I'd mopped the last trace of egg from my plate with the bread, pushed the last crumb into my grateful mouth, he told me I'd a choice. Black tea, port wine or whiskey?

I said port.

The first sip woke my mouth. The second coated my throat and all the way down to my stomach with a fierce glow. I was ravenous still. I could have eaten three more eggs in quick succession. Just the one was nearly worse than not eating anything at all. 'I feel so greedy, I'd eat the whole world if I could.'

'I like you that way.'

He pushed the plates aside, refilled our glasses, lit two

cigarettes and passed me one. 'Now,' he said. 'We could go up to the parlour, but the windows have gone. Or we could go to bed.' His face intent on mine. 'We'd be warm up there.'

'What about the others?'

'No one can come 'til morning.'

'I did.'

He lifted the hair from my neck. 'You're different.'

'I need a bath.'

'I think we can manage that.'

He dragged out an old copper hip bath from the scullery, half filled a large pan with water, and the kettle. Asked me to lift them to the stove.

'Shouldn't we fill up the pan?'

He waved his hand, no. How stupid I was, with tiredness. I'd have to do the pouring, when the water was hot.

Paschal curled up on a cushion in the corner chair with a contented sigh. I went over to the dresser, the low-burning lamp.

'Are you cold?' Hubie asked. 'I could open the door of the stove if you want, but the water will take longer —'

'No. I couldn't bear it. I don't think I'll ever be able to face a fire again.'

'Wait 'til winter, you'll be glad of it then. Come here.'

I squashed into the straw chair beside him, curled my legs up, leaned into his arms. His ribs rose and fell in a steady rhythm that was easy to match. It was calming, to simply sit there and breathe, together. To wait for water to come to a boil.

Steam rose from the water. 'That's hot enough.' I got up and emptied the pot into the tub. 'Are we sure they won't be back tonight?'

'Not hardly. It's after midnight.'

Shy, even in the lamplight, I took off my clothes. Tested the water, and sat into it, my knees drawn up to my chest.

The tub was a tight fit. Designed for a child maybe. But I was glad to bend forwards and show him my back. He immersed a flannel in the water and squeezed it, letting the drops fall to my spine.

I drifted in a jewelled boat while he washed my back, then dabbed my face clean, avoiding the dressing. He put his lips to it instead, as light as breath. He soaped my chest and under my arms, ran the soapy cloth down my legs, along my feet and back up to my neck, squeezed water from the cloth to rinse me. Then he leaned in, to kiss me. My wet arms went up around his neck. He wrapped me in a towel and I was standing against him, falling into him, when there was a whoop and a splash, and waves of water sloshed over the sides of the tub. Paschal bobbed up with soapsuds on his head. He rubbed his eyes and chattered, took up the flannel and twisted it, wrung it out, tutting at the sudsy water.

We had to laugh. Hubie made me sit on the chair wrapped in my towel, put Paschal on a ladder-back wrapped in his, and dragged the bath to the back door. It shrieked across the stone flags. He tipped it out, one-handed, on to the grass.

'Where there's a will,' he said, holding out his good hand. I put mine into it and got up to follow him upstairs, with Paschal, chattering, behind.

Hubie's eyes were warm and dark, like rare, fabulous stones, tiger's eye or topaz. I stood in front of him, unsheathed and bare. The feel of air on my skin was different when he was there. Those honeyed eyes passed over me, cupped the air and moulded it around me, changed it. I dropped my chin. My hair slid around my shoulders, fell down my back.

'You're beautiful.'

'Thin as a stick,' I said, quoting Florrie. Odd, to think of Florrie now – her blighted, postponed wedding. All this still ahead of her.

'Curved,' Hubie said, calling me back. 'Like a scythe. Come here. Slay me.'

He'd planted something in me. Rooted behind my ribs, its shoots stirred. I was pinned to the bed by pleasure, a melting lassitude, my bones like jelly. All my life I'd walked around inside my skin not knowing what it was, what it opened to. I didn't know what my body could do or want. How easily it could break. 'Why does no one ever say?'

'Maybe there are no words; we can only go around it.' He drew a narrowing spiral on my stomach.

'Strange how shy and stubborn words can be when you try to hook them to ideas.' Alanna's paper dolls came to mind, the flimsy tabs, how interchangeable they were.

'So I'm an idea, am I?' His hand stopped over my navel, rested there, called up a pulse I'd never known before. 'What are you thinking now?'

'That you'll leave. When this is over, you'll go back to your own people in the country.' Maybe even tomorrow.

'Will you miss me?'

I wrapped my legs around his and laid myself along the length of him, pinning him to the sheet.

'I found out what happened to your Peace Man,' he said later, when we were quiet again and Paschal was snoring on top of the wardrobe. 'It's not good.'

Cold crept through me while he told me that a priest saw Skeff's body when he was called to administer the rites to a dead boy who'd been told to kneel down in the street and pray while an officer shot him in the head.

Like a kick, it would have been. Sudden. I pulled away from him, sat up.

'There's a lot of bluster, but I heard your man who did it is off his head.'

264

'He should be shot himself.'

'It's just the one story. There's fault on both sides.'

'You don't know this man. Everyone loves him. This is a bad, a rotten thing to happen.'

He gave me an ironic look. I went on, defiant. 'We're all worse off, if something's happened to him.'

'Not just him. There were others. Journalists. The twist of it is, they wrote for government-friendly papers. Which only goes to show, your man wasn't thinking straight. They're trying to smooth it over, but another officer reported it.'

'Don't.' I hated his brittle, flippant tone. It made him sound like someone else, someone I would never know or want to, and that hurt nearly as much as the idea of that big bear of a man and his untidy beard, of all people, having been killed. Even children used to tease him in the street. 'This is the worst,' I said. 'The worst they could have done.'

He pulled me back down against him. 'You don't know what the worst can be,' he said into my hair.

'Con says there's not enough coffins. They're burying people in gardens, storing bodies in halls.'

He went very still.

'What?'

'One billet we were in, they were busy making coffins outside our window. All night, they were at it. And in the morning they were stacked against a fence we had to march past. Those coffins were for us. That crowd out there' – he gestured towards the window – 'the things I've heard people say – you'd think they invented sacrifice. You'd think they'd never heard that a million or more young men have sacrificed themselves already.'

I told him about the soldiers who'd stopped Vivienne and me. His good hand stroked my arm and calmed me. Through the empty windows, fog crept into the room to listen to me tell about the hatred in the soldiers' voices. How that private had smelled, the rough feel of his hands. These were men that Liam and Hubie might have loved, out there in Flanders. Their companionship, friendship, brotherhood – whatever it was that bound them – had kept Liam safe, up to a point. Then it destroyed him.

'It was the strangest thing. Liam was there. For real. I felt his hand on my mouth. Telling me to be quiet and not provoke them.'

'Good advice.'

'You don't believe me.'

'You'd be surprised what I believe.'

'Do you believe that he's still with me?'

'Why not, if you carry him?'

'I thought I saw him once. I hear his voice, in my mind.'

'Did Liam ever mention Thatch Doyle to you? An abrasive man, face like a ferret, but handy in a fight.'

Yes, he had. *I saw my first corpses today. We moved into some German trenches that had been cleared by shelling, came to a place partially blocked by a spill of earth. Made our way around it and there they were. One lay across another's lap, a pietà. Their uniforms in shreds. Skinless faces. Empty sockets for eyes. The seated one still wore his helmet. The most surprising thing about them was their teeth, ordinary in the strangeness. Grinning. Waiting for us to get the joke. Doyle worked the jaws, made them speak obscenities. No one laughed. He gave it up soon enough and set about burying them with the rest of us.*

I'd imagined worse. The dead have no power here.

'There weren't many officers could box, but Doyle was good. Quick on his feet. One day after a skirmish – one of many that played out exactly the same that winter, gain ten yards in the morning, lose them all by nightfall, lose at least one man in each – I saw Doyle, leaning against a tree, during the roll. As close as you are now. But he didn't answer when his name was called. I looked right at him and said his name again. The third time I said it, he went.'

'Went?'

'One minute he was there. Then he wasn't. One of the men brought up his tags and his notebook, taken from his body an hour before. But I saw him.'

That night was a candlelit cave or a chapel. Gold and amber lozenges roamed the walls. Only a river I loved lay between us and a ravening, roaring beast, all red and black billows, snapping and loud, crushing buildings and stealing air. This flame was of a different order. When I held my glass to the candle, it kindled to shapes, a tongue, a globe that broke apart. He tilted his head and looked at me. I felt peeled, raw. My hair sat, heavy, between the bones of my shoulders.

When he touched me, I had the strangest sense that he was making me flesh, making me real in the world again. Making the world real.

'There's something I have to ask you. Tell you. About Liam. Something he did.'

It was all in a letter, the last one before the terse, two-word message: *No more.* The one that told me he didn't want to come back. The one that explained his long silence to Isabel, a silence I didn't break for him, because it would have felt like a betrayal.

I'd told no one. Not Isabel, not Dad, not even Eva. I couldn't hold it in any longer. It poured out of me.

All leave postponed, we went up the line again. Something was up. Transports rolled night and day, moving artillery, the horses struggling through muck. Then a bombardment. Hell on earth. Three days, it lasted. I was in a hole with three others, all dead. I'd lost my bearings. The earth out here's been wrenched inside out – hills become pits, heaps of muck where there used to be trench. Bits of men strewn around and all landmarks blasted. There's no knowing which direction to take for your own line, which would bring you to theirs. You could jump into a trench, thinking yourself safe, and land bang in the middle of a nest of

Germans. I was parched, tongue rasping with thirst. Sporadic fire in the distance, the fight burning itself out. There were trees nearby. I crept in, for shelter and to take my bearings.

I leaned against a trunk for breath. When it steadied, I saw a field-grey uniform, not thirty yards away, and over it a ruddy farmboy's face, staring at me. My pulse throbbed so hard in my ears, I thought they'd burst. Neither of us moved. His eyes wary and alert, as mine must've been. Blood on his chin. He held out his two hands. His rifle in one of them, held by the barrel, harmless as anything. No blade. He took a backward step. Away. Then another. We could let each other be, go our separate ways. All this was in his eyes. He turned his broad grey back to me. It came to me then that if I let him go he could use that rifle against anyone, any of the men, Doyle or Wilson, or the priest. That's when I raised mine.

I thought I'd missed. He lurched, stopped still. I thought he'd spin around and shoot me in return. I wished he would. I'd have ripped my heart out and held it towards him for a target, if he had. I prayed for the shot that would end it all. Instead, he crumpled. Six feet of Imperial uniform. Folded up and fell.

I sat beside his body. Night crept in. Some men from my company found me, brought me back. I began this day a soldier and finished a murderer. I could be dead myself, for all I know. If so, I'm not writing this at all, but dreaming it. I can say what I like. Nothing will change.

The brother you thought you knew is gone. All the love in the world won't bring him back. This *is life, now. Hardly worth fighting for.*

A pulse throbbed in Hubie's neck. When I couldn't stand his silence any longer, I said, 'Well? What do you think?'

'Nothing.'

'Nothing? He killed a man who was no threat to him.'

'And?'

'And – I think he put himself in harm's way because of it.'

'Do you, now.' He lit a cigarette. Didn't offer me one.

'I think it was himself he killed, when he fired that shot.'

'Stop it!' he roared, making me jump. His eyes bulged. His voice was a splintered thing, bouncing off the walls. 'Stop!'

I kept my head down. After a while he said, hoarse but calmer, 'Does it make you feel better, to think that?'

'Of course not.'

'Good, because it doesn't make one damned bit of difference. How many men do you think he might have killed in, what, six months of fighting?' The scorn he showed us all at first was back in his eyes; he was blind with it. 'I'm sure he didn't know. This one – yes, he could have let him go. But what he says is true. That same soldier could have gone on to kill me. Or Jonesy. Or a hundred others. Kill or be killed, is the logic of it. Liam's loyalty was to his own, not to some peacetime code or other. He knew that.'

'Then, why? Why would he stand up like that, with the flares lighting up the sky the way you say they were?'

'A moment of madness? Maybe he wanted to pull down the sky and smother the whole filthy war. Choke it to death and bury it. Maybe he forgot, for a split second, where he was and what might happen. Maybe he thought luck was on his side. We'll never know. Multiply that unknowing by a million. What does it change? Nothing.' He took a long breath. 'Whatever hellish frame of mind he was in, it's over. If he brought it down on himself, at least he took no one with him.'

I left the window, the dark grass and knotted trees, the canal, the sentries. Slipped into bed beside him, as naturally as though I'd been doing it all my life.

Until now, I'd barely been aware of my body, other than as a shell to carry me around, needing minimal care and attention to keep it fed and clean. Now it was wide awake. It rushed forward, pushed past me in this strange matter of love, of loving him – what else could I call it?

'Something bigger is dying out there,' he said into the floating, half-sleeping dark. 'And we'll never know what it was.'

'I thought you were asleep.'

He raised himself to sitting, propped by pillows, struck a match. His features swam towards me and away. The sweet smell of a fresh cigarette. I wondered what time it was. Hard to judge, in those dim hours, half-night, half-morning. Somewhere a bird sang, a sweet triumphant note that settled it. Another day. What would it bring? We fastened the wooden shutters across the gaping, unglazed window-frame and we were back in our own black cave, the rage of the fires shut out.

My parents could have been among the refugees, about to lose everything to fire. It's true they planned to move, but that would have been a matter of packing what they wanted to save, books and photographs and letters, long discussions and sessions of do-you-remember-this? Fire would destroy it all. Every trace of Liam. Eva as a child, before she challenged them. Matt, the petted baby of the house.

'That world has gone,' Hubie said. 'Have you not listened to anything I said?'

He slid his thumb along the underskin of my forearm. 'Once I could have circled your waist with my two hands.' He held me by the wrist instead, loose as a bracelet. 'Come away with me, Katie. Let's leave this godforsaken place and not look back. We'll go somewhere new.'

'Where?'

'I've been thinking about Canada.'

A sun rose through the word. A place of light and snow, long hard winters. 'Why there?'

'There's room there – and to spare – for anyone who's willing to work.'

'It's so far away.' I looked at the shape our hands made, braided, on the sheet. 'Liam was never there.'

'Has it occurred to you that Liam might not be haunting you, that it's the other way around?'

Everything stilled. This was the heart of it. One way or

another, there was the rest of my life to face. Keeping pace with me in that queer way I was getting used to, he asked, 'What do you want, Katie?'

Again I couldn't answer his question. 'What will you do?'

'There's a whole new world out there, waiting to be built. I can't do the building, but I know about planning, and moving men and equipment, and materials. I have ideas, designs, in here' – he tapped his forehead – 'for machinery to make the work faster and safer. I can't make them myself but I'll find people who can. I'll find someone to back me. They were fine men, the Canadians. Clean, brave fighters and practical. I could get on in a place that breeds men like that. If it doesn't work, I'll try something else.'

'I wish I was like you, ready for anything.'

'What are you waiting for, permission? You won't get it. Believe me, our society has more murderous concerns than deciding whether or not to let a young lady take a job in a shop.'

'Don't mock.' I groaned and buried my face in his shoulder. 'When you say it – you make everything seem easy. As if nothing matters but what you want.'

'It would be a good time for a person to disappear,' he said.

'Don't.' I was thinking of Matt. How his departure would make mine more difficult. But, if I stayed, I'd have to pretend that none of this had happened. I'd have to unlearn all I'd learned. And Eva. What lay ahead for her, what might she need from me?

Hubie stroked my arm, quite roughly at first, but then he slowed, his touch lighter, questioning. 'I forget where I am sometimes. Have I ruined you?'

I laughed. Then I stopped laughing.

He patted my shoulder, alarmed. 'There,' he said. 'There.' Threads of flame in his eyes. His missing, ghostly fingers quickened on my skin.

He'd got it wrong. He thought I was crying for lost innocence, or virtue, words without colour, muscle or sinew. Words that would never bleed. I was crying because there could be no more pretence. The people who had died were dead. Every morning that I woke, I could get up or not, eat or not, admire the day or not, and it would still be true. Liam would never come home. There are things that can never be undone, thresholds to be crossed in one direction only.

Friday, 28 April 1916

I dreamed I was an island, a stony beach. The sea rose and showed itself, then sank back, sighing. It pushed at the shingle, the land a wheel it wanted to turn. It sucked the shore, shrugged and turned away, biding its time.

In that grey moment before day begins, when light is still a veil you could part with your hands and pass through, I woke, tasting salt. The air was autumnal, heavy with bonfires. But there'd been no summer yet. A stair creaked and I was wide awake, rigid with fear. Someone creeping in? No, the house settled.

There was no one there, but soon enough, too soon, there would be. I moved closer to Hubie, laid my body against his. He stirred. I closed my eyes and let my body do the seeing, felt his skin bloom and come alive against mine. 'If there was no light, ever again,' I said, 'would time stop?'

He rolled over. 'We wouldn't know what time was.'

I moved under the sheet so that we were length to length. I wanted the cup of his shoulder to fit my palm like a warm egg. The fan of his ribs, the taut button of nipple springing to my mouth, the feel of his hair when I spread it the wrong way with my fingers.

I couldn't imagine returning to a life without these strange, delirious nights, or quite believe that other people lived them too. How does no one blush when they use their hands to prepare food, write letters, open doors? How do they hide their wild undernature, their inventive nocturnal selves, put on their clothes and go out about their business?

Liam wrote that he started each day wondering if he'd see

its end. *Our days lie ahead of us, already formed, waiting for us to do their living for them. Our lives live us, I think, rather than the other way around. War is the life that has chosen me. It was always waiting for me to step into it, like a pair of new boots, tight fitting. Or a skin. Once you put it on, you'll never get it off.*

This was a different kind of choosing, a new learning, savouring the mysteries of something as everyday as skin, its changing textures and appetites, its conflicted nature bringing us together and holding us apart at one and the same time.

After a while I got up and opened the shutters. I wanted to see Hubie's face. Outside, the morning was greasy and dense, yet I could see blue in it, as through a thick veil. There was a sour black smell.

'The fires must still be burning,' he said. 'Come back to bed.'

A person could lose herself in the flaring petals of his irises, intricate layers of jewelled colour, every shade of green and gold and brown, the dark well of his pupils.

'Say you'll come away with me, when this is over. If you stay, you'll squander your life on what other people want from you.'

'And if I go? Wouldn't I be giving it to you?'

'I'd hope not.' He gathered my hair and rolled it around his hand, like a bandage, held it at the back of my head so I had to face him. 'We could have a life of our very own making. Think of it, Katie. A place where people make special shoes and walk out on fresh snow. Where you can pace out a stretch of land and call it yours, so long as you're willing to work it.'

He was a stranger.

He was another self.

He was so close. It wasn't close enough. Every hollow in me ached for him to fill it.

He saw and said things other people never would.

It could be a life's work, learning to see what's right in front of you. You'd need companions who took you seriously.

On the windowsill, Paschal hopped up and down and pointed. He jumped to the bed and back again, chattering.

I went to see. Through the murky light, two figures holding hands moved slowly under a sky like a bruise, like spirits crossing from one world to the next through fire. A child skipped along beside them, her hands free, in the pattern of a hopscotch. Two feet, one foot, two feet. Hop, hop, hop.

My heart kicked. 'It's Dote and May – and Tishy. They've come back.' A stab of loss, then panic: we'd be discovered.

Someone stepped out from under a tree, one of the neighbours. Dote and May stopped to talk. Tishy went to the edge of the canal and threw something into the water.

I hurried into my skirt and blouse, dragged a brush through my hair at the mirror. Hubie stood behind me. 'You look fine.' Our reflected eyes met. I couldn't prevent my mouth from curving into a smile that lifted my chin and squared my shoulders so that I stood taller. Looking at him gave me such satisfaction. If time pinned this exact moment, fixed it like a moth to a frame, our privacy unbroken, I'd be left leaning into him forever, my spine dissolving, his face looking at mine, taking me in, the two of us wide open to each other. It was enough.

No, it would never be enough; it was only a beginning. Already, satisfaction turned towards wanting. 'Don't look at me like that when they come in. They'll know.'

He kissed the top of my head. 'Think about what I said. We'll talk, later.'

I splashed myself with Dote's cologne and followed him downstairs. We heard the gate, the sound of feet crunching broken glass. They'd have news we might not want to hear. War was the same story told over and over, only the names would change. I wondered was love like that. I'd never know if I walked away from it.

Hubie opened the door and went down the steps. I disliked the sight of his back moving away from me. How could I let him go? Beyond him, across the road, the canal was full, full as I felt, brimming and ready to spill. The air smouldered, hard to breathe. Chunks of charred matter and singed paper a black snow falling. So many disembodied words flying free, they made my head swim. I plucked a tattered scrap from the air. It turned to dust and soot in my palm. Imagine manuscripts, like Dote's, all the years of work and thought and dedication lost. Imagine all the proofs of your existence gone – who you were, everything you'd ever done, or planned to do. Everything lost, everything starting again.

A breeze sounded in my ear, *choose*. Somewhere, someone wept, as well someone should. I wished for rain, to wash away the smoke and murderous grime of the coming day. Going down the steps after him, I breasted the smutty fog as swans breast water. There was the full span of my foot, there my weight and there the solid ground.

Author's Note

This is a work of fiction, and its main characters and their predicaments are wholly imagined. But it is set in a very particular time and place, against the backdrop of two great conflicts, and I have relied on many sources, published and unpublished, to help me depict its settings and atmospheres. Vera Brittain's books are an essential resource for anyone interested in the Great War, and in particular its effect on soldiers' families. *Letters from a Lost Generation* was invaluable to me in trying to think my way into the mindset of a soldier. The scene in which the Crilly family receives Liam's personal effects has its origins in Brittain's account of Roland Leighton's effects, although she is far more eloquent and expository than I am. Other sources on the Great War that I have found useful include Myles Dungan's *Irish Voices from the Great War*, Correlli Barnett's *The Great War*, Robert Graves's *Goodbye to All That* and *The Ways of War* by Tom Kettle and Mary Sheehy Kettle. The exemplary firstworldwar.com was invaluable.

James Stephens's *The Insurrection in Dublin* is a contemporaneous account of the Easter Rising by an eyewitness; other first-hand accounts are contained in Roger McHugh's *Dublin 1916* and Alfred Fannin's *Letters from Dublin, Easter 1916*, among others. Max Caulfield's *The Easter Rebellion* remains one of the most vivid fact-based accounts, while Charles Townshend's more recent *Easter 1916: The Irish Rebellion* is authoritative and comprehensive.

Sean J. Murphy's article 'The Gardiner Family, Dublin, and Mountjoy, County Tyrone', available on his website, provided the basis for the lecture Katie and Bill attend in the Mansion House.

Two evocative books that helped me to think about Dublin's atmospheres during this period are *Dublin 1911*, edited by Catriona Crowe, and Christiaan Corlett's *Darkest Dublin*.

Acknowledgements

Anne Enright saved this novel from the shredder not once but twice. Blame her. A residency at the Centre Culturel Irlandais in Paris turned it inside out and lit it from the inside. Huge thanks to everyone there, especially Sheila Pratschke; and to Gail Ritchie, fellow resident, with whom I shared many adventures in Paris graveyards and late-night conversations about dead soldiers and history's many forms of amnesia. A bursary from the Arts Council/An Chomhairle Ealaíon arrived at a crucial moment: many thanks to them.

Thanks to members of writing groups past and present for their patient encouragement, and to the loyal readers of early drafts: Sheila Barret, Celia de Fréine, Catherine Dunne, Simon and Vanessa Robinson. Also to participants at the 'Women, War and Letters' conference in the University of Limerick in 2012, and in particular its organizers, Tina O'Toole and Meg Harper. Anna South gave generous and practical advice when I needed it.

For information, books, sources and enthusiasm, I am indebted to: Robert Towers and Mary Fitzgerald, Dermot and Maura Hourihane, Davis Coakley, Ronan Fanning, Tony Farmar, Kate Lochrin, Martina Devlin, Luz Mar Gonzalez Arias, Sheila McGilligan and Ann Marie Hourihane. For help with sources: the Royal College of Physicians of Ireland, the Research Reading Room at Dublin City Library and Archive (Pearse Street), the National Library of Ireland, the National Museum of Ireland at Collins Barracks (especially Enda Greenan), the Imperial War Museum (London) and Gerard Whelan at the Royal Dublin Society Library and Archives.

Pearse Quinlan at Mr Fax was an indefatigable supplier of paper and toner at crucial moments.

Thanks to everyone at Penguin Ireland, especially Brendan Barrington, who put manners on it as only he can. Also to Donna Poppy for her keen eye and attention to detail.

It can't be easy to live with someone who's hatching a novel. Simon, Zita, Emma, Nessa, Peter, Eoghan and Ryan did so with grace and good humour, and Isabella arrived just in time to help us see it off.